SUBDIVISION BATTLES OF THE DEAD AND UNDEAD

THE WARLOCK'S HOMEOWNERS ASSOCIATION (BOOK I)

A.J. Renwick

Plotworks Publishing

ISBN (electronic): 978-1-960936-43-1

ISBN (print): 978-1-960936-44-8

CONTENTS

ONE

On a cold night in the middle of June, at exactly 10:57 pm (though when the story was retold, the time would be changed to midnight for dramatic purposes), a dead man strode into The Clover Motel.

A brown messenger bag hung from his shoulder, and beneath his arm, he clutched a black chrysalis. It shimmered with iridescent light and radiated with the heavy heat of the underworld.

Bartholomew Whitlock wasn't dead in the traditional sense, or even the untraditional sense. His heart still beat. His breath was steady. He had no desire to moan, hold his arms stiff before him, or eat brains. His death was a metaphorical one.

Gone was Bartholomew Whitlock, exalted among the Acquisitions Department of The Bearded Syndicate, in his place was—

"Bartholomew *Bartlow*?"

Rebecca Willis, the woman stuck working the night shift at the motel's front desk, peered at the identification card through a pair of pink-rimmed spectacles. Had she looked closely, she might have noticed a curious sheen on the plastic, like it was turning brown in a pattern of lines and dots. But the news was reporting on a plane crash, and Rebecca took a morbid delight in listening to tragic stories, even if only so she could inform her husband the next day and chide him for his lack of empathy when he remained indifferent. She was eager to get this new guest checked in so that she could get back to the television.

Still, she attempted to make what she considered polite conversation as she typed Bartholomew's information into the old computer. "I'll bet school was tough for you."

Rebecca cracked a sympathetic smile and looked at the man before her desk.

He stared back, dark eyes serious beneath a pair of thick black brows that matched the curls on his head. His lips were drawn in a tight thin line. "No," he said, "I was an excellent student."

Rebecca stared at him. There was something unsettling about his voice. In the moment, she couldn't place what it was, but when she recounted the meeting later, she'd realize. Though Bartholomew's face was smooth, not a day over thirty, he spoke like a radio-announcer who was pushing seventy.

"No, I meant— Right, well..." Rebecca waved her hand in dismissal and continued entering the information. "And do you know how long you'll be staying with us, Mr. Bartlow?"

"Who? Oh that's me." He nodded. "No, not yet. But I'll need a pet-friendly room. I'm about to get a cat." For some reason, he shifted the black chrysalis in his arm as he spoke. An arc of light shimmered around it, as though it were wrapped in a rainbow.

Rebecca blinked. She'd never seen anything like it, which wasn't surprising. Most people, even magical and undead ones, hadn't.

"Very good, Mr. Bartlow. Pets are only allowed in rooms on the first floor. We have one still available." The Clover Motel in fact was mostly empty, but Rebecca had been instructed to say otherwise by her boss, who was under the mistaken assumption that the lie gave the establishment an air of desirability. "We'll keep your credit card information on file until then. Wi-Fi password and information are in a binder on the side table when you go in. Room is right down the hall, second on the left. Here's the key."

She dropped it into Bartholomew's waiting hand. Like the rest of his body, his fingers were long and thin. Unlike the rest of him, they had a tendency to twitch like the limbs of a dying spider. They curled around the key with a snap.

He turned, took two steps toward the hall, and stopped. His fingers flitted into his pocket and retrieved a green bill.

As a habit, Rebecca's interest in guests ended the moment the room key was exchanged. She'd already begun switching the computer tab back to the news. However, the glint of green caught her eye.

It wasn't often that guests bothered to tip her.

And it wasn't a one-, or five-, or even a ten-dollar bill that Bartholomew was crinkling in his fingers. Rebecca recognized Benjamin Franklin's shiny forehead, and even if she hadn't, the two zeros beside it could have only meant one thing.

Bartholomew had her interest once more.

He rested the hundred dollar bill on the desk. "If someone with a beard shows up, tell me."

"Absolutely!" Rebecca grabbed the money before Bartholomew could change his mind. She would have responded just as eagerly to a ten.

Of course, she would have been just as inefficient if he'd given her a thousand.

Two bearded men would visit the motel in the next week, and Rebecca would inform Bartholomew about neither. Not due to malice, but because the entire encounter slipped from her mind, replaced instead with facts about the night's disaster.

The private plane had exploded mid-air, killing three individuals: the pilot, co-pilot, and a single unnamed passenger. His face flashed across the screen: a man in his thirties with a black beard, long, slicked back hair, and dark eyes that seemed strangely familiar.

I bet he'd be handsome if he shaved, Rebecca thought, and then immediately imagined a new, and incorrect, face for the deceased passenger, which drew more than a little inspiration from the hero on the cover of a romance novel that currently waited beside her bed.

It would be years before she realized that she'd rented a room to a dead man or remembered Bartholomew's request. And even then, it would be only for a second before a bearded man plucked the memory from her mind.

Two

"**D**amn it!" Blood dripped from Bartholomew's chin onto the sink. He stared at the accursed instrument in his fingers and flung it across the small bathroom of the motel room. "A plague upon your family!"

The disposable razor crashed against the glass shower and dropped to the tiles. It didn't have any family as far as it was aware[1] so was forced to take the brunt of the curse itself. Its bladed head snapped from the rest of its body.

"Stupid invention," Bartholomew muttered, ripping a piece of toilet paper from the roll and dabbing his chin. "What's wrong with a pair of scissors?"

He tossed the bloody paper into the bin along with the rest. It was his eigth nick for the morning, which was two more than yesterday.

An individual with high emotional intelligence would have deduced that this was the result of nervousness. Today was the final day of Bartholomew's scheme. Once all went according to plan, he could stop looking over his shoulder for beards and settle into an easy retirement.

---

1. Which was very little, considering it was an inanimate object.

However, Bartholomew had been called over-confident, wily, and a downright miserable pain-in-the-ass. No one had ever accused him of being insightful.

In his estimation, the source of the many bloody spots on his face was obvious, and the culprit lay defeated on the tiles, snapped in two. He felt no remorse as he scooped up its broken remains and tossed them in the garbage.

A shimmering light flashed beneath the bathroom door.

Crack!

It sounded like someone was preparing to make an omelet for a giant.

Bartholomew's heart quickened with unfamiliar excitement. Were he the type, he might even have smiled and rushed into the main room.

But his familiar would read far too much into that. He'd begin to think Bartholomew had missed him!

Instead of racing out of the bathroom like an overeager puppy, Bartholomew made an effort to slow down. He fiddled with the top button on the collar of his gray shirt, shifted the knot on his maroon tie, and combed his curls. His fingers itched for styling gel and clips, but he had no beard to adorn, and the slick-backed, wet-hair look belonged to another man.

Bartholomew Bartlow embraced his curls.

Unfortunately.

All the while he waited, hoping he'd hear a meow, or a purr, or a cheerful voice inquiring after his health. But nothing came, and the longer that there was no sign of his familiar wanting to greet him, the more annoyed Bartholomew became.

Eventually, he was forced to accept there was nothing left for him to do in the bathroom. He'd combed his hair so long, the damn curls were starting to frizz.

Bartholomew spun around, faster than usual though he'd have been loath to admit it, opened the door, and stepped onto the dingy brown carpet of the main room.

It served as bedroom, kitchen, and temporary study. A queen size mattress with straight black sheets and carefully arranged pillows lived beneath a low hanging bulb. The light shade, and much of the rest of the room, had been covered with dust when Bartholomew first arrived. He'd had to dedicate most of his first day to cleaning before he was able to get anything done.

In addition to the bed, there was an empty silver mini-fridge in the corner, a gray counter with a kettle, and a desk on the opposite side. Displayed in its center was a smooth black box, open to reveal five glass vials within. Each held a different colored ink: brown, white, blue, pink, and indigo. The first was almost empty. The second nearing the same level.

Bartholomew's eyes scanned the carpet for signs of a cat.

"Oy," a cheerful voice barked from beneath the desk. "Bart, come here!"

"I'm the warlock. I give the orders," Bartholomew reminded his familiar. When no apology followed, he sighed and stepped forward rationalizing the decision in his mind. It wasn't that he was acquiescing to his familiar's command. He needed his inks.

However, his dark eyes turned downward as he approached.

Beneath the desk was the black chrysalis. Its rainbow of colors had been dispelled, replaced with a large split in the middle like a lightning scar. A pair of deep brown eyes peered out from within. Beneath them was the hint of a pink tongue.

"You're obviously finished," Bartholomew said. "Why haven't you come out yet?"

"I was waiting to make an entrance." There was another boom of thunder as half of the chrysalis fell to the floor. A small, fluffy black creature pranced out, tongue lolling from its mouth, and tail wagging like a hyperactive pendulum.

Gizmorgoth of Darkness was one of the great demons of the underworld. His powers were vast and mighty. He could enter nightmares, summon darkness and flames, torment the soul with visions of its greatest fear. None of his caliber had ever chosen to bind themselves to a warlock. When he'd appeared as a black crow on the shoulder of this scrawny unknown warlock barely two decades old, he'd shocked most members of The Bearded Syndicate.

They would have been just as surprised had they seen what the great demon had done now.

Gizmo had changed forms.

He'd cloaked himself in the chrysalis and fed off his own magic to alter his shape. The process had leached his power. It might take another century for him to return to full force.

It was a dangerous, but necessary precaution.

Tales of a man with a black crow might travel and tempt The Bearded Syndicate to investigate Bartholomew Whitlock's death more closely.

No one would notice a man with a pet cat.

Except that Gizmo was not a cat. He was the sort of small, fluffy black creature that would tempt barren middle-aged women to put him in a stroller and push him around a mall, the type of animal that could whine and yap at a pitch that threatened to break glass, the kind of pet that was dumb enough that it would chase its own tail in circles, try to chase balls that you only pretended to throw, and happily sniff someone's butt.

"Bahaha!" A loud deep laugh exploded from Gizmo as he stared up at Bartholomew. "Look at you! I didn't realize you looked like a child still without your beard! You'll barely pass for thirty."

"It's the curls," Bartholomew muttered, before remembering that he was the one who should be shocked and indignant, not his familiar. "You're a dog!"

Gizmo barked. It was as high-pitched and annoying as Bartholomew had feared.

"We discussed this. You were supposed to become a cat. Who ever heard of a warlock with a yorkie[2] for a familiar?"

"Exactly! No one will ever suspect. And anyway, this form suits me better." He trotted on the spot, bending his knees and lifting his toes high as though he were a pedigree stallion on parade and not the warped, ineffectual descendant of a wolf. His big brown eyes stared up at Bartholomew, hoping for a compliment even though he knew well enough that none was coming.

"Just don't bark. We have a property to purchase today, and I doubt they're keen on noise." Bartholomew pulled an uncomfortable plastic chair toward the desk and sat before his inks.

Gizmo stretched his front paws onto the warlock's knee and stared up at his chin. "Are they keen on blood? You look like got in a knife fight with a pixie."

"I'm fixing it now." Bartholomew scowled at his familiar before opening the desk's top drawer. Within was a black quill, scraps of paper, and a necklace with an onyx eye set deep in the center of a golden

---

2. Gizmorgoth of Darkness had in fact modelled his new form on a Pomeranian and poodle mix, and he might have been offended by this comment had he not been more impressed to discover that Bartholomew knew the name of any toy breed at all.

sun. The Amulet of the Impaler had been Bartholomew Whitlock's final acquisition for The Bearded Syndicate. He'd found it guarded in a catacomb beneath the city of Bucharest. It had taken over a month to bypass the enchantments and return home with the treasure. And all that time, Bartholomew and Gizmo had wondered: what if they kept it for themselves instead?

Not that a warlock and a demon had much use for the amulet, but it was worth a fortune to the right buyer. Bartholomew was tired of taking orders from the leaders of The Syndicate, and Gizmo had never approved of the organization. The dream of freedom snaked its way into both their minds.

And when Bartholomew was tasked with delivering the amulet to a wealthy buyer[3], they seized their opportunity.

"You're not using runes to fix it, are you?" Gizmo objected as he saw Bartholomew pull the quill from the drawer. "We only brought a limited supply of ink."

Bartholomew ground his teeth as he dipped the nib into the vial of white ink. He was positive that other familiars didn't speak to their masters this way. "Otto can send more," he said, shaking Gizmo off so that he could focus on his task. Runes required precision. One wrong stroke or a symbol in the wrong color and you'd find yourself with an explosion, or even worse, a wasted set of ink.

The familiar's small paws tapped against the carpet as he pranced in circles around the room. "Have you heard anything from Otto? Did he find a buyer?"

---

3. And robbing his mansion, of course. The Bearded Syndicate weren't going to send their acquisition specialist out as an errand boy without putting him to good use.

Otto Mills was either the second or third[4] conspirator in Bartholomew's retirement scheme. Describing him as a friend would have been a step too far in Bartholomew's estimation. Otto was more of an intriguing acquaintance, one of the few warlocks who managed to operate on the fringe, talented enough to survive but wise enough not to overstep his bounds and anger The Syndicate. Where Bartholomew couldn't sell lemonade to a man crawling across a desert, Otto had a long list of seedy black-market contacts. He'd agreed to find a buyer in exchange for an even split of the profits from the amulet's sale.

"There's a few interested parties," Bartholomew answered without averting his gaze. His fingers swirled the quill in his hand, creating smooth curves along the paper. The white ink was difficult to spot on the page. There was no way to doublecheck the runework.

Bartholomew trusted himself. He pressed the paper to his cuts. One by one, the skin began to heal.

Part of him was relieved that nothing had gone wrong. A louder part insisted he'd never been concerned.

"That sounds like a no," Gizmo said, dropping into a sploot on the carpet behind Bartholomew. "You ought to just stick some plasters on your face instead. Otto isn't going to buy you supplies out of pocket. He already gave you part of your share upfront so you could get somewhere safe."

"I'm well aware, Gizmo," Bartholomew snapped. He'd lived a century and a half, yet the familiar lectured him like a child. "Why do you think I'm taking care with my appearance today?"

---

4. The discrepancy depends on who was asked. Bartholomew, who didn't count Gizmo as a person, would have called Otto the second conspirator and his only accomplice. Gizmo, who did count himself, saw Otto as the third.

Gizmo's ears pricked up higher. He tilted his head, black and fluffy and with features very similar to a teddy bear. His tail rose to the alert. "You've found somewhere safe for us to retire?"

"For *me* to retire." The distinction seemed important to Bartholomew. He'd been the one doing most of the work. Gizmo just loaned him power. "And yes, I have." He paused, trying to build a sense of dramatic tension before revealing the home he'd found.

"Where? Europe? South America? Say we're not just going to Canada." Gizmo's yapping ruined the moment.

"No, we're—ugh." Bartholomew clenched his jaw and shoved the cork back onto the white ink. Had he really missed Gizmo? The familiar only ever managed to talk through significant moments.

With a scowl, Bartholomew spun around to face the small, black-furred, pink-tongued, tail-wagging dog. "We're going to the last place anyone would look for me," he snapped. "The suburbs."

THREE

Mill Run Heights was a small subdivision two hours north of the city. It consisted of one hundred and forty-four cookie cutter houses with white walls, red roofs, and manicured green lawns, all arranged in neat rows across fifteen rectangular blocks[1]. According to the ordinances of the development, no home was permitted a basement or a fence, permissible garden plants were limited to select native species, and all visible decorations had to be approved by a committee.

In short, Mill Run Heights was dull, boring, and mundane, the antithesis of magic. Anyone with a hint of creativity or uniqueness would shudder at the thought of a shared swimming pool that had little old ladies instead of life-guards, though they were passionately devoted to saving people from the horror of crumbly foods, sticky popsicles, or splashing children; flee in the face of monthly barbeques with loud-mouthed men who boasted about the cost of their grills and parroted stock market predictions that they'd googled the night before; and be repelled by the sight of the stay-at-home mothers, marching the perimeter every morning in matching tracksuits and

---

1. As everyone knows, rectangles are the least magical of shapes.

high ponytails while they discussed the latest parenting faux-pas of one of their members[2].

No warlock in their right mind would venture into such a place willingly.

Which made it the perfect place for a dead one to hide.

Their taxi stopped before a two-story building, almost identical to its neighbors. The red doors opened to a living room. Couples milled about within, talking with their heads close and pointing to the ceiling and floors as they attempted to re-envision the space. A sign stuck in the center of the lawn showed a short-haired brunette in a sensible gray suit, smiling beside the words *Open House*.

"Number forty-two A," the taxi driver announced from the front seat. "Looks like a popular place. You thinking of throwing your hat in the ring?"

Bartholomew's lips tightened, and he gave the driver a suspicious glance. He looked like a thin, clean-shaven boy, but The Syndicate had spies everywhere. "I haven't got a hat. Are you suggesting I look like someone who should?"

"No, sir," the boy stammered, thrown off by the harsh, old voice that snapped at him. "I only was asking, if you were hoping to move here."

---

2. When Bartholomew had first visited Mill Run Heights, he'd overheard them discussing a disastrous birthday party which had featured gendered balloons, cancelled artists, and a gluten-full cake.

Bartholomew scowled. The driver was far too nosy for his liking. Without answering, he shoved a hundred into the boy's hand[3] and climbed from the car.

"So long then! Thanks for not hitting the brakes too hard," Gizmo said cheerfully[4] and jumped onto the pavement after his master. He looked around the street, and his tail appeared to be having a seizure. "This looks nice!"

Bartholomew had been checking the interior pockets of his suit for his inks and quill, but at the familiar's words, his fingers fumbled the feather. It floated to the green lawn beneath the sign.

"No, it looks terrible," Bartholomew grumbled, scowling at his familiar as he was forced to bend over to collect his quill. Gizmo never understood. "That's the point. No one will look for us here. Now, don't talk when we get inside. Dogs can't speak." His countenance grew darker as he saw the cheerful, fluffy black demon at his heels as they walked up the four steps to the door. "I don't know why you chose that form."

Gizmo barked. As far as he knew, cats couldn't talk either, nor could they follow commands, or walk around off leash without drawing

---

3. Considering the trip cost half that amount, this was a rather generous gesture on Bartholomew's part, though quite accidental. He had little experience with taxis and less with paying. But given his sour demeanor and his familiar's later error, few would argue that the poor driver didn't deserve the tip.

4. Gizmo, who had even less experience interacting with humans than Bartholomew, didn't notice the wide-eyed, slack-jawed stare that followed his comment. Though unlike his master, he would have felt guilty to know that the driver would later confide of the experience to his friends and henceforth be considered a bit loopy thereafter.

attention. But he wasn't one for arguing[5], and the interior of lot 42A was far more interesting to the demon, who'd visited many a warlock den, haunted mansion, and cursed cave, but very few suburban homes.

To the average person, its layout might have been unremarkable, but Gizmo was amazed by the sense of space in the large room. The bottom floor was open plan. No walls separated the granite kitchen counters from the mahogany decked dining area or the gray couches of the den. Only the powder room was sectioned off.

Upstairs were the bedrooms. Gizmo overheard a couple speak of them in plural, and immediately dashed up the stairs to see for himself[6].

Bartholomew remained below. He scanned the crowd until he found a pair that weren't a young couple, giddy with the dream of owning their own home and blissfully unaware that between a mortgage, taxes, and the inevitable cost when just about everything broke, it would have been cheaper to rent.

In the corner of the kitchen were two women. The first was a short woman in a baggy shirt, with gray streaks in her bun and circles beneath her eyes. Beside her, dressed in a flared navy skirt, with brown hair held back with a gold clip, was the realtor. Bartholomew recog-

---

5. Unless he was in the mood for it.

6. To fully understand, Gizmo's excitement, it's important to note that since rising from the underworld, he'd been forced to share a room with Bartholomew. They'd lived in a small, single room apartment in the city, and though their job saw them housed in many luxurious manors, no one had ever offered Gizmo his own room as it was customary for a familiar to share with his master, and he'd have hated to seem rude by requesting one. But the idea of having his own space very much excited him.

nized her from the sign and correctly deduced that the woman with her must have been the one selling the house— Heather Anderson.

He'd done his research on the property. Mill Run Heights, Number 42A, belonged to an elderly gentleman by the name of Clifford Anderson. He'd lived in the property for fifty years, the past ten of which he'd lived alone, dedicating himself to the neighborhood as president of the Home Owner's Association. Everyone assumed he'd have died on the property. However, after a recent stroke, his daughter had convinced him to move to Dallas and live with her family down there. He'd gone ahead, and she'd remained to collect his belongings and oversee the sale.

Which meant it was Heather that Bartholomew needed to speak with now.

He sauntered toward the two women and cleared his throat.

Both turned and assessed the man standing before them.

Heather would remember the boyish curls that formed ringlets by his ears, the intense gaze, unnerving and intriguing at the same time, and the tight set of his lips. They gave him the permanent appearance of a man who'd bitten into a lemon and ruined what she might otherwise have considered a handsome face.

The realtor, whose full name was Karen Archer, was less offended by Bartholomew's sour expression. She thought he was handsome[7], though perhaps too thin for her taste. Her main impression of him, however, was that he was rather fidgety, for his fingers flitted before him like he was weaving a web.

Both women noticed and would remember that Bartholomew was tall and impeccably dressed.

---

7. Though she would soon deny this fact, especially to herself, as Bartholomew's personality revealed itself.

"I'll take it," he announced, and followed up the bold statement with his offer[8].

"Oh, um, that's—" Heather, who was sleep deprived, exhausted, and simply wanted the entire process to be finished so she could return to her husband and kids, struggled to find the appropriate response.

"Thank you for the offer, Mr—" Karen paused, waiting for Bartholomew to supply his name.

"Whit— Bartlow." He cleared his throat. "Bartholomew Bartlow."

Karen frowned. She'd mistaken his initial fumble for a flirtatious attempt to call himself witty and was deciding whether to judge him for it or simply be relieved that he'd reconsidered before embarrassing them all. At any rate, it meant that she didn't dwell much on his actual name or start questioning what kind of parent would have named their son something that shortened to Bart Bart[9].

"You won't get a better offer," Bartholomew said, addressing his statement to Heather.

"Excuse me, Mr. Bartlow," Karen answered for her client, crossing her arms and stepping between the two. She stuck her chin forward and narrowed her eyes[10] "This is a prime piece of real estate. Mill Run Heights is the ideal place for a young couple looking to start a family, and Mr. Anderson kept his home in pristine condition. We've already

---

8. The vast majority of the money in Bartholomew Bartlow's account was considerably below the asking price.

9. And to Karen's credit, even if she had questioned it, she would have done so quietly and to herself, for she had a special sympathy for people with unfortunate names.

10. Which were brown, if it's of interest to you. It certainly wasn't to Bartholomew, who would have no idea what color Karen's eyes were for many years.

had better offers than yours, and I expect we'll be flooded with more before the end of the day. But if you'd like to purchase something more in your price point, I'll be happy to help you."

This last part was, of course, a lie. Karen could already tell that Mr. Bartlow was the type of person you helped out of a sense of unavoidable moral obligation or desperate financial need, not because it would bring any semblance of joy.

Still, she held out a business card, certain that she would regret it.

Bartholomew's fingers, acting of their own accord, plucked it and slipped it into his pocket without looking at the realtor.

"The decision is yours, Miss Anderson," he said. His height meant that Karen's body did little to stop him from seeing Heather. Indeed, Bartholomew barely noticed that the realtor was there. "I'll be here an hour. Come find me when you're ready."

Karen scoffed as Bartholomew sauntered off once more. She turned to her client. "Can you believe? The nerve of that man?" At least, she thought it would make accepting a better offer all the sweeter.

Until fifteen minutes later, when the complaints began, viewers started shouting, and both of their previous offers were withdrawn.

FOUR

As you might well have guessed, Bartholomew wasn't standing idly in a corner those fifteen minutes.

He'd fully expected that his offer might be rejected, in fact, he was pleased when it was. It would have been a shame to come prepared for nothing. Plus, an initial defeat made his gloating all the sweeter when he eventually got his way.

While couples cooed over the large windows and debated the necessity of the master bathroom's bidet, Bartholomew slipped behind them unseen, quill in his hand.

In his former life, the warlock's talent as an Acquirer had been undeniable though the reason for it had been much debated. Many[1] attributed his ability to Gizmo. This assumption was not without cause. Having a great demon as a familiar provided a considerable boost to Bartholomew's magic. But a few dissenting voices claimed that there was more to it than that.

Bartholomew was too sly, too presumptuous, too damned sure of his own brilliance. All his years spent ignoring the rest of them, locked in a room pouring over books, had lead him to discoveries.

---

1. Though notably, not Bartholomew himself.

And there was only one thing warlocks sought to learn: runes.

The forgotten language of magic was the doorway to their enchantments. But, unsurprisingly given the name, few symbols remained common or even uncommon knowledge. When a warlock had the wit and talent[2] to discover a rune, he treated it like the last chocolate in a box. He might feign ignorance (*I've never heard of chocolate, much less held one trapped in a box.*), or force everyone to watch in jealousy as he indulged (*Oh, mmm, this is the best chocolate I've ever had in my life. I'll just let it melt on my tongue for the next ten minutes.*) But one thing was certain: A warlock with a secret rune never shared it.

Bartholomew Whitlock, and therefore by extension Bartholomew Bartlow, knew several and, equally important, he knew the best inks to write them in[3]. There were, after all, some benefits to spending two decades with no friends[4], locked in a library with a set of dusty old books, a dripping quill, and a fluttering set of fingers.

He knew runes that could force traps and secrets to reveal themselves, runes that could reach into the past and guess at the future, runes that could change what a person saw.

And he put all of this knowledge to use in Mr. Anderson's house.

Bartholomew wove three symbols into a large rune: a blue for *show*, a pink for *past*, and a brown for *worst*. He painted it beneath the bath-

---

2. Or, in most cases, the dumb luck and bullheadedness.

3. If runes were doorways to enchantments, then ink was the key to unlock them. Otherwise, you might end up doing something silly, like writing a healing rune in indigo or a stability rune in brown.

4. Except of course for Gizmo, though Bartholomew would be aghast to learn that his familiar considered them such.

room cupboards, on the walls in the bedrooms, under the banister of the staircase, and wherever else he could flit his quill without being noticed. The more the ink sank in, the more the appearance of the previously pristine home began to shift.

"There's black mold under two of the sinks," one girl whispered to her partner. She'd majored in biology and taken an undergraduate course in mycology. He'd studied marketing and finance, so naturally needed to double check her assessment by going to one of the bathrooms himself.

"Holy—" He coughed and slammed the cupboard door. "There's no way we're buying this place at that price just to spend a month getting that removed.[5] His voice was loud and annoyed. It traveled beyond the confines of the bathroom, and soon all of the would-be-buyers[6] were hunting for imperfections in the building.

"Oh my God, the stairs are broken!" One of them gasped and pointed to a section of the banister that appeared to be rotting. "Are those termites?"

"There's grout on the tiles in this shower," someone else complained, and soon more voices of dissent swept through the house.

"This wall looks like someone's punched it."

"I think a rat's taken a poop under the bed."

Bartholomew pulled a gold pocket watch from the top pocket of his suit. One side of his lips tilted upward so that there appeared to be a vertical pink slash across his face. It was, in fact, his version of a smile.

He watched the seconds tick past, listening to the frantic footsteps of viewers as they hurried from the house. In the kitchen, Karen's voice

---

5. For any concerned reader, please be advised that it does not take one month to remove black mold.

trembled with poorly concealed panic as she tried to reassure Heather that everything was fine even though both previous offers had been rescinded.

"It's a great place. We just did an inspection, there's no way we could have missed—"

"Well, obviously, we did. It isn't in good condition at all," Heather said. She'd swept through the house, seen the many issues that had suddenly arisen, and arrived at the only logical conclusion her sleep-deprived mind could draw. "Maybe all the people moving around in here just made the problems clearer."

Karen, who had significantly more experience in showing houses, shook her head. "No, black mold doesn't just appear overnight." She looked around the room and saw Bartholomew, leaning against the corner, staring at his pocket watch with an unquestionably smug expression. "He did this." She pointed toward him. "He sabotaged everything."

Ah, that's my cue, Bartholomew thought, and he pocketed his watch and stepped forward, holding his arms open in what might have been a display of innocence if he'd managed to fake humility. "You think I slipped in here with rats and termites in my pockets just to plant them in the house?"

Everything about his tone suggested that this was exactly what Bartholomew had done. Karen wanted to scream *yes,* but it was so absurd that she was forced to swallow the suggestion. Logically, she couldn't see how the man before her could be responsible for the sudden appearance of the house. But something in her gut insisted that he was.

"Of course not, Mr. Bartlow," Heather said, giving her realtor a look that meant *keep quiet.* "I imagine you noticed the issues before you made your offer and that was why you were so confident, correct?"

It was such a delight when humans explained his actions for him. That was the perfect excuse.

Bartholomew scoffed as if he had always intended it to seem that way. "Obviously."

A feeling of relief washed over Heather. "So your offer still stands then?"

"What? No." Karen's eyes widened. She leaned toward her client. "You can't seriously intend to sell to this man. We can fix up the house and get you twice as much."

This might have been enough to ruin Bartholomew's plan had Heather been a woman desperate to make a dollar. But her husband was a chemical engineer who made enough that he could've comfortably supported a family of ten. She had no interest in extending her stay and just the thought of haggling with contractors made her stress levels rise.

So, despite Karen's whispered objections and silent fury, Heather accepted the warlock's offer.

And one week later, Bartholomew Bartlow was the proud owner of his very first suburban home.

FIVE

Bartholomew scowled at the empty open space that was his new house. He hadn't realized the furniture wasn't included in his purchase and was currently feeling rather cheated. Most of the advance Otto had given him had vanished in the purchase. Bartholomew might be stuck sleeping on the floor if his accomplice didn't find a buyer for the amulet soon.

At the thought of the precious item, his hand slipped into his suit. His fingers flitted over the bottles of ink, creeping down to where the gold necklace was zipped into the silk blue lining.

"Oh boy, Bart!" Gizmo shouted as he zoomed in circles in the center of floor. "This sure is exciting! I've got so much room to run. We should make an obstacle course."

Bartholomew scowled at the ankle-high black powder puff of a demon. He didn't understand his familiar. Gizmo used to be able to fly. What fun was running with teeny little legs? At least as a cat, he could've climbed trees.

"We're going to fill it with as much furniture as we can find once Otto pays us," Bartholomew grumbled, staring at the cream walls on the far side of the living area and feeling his skin crawl. He missed his cramped apartment in the city, so full of books and supplies that he'd barely had room to walk. The absence of things made him uneasy[1]. "Nobody needs this much space."

"Quite right," Gizmo said, stopping suddenly and tilting his head. "Perhaps I should take the large room[2] upstairs? Just so you don't feel uncomfortable, I mean." He trembled as he waited for a response.

"Yes, fine." Bartholomew flicked his hand in dismissal. He was barely listening to the familiar. Something had caught his eye through the large window beside the door.

Someone was walking toward his house.

"Okay!" Gizmo's tail thumped against the floor with the fury of a metronome attempting to keep up at a rave. He'd had his eye on the massive bedroom since their first visit to Mills Run and was already beginning to imagine how he might decorate his new space. Visions of plush pillows, buckets of bones, and a stuffed squeaky unicorn filled his mind.

Bartholomew pulled his hand from the amulet and up to his quill. His fingers tapped the feather as he approached the door.

He pulled it open.

A man in a blue baseball cap stood on the step, his hand poised to knock. He wore a gray t-shirt and a pair of jeans. There was a set of papers in his hand.

---

1. Although this might seem strange to the average person, this feeling was quite common among warlocks, who tended to spend large swathes of time hiding in libraries and scheming in underground dens.

2. Most people would have called it the master bedroom, but Gizmo was careful to avoid that term lest it make Bartholomew suddenly insist on claiming it for himself.

"Oh, you're quick on the draw." He laughed and extended his arm with a smile. "I'm Dan Miller. I live over in 46A, right beside the park. Nice to meet you, neighbor."

Bartholomew's eyes narrowed at the offered hand. The use of the word *draw* seemed an obvious allusion to runework. But he'd vetted the area beforehand. The Millers were your typical suburban family: husband, wife, and three children. Except that instead of being gainfully employed, Dan spent his days at home fiddling with computers[3]. Could a bearded stranger have bribed him to spy on his new neighbor?

"Who sent you?" Bartholomew asked, ignoring the offered hand.

Dan stared at him, brow furrowing beneath his cap, trying to process a number of things at once. He'd never had anyone decline a handshake before, which had thrown him off, but beyond that, there was Bartholomew's voice. From his smooth skin and full head of curls, Dan had placed his new neighbor at about thirty, but he sounded like an old man, shaking a cane and yelling at kids to get off his lawn.

Finally, he at least wrapped his head around the question. "Oh, you think I'm only here because my wife sent me." Dan laughed. "I'm not one of those guys. I'm always excited to welcome someone new to Mills Run. Although, I must admit that I do have an ulterior motive this time."

Ah ha! Bartholomew thought. *I knew it!*

Dan separated one of the pages from his bundle and held it out.

---

3. Dan Miller was a private contractor who worked from home designing custom blockchain for company websites and applications. However, given that Bartholomew's formative years occurred at a time when most streets were lit by torches and horses were more common than cars, he can probably be forgiven for not understanding this.

As matter of course, Bartholomew didn't accept things from strangers[4]. It was too easy to mark them with runes and lay traps for the unsuspecting. But he craned his neck further through the door so that he could get a better look at the paper.

It was a bright orange flyer with an image of Dan Miller smiling on the front. Above him was a nonsensical question: **Want more fun for Mills Run?** And beneath it read: **Vote Dan the Man for HOA President.**

"Hoe-Ah?" Bartholomew's eyes narrowed, and he attempted to sound out the letters.

"The Homeowner's Association," Dan explained, still smiling. "Mr. Anderson who used to live here was the president, and he did a great job, but—" He leaned closer, a guilty expression on his face. Dan wasn't the type who liked to speak poorly of anyone, but he whispered, "He was old, you know? A bit out of touch with some things. There's a lot of rules that we'd love to change. Do you know I can't even put a trampoline on my lawn for the kids?"

"That's ridiculous," Bartholomew said. He was speaking about the fact that Dan wanted to purchase a trampoline in the first place. In Bartholomew's opinion, children ought to have been kept indoors, preferably out of sight, where they could read books and study. Once they'd educated themselves to a level capable of rational thought and engaging philosophical debate, they could emerge[5]. But they'd certainly have no use for anything as frivolous as a trampoline.

---

4. Or, truthfully, most acquaintances.

5. In Bartholomew's estimation, this meant that more than half the population would never leave their houses. He considered this an additional benefit as opposed to a flaw.

Dan, thinking he was speaking to a normal person and not a hundred-and-fifty-four year old warlock, assumed that Bartholomew was agreeing with him. He grinned. "Exactly. Thanks, uh..." He paused. "Sorry, I didn't catch your name."

"Bartholomew."

"Well, it's great to meet you, Bart. Do you mind if I call you that?"

"Yes."

Dan, who asked because he knew it was the polite thing to do and not because he actually expected an objection, didn't hear the response. He continued talking, a broad smile on his face. "I'm thrilled to have some more young people in the community who get it. You know, we're having a barbecue tonight. You should stop by."

Bartholomew, who had never been invited to an event that wasn't work related, was so confounded by the invitation that his hand jumped out from within his jacket and accepted the flyer when Dan offered it once more. The feel of the paper in his fingers shocked him, and he stepped back and slammed the door at once.

Gizmo sat behind him, head titled to the side and tail vibrating once more. "He seems nice. What should we wear to his party? I saw a dog on a television show with a bowtie. Do you think we could buy me one?"

"No."[6] Bartholomew scowled. "And what are you talking about *we*? I didn't hear him invite you." He walked toward the kitchen where he'd left his single brown bag of belongings. At least, the counters gave some semblance of a blockade from all the emptiness.

---

6. The warlock regretted this answer almost at once. A bowtie might have given Gizmorgoth an air of formality that his current form seriously lacked. However, Bartholomew hated television and had an immediate negative response to anything related to one.

"Well, he didn't see me or I'm sure I'd have been included," Gizmo said, trotting at Bartholomew's heels. "And it would be terribly rude for you to leave me behind and go have fun without me."

"Parties aren't fun," Bartholomew objected. He could think of little worse than milling about among a large group of people who would expect him to engage in discussions on trivial matters like which magazine model wore the prettiest outfit or which ball-thrower kicked it furthest.

"Do you mean we're not going to go?" Gizmo's ears drooped. He lay flat on his belly, chin on his front paws, staring up at Bartholomew with big eyes. It was objectively adorable.

Perhaps even the warlock might have felt a twinge of guilt had he looked down and seen the demon's sad but hopeful face. But Bartholomew had retrieved a notebook and pen from his bag and was writing a message.

"We don't have time for socializing with humans," the warlock said. He ripped out the page, folded it, and slipped it into his pocket.

Gizmo whined in disagreement. The sound grated Bartholomew's ears. "What else do we have to do? You've already hung up your spare suits, and you've only a few books and your inks to unpack."

Bartholomew snorted. He could have given the familiar a long list of things more important than a party, starting with securing the perimeter of their new home and ending with cutting his toenails. But in order to draw protective runes, Bartholomew would need more ink. There was only one way he could think to get that.

"We're going to deliver a message to Otto."

SIX

In the modern world, there are a number of efficient ways of communicating across long distances while masking your location: there are apps on tablets, burner phones, laptops with VPNs. Any of these would have been better than what Bartholomew and Otto had arranged.

To the northeast of the city was a small nature reserve. In the center of it was an old oak tree with a large hole that had once been home to a family of squirrels. The two warlocks had agreed to leave one another messages within.

"But I thought you told Otto that you were leaving the country," Gizmo said, trotting at Bartholomew's heels across the soft grass.

"I did," the warlock said, pulling the hood of a bright yellow raincoat over his head. He'd purchased it at a shop near the entrance to the reserve as an extra precaution. Members of The Syndicate seldom went for strolls in the woods, but there might be some other creature who'd recognize him. He couldn't risk rousing suspicion[1]. "As far as Otto knows, I'm settled in China by now."

"And flew all the way back just to put a letter in a tree?" Gizmo didn't see how that could make any sense.

Bartholomew rubbed his temples, frustrated by his familiar's question. He didn't notice the bold chipmunk creeping along a log, trying to catch a better glimpse of the face beneath the yellow raincoat.

But Gizmo did. He bounced forward and released a ferocious *yip, yip, yip.* The chipmunk turned tail and fled in fear, much to the demon's delight. His powers may have been diminished, but Gizmorgoth of Darkness could still vanquish his foes. He looked up at Bartholomew, hoping for[2] a thank you. A nod of recognition would have thrilled him.

Bartholomew groaned. He could think of few noises more annoying than Gizmo's bark. "Obviously, I wouldn't fly back from China. I'd use a teleportation rune to send the letter."

Despite the warlock's utter lack of appreciation, Gizmo continued to scan the woods for more attacks. Something about this arrange-

---

1. Unfortunately, though it didn't occur to Bartholomew, if you want to walk unnoticed through a nature reserve, wearing a three-piece suit with a bright yellow raincoat is not a good idea, particularly when it's sunny. Three school-aged boys followed him laughing for a good ten minutes. Two young women assumed he was having a psychotic break and debated calling the police. And he was the chief item of gossip among the squirrels, chipmunks, and deer for the next month.

2. Though admittedly not expecting.

ment still wasn't making sense to him. "But you don't know any teleportation runes."[3]

Bartholomew scowled. He didn't like to be reminded of what he didn't know. "But Otto will assume that I do. It's quite clever, don't you see? He'll think I'm even more powerful, which will make him afraid to betray me to The Syndicate."

Gizmo nodded, not because he did see, but because it was a natural movement for his head to make while trotting. "I don't know why The Syndicate would go asking Otto questions about you when you're already dead."

"That's because you don't think," Bartholomew said, turning his head to either side and trying to remember where precisely the oak tree in question was. "What if Otto slips up and gets caught trying to sell the amulet." He tried to remember the directions he'd memorized. *A hundred paces east, then a forty-five degree turn clockwise, and another fifty-five paces.* That was right! He turned east again, and continued explaining the situation to his familiar. "The Questioners aren't exactly known for their polite conversation. Otto might rat me out, and they'll come looking at once."

Another twenty-one paces, and Bartholomew saw the oak, leaves broad and green. There was a hole in the center of its trunk, six feet up from where one of its roots rose free from the earth. He hurried forward, forgetting to act aloof for the moment, and peered in.

He hoped to find a message from Otto already inside. Maybe he'd already found a buyer. Then, Bartholomew could stop worrying

---

3. And even if Bartholomew had, he still wouldn't have known the runic name for the oak tree in question, which he would have needed if he wanted to teleport a letter into its trunk from halfway around the world.

about how he was going to fund his retirement and start focusing on stockpiling furniture for his new home.

A small slip of paper waited for him in the tree. He pulled it out eagerly. But all the note said was: *Good luck, my friend.*

Useless! Bartholomew ground his teeth and shoved the message back into the tree along with his letter. What was Otto doing wishing him *luck* anyway. Did he think Bartholomew was so inept that only a fluke would allow his plan to succeed?

Beside him, Gizmo was still trying to wrap his head around how exactly leaving messages in a tree was a good idea. "If Otto tells the Questioners that you're alive," he said as they began heading back toward the entrance to the reserve, "then won't he mention how you've been communicating too? And then, wouldn't The Syndicate send the Correctioners to stake out the woods? And then, wouldn't they see when you came into the reserve in person? And then—"

Bartholomew groaned. For the rest of their time in the reserve, he was forced to endure his familiar's barrage of questions. All in all, the warlock considered the trek a miserable experience.

But he ought to have seen it as a victory. For Bartholomew made one very wise decision on his first visit to the reserve. And had he only gone the once, his retirement might have been as peaceful as he envisioned, for despite the attention he attracted, no one recognized Bartholomew as the dead man from the news.

Alas, the warlock had spurned luck, and she would eventually return the favor.

SEVEN

It took two busses and a few miles of walking to travel between Mills Run and the nature reserve. Bartholomew and Gizmo stopped for food along the way, much to the demon's delight. He devoured a scoop of dog ice-cream and strutted across the sidewalk with a dried pig's ear between his teeth, so large that the familiar had to hold his head back to stop it dragging on the ground.

Meanwhile, the warlock's fingers patted and poked at his wallet. It had grown thin, too thin.

"Don't expect any more of those," Bartholomew said, scowling at his familiar as they walked from the bus stop toward the Mills Run entrance. Gizmo, parading with his pig ear proudly in his mouth, looked far too happy for the warlock's liking. Their situation was desperate. The familiar should look as miserable as his master felt. "They're an expensive and unnecessary indulgence.[1] I can barely afford to feed myself."

---

1. The pig's ear in question had cost less than four dollars. Although still poorly versed in human pricing systems, Bartholomew recognized that this was not much in the grand scheme of things. But it would have given him some comfort to make Gizmo feel guilty.

Bartholomew looked at the fluffy, little demon, waiting for an apology.

"Buhr yuhr an ack-eye-ruhr." Gizmo said.

"Squids!" Bartholomew cursed. He bent over and snatched the pig's ear from the familiar's mouth. "What are you saying?"

Gizmo pouted[2] and stared up at the pig's ear, now well out of his reach in Bartholomew's hand. It wasn't often that he missed his powers, but had he the capability to burn the warlock's hand and force him to drop the treat, he would have done so in a heartbeat. "I said," Gizmo repeated, "*but you're an acquirer*. We don't need money. You can just acquire food."

"Oh really?" Bartholomew sneered and held up his hand to block the sun, which remained stubbornly high despite the late hour. "You think we'll stumble across an enchanted dungeon where someone hid a refrigerator full of steaks."

It was just then, that the smokey scent of barbequed chicken wafted into their nostrils.

"Well..." Gizmo started to say.

"Don't you dare."

They turned the corner onto the small green space, which had been designated as a park*ette* by the previous HOA president[3]. Before them,

---

2. Which is an expression that needs no description to any dog owner.

3. Mr. Anderson had given himself perhaps a few too many pats on the back for thinking to use a diminutive suffix to distinguish the small green strips on either side of the community center from the official Mills Run parks, which were just across the street. There were another six plots of land in the subdivision that had been allocated as protected wooded areas in order to appeal to eco-conscious home-buyers. Mr. Anderson's attempts to relabel them as *woodlets* had failed.

on the opposite side of the street, the source of the smell was evident: the Miller's Barbecue Party.

A group of far too many children[4] darted between lawn chairs, knocking paper plates from tables while laughing and tagging one another with their hands. Mothers, many with toddlers clinging to their necks or dishes in their hands, hurried behind, cleaning the mess, and shouting at the runners to slow down and be careful. When their instructions were inevitably ignored, they turned to commiserate with whoever was nearest. Gathered in the corner, were the men. Their backs were turned to the chaos, forming a protective circle around the smoking black grill.

Before it, Dan Miller grinned, tongs in one hand and a bottle of beer in the other.

Bartholomew stopped on the opposite side of the street. His desire for free food grappled with his hatred of people. There was still money in his pocket. He wasn't starving yet. It couldn't possibly be worth it.

Unfortunately, he hesitated a moment too long.

Dan turned and saw him.

"Hey, Bart!" Dan's smile grew larger. He stepped away from the barbecue, waving his tongs in greeting and, to Bartholomew's horror, began to cross the street. "Come on over." He clapped a hand on the warlock's shoulder and led the way.

Bartholomew was too confounded to resist. Gizmo barked in excitement and followed at their heels.

Dan glanced down at the small fluffy black dog. A number of questions crossed his mind. It wasn't often that he met a six-foot-three, single man in his thirties who lived alone with a toy poodle mix.

---

4. Bartholomew estimated about thirty. There were five.

But because he thought it would be rather rude to ask, Dan kept his questions to himself and instead jumped to the wrong conclusion.[5]

"You have got to meet my friend, Edward. I think you two would really hit it off.[6]" Dan's smile grew broader. He fancied himself an ally, and was now more determined than ever to make Bartholomew feel welcome in Mills Run. "Is this adorable little fellow okay with kids?"

It took Bartholomew more than a while to realize who Dan was talking about, and even then he was skeptical. No one had ever before called Gizmorgoth of Darkness, the great demon, an *adorable little fellow*. "Him?" The warlock pointed to his familiar. "Gizmo?"

"Oh, that's his name. Well, hi there, Gizmo." Dan bent down in the road, speaking to the demon as though he were a baby. "Aren't you a cutie?" He rubbed the top of the confused familiar's head, then looked up at Bartholomew. "Gremlins fan, eh?"

"I have absolutely no idea what you're talking about."

Dan, who once again mistook his new neighbor for a normal person, assumed this was a joke and laughed. "Well, once he's good with kids, he's welcome to come to all the barbecues too. One of the other couples bring their yorkie sometimes. Maybe they can play."

---

5. Of course, it Dan Miller's defense, it would have been even stranger if he'd jumped to the right conclusion.

6. Edward Price was a graphic artist who specialized in creating custom characters and sprites. Given his introversion, love of reading, and talent at drawing, Bartholomew probably would have liked him, at least as much as the warlock liked anyone. But given that Dan knew little about his new neighbor, he had no way of knowing that this would be true. Edward was just his only gay single friend.

Bartholomew, who still didn't know that his familiar was not currently a yorkie, thought to himself, *Oh, great. Just what I need. Two of them!*

Dan straightened and began shouting introductions to his friends as he continued to push Bartholomew forward. "This is 42A now, guys. Bart and his dog, Gizmo!"

"See? I told you I'd be invited too," Gizmo said, puffing his chest out as he walked.

Bartholomew's eyes widened. He bent down, grabbed the familiar, and stuffed the pig's ear into his mouth. Under his breath he hissed into Gizmo's ear. "Dog's don't talk, you idiot."

Thankfully, Dan and his friends were loud. Once the introduction had been made, they'd all started speaking at once, welcoming Bartholomew to the neighborhood with a mixture of genuine friendliness, bad puns, and tasteless jokes. They hadn't noticed the demon's voice mixed in with their own.

But someone else had. Someone who none of them had noticed.

EIGHT

S itting in the boughs of a maple tree at the edge of the property was an eleven-year-old girl with big square glasses, flat black hair, and cheeks that had never lost their baby fat. Her name was Sarah Anne Miller, but she was currently going through a phase where she introduced herself as Aurora Moon. It was far more unique and beautiful and better suited to an eccentric individual such as herself. Certainly, it was better than *Sarah*.

Eccentric had been one of the words in her vocabulary list last year and by far her favorite. It made Sarah think of clever old ladies who took their cats on strolls, handsome men who walked barefoot to be closer to the earth, and women with secretive smiles who kept collections of discarded socks. Fascinating people with fascinating lives.

Almost immediately, that word came to represent everything Sarah aspired to be. So while the other children, who were not her friends despite what her parents insisted, ran about playing pointless games of tag and hide-and-go-seek and what's the time Mr. Wolf, Sarah hid in the maple. She had a brown faux-leather notebook, which she'd requested for her birthday last year, and her favorite sparkly purple pen. Not pink, obviously. That was the color most girls liked. Purple was unique and individual, like the name Aurora Moon[1]. She intended to listen to the wind and write the poetry that it whispered to her. Though so far, she had only practiced the words *Aurora Moon* in a variety of different handwritings in the front of her notebook. But her muse had been interrupted by the sudden appearance of two strangers at her family's barbecue.

Eccentric was precisely the word Sarah would use to describe Bartholomew Bartlow. Despite the heat, he wore a black suit, a cream colored shirt, and a blue silk tie that matched the lining of his jacket. It was sunny, but there was a yellow raincoat in his arms, and his fingers tapped against a dried pig's ear as though he were composing a piano symphony in his head.

And beyond all that, his dog could talk.

Sarah had heard Gizmo's voice, clear and cheerful as he trotted across the street. If a talking dog wasn't eccentric, then she didn't know what was!

And suddenly, Sarah knew what to write. While her father and the other men laughed and joked around the grill, she listened from the tree, scribbling everything her new neighbor said in sparkly purple ink.

---

1. This was an accidentally apt comparison on Sarah's part. Purple is one of the most common favorite colors among women, losing by only a small margin to blue. And the name Aurora was currently one of the top 50 most popular girls' names. Sarah would have known all this if she'd ever researched either, but it's lucky she didn't. She'd have wanted to change her name to something dreadful like Hortensia Thimble and would have insisted her favorite color was orange, which she actually quite disliked on account of how terrible it looked with her complexion.

Bartholomew had no idea that his words were being recorded nor that he'd gained an admirer[2]. He stood amongst the men, gnawing on a delicious drumstick of chicken that Dan had slathered with his secret sauce[3]. It tasted so good that the warlock almost didn't regret attending. Though he did wish parties came with more food and less people. There was far too much talking, and while Bartholomew could tune out the tedious discussions about pre-school, and football, and market fluctuation, it was difficult to remain silent when questions turned to him.

"So, where you from, Bart?" Joe Baker[4] asked. The widow-peaked, baseball enthusiast lived in house 18B, near the entrance to Mills Run Heights. He was in his late thirties with two sons and one of the regulars at Dan's barbecues.

Sauce dripped from the corner of Bartholomew's lip and onto Gizmo's pig ear. The familiar happily stopped chewing long enough to lick it clean, while the warlock dabbed the rest with a napkin and considered his answer. Bartholomew Whitlock had been born in a large manor in New Hampshire before discovering his talents, meeting Gizmo, and moving to the city. Bartholomew Bartlow's identification card said that he'd been born in Illinois. Either way, he couldn't see

---

2. Not a romantic one, it should be noted. Sarah intended to live her life as a spinster, either in a cottage in the woods or an old theater that had been renovated into an apartment in the city. She would adopt five children, all of whom would be eccentric souls like herself, and each would have a special talent, so they would produce books and plays together. She also wanted a pet chinchilla.

3. It was a bottle of store-bought barbecue sauce that he mixed with ketchup.

4. Who, contrary to his name, was a Systems Analyst at a nearby firm. There, he went by Joseph.

what business it was of a man whose very last name hid the truth of his profession.

"Mills Run Heights, forty-two A," Bartholomew said, his lips tilting upward in a slashed smile. There was a dangerous glint in his eye that dared Joe Baker to ask again.

He was going for intimidating and off-putting, but in a way that struck the men with fear and awe. Instead, he was greeted with a round of laughter, and William Lee[5] clapped the warlock's arm. "I love it! Already a man of the community. What do you do, Bart?"

Bartholomew stared at the hand on his arm. Why did these men keep touching him? They were going to get sauce on his suit.

"I'm retired," he said, sliding away from William and accidentally bumping shoulders with Norm Jeffries[6] instead.

That earned another laugh.

"No, seriously," William tried again. "You work for a company in the city? You look corporate." He gestured to Bartholomew's suit.

"Certainly not." The warlock didn't want his neighbors associating him with the city in any way.

The men began exchanging looks that Bartholomew didn't understand. After a moment, Dan gave an awkward laugh. "You saying, you're seriously retired? At your age?"

Bartholomew's fingers tapped against his chicken bone. He was growing weary of all this prying. "I'm older than I look," he said. "I'm seven—" He looked down at Gizmo, who shook his head. "Fif—" He saw the skeptical faces of the men. "Thirty-five," he said with a sigh.

---

5. Another barbecue regular, whose family lived in 21B.

6. Norman Jeffries was the architect who had designed Mills Run Heights. He was also one of only six black men who owned property in the development.

"And already retired! Seriously, what did you do? I gotta change professions," Joe said.

Bartholomew ground his teeth. It was high time he left this party, and he had no intentions of attending another anytime soon. He glanced at Dan. "Is there more food inside?"

"Of course, yeah. I should've shown you right away!"

Dan, a more gracious host than Bartholomew perhaps deserved, smiled and led him to the kitchen[7] where a spread of casseroles was displayed on the counter. "Don't mind the guys. We're all just excited to have a new neighbor. But your finances are your own business. Help yourself."

He left the warlock and familiar alone in the kitchen.

Bartholomew rested Gizmo on the counter beside the dishes. The demon dropped his pig ear atop a dish of tuna casserole and sank his muzzle into the pasta.

"Creamy," he said.

Bartholomew wasn't interested in heavy ceramic dishes with half-eaten casserole. He found a reusable shopping bag folded beside the sink and began hunting through the cupboards. They were full of snacks and easy-to-make meals: macaroni and cheese, animal crackers, pudding cups. He flung a selection into the bag and then turned his attention to the fridge.

Jackpot, he thought.

---

7. Despite the Millers living in the largest, four-bedroom model, the kitchen and living space were Identical in design to Bartholomew's own. However, the Millers' kitchen was full of children's sippy cups, plastic plates and sporks, and the area beside it had a variety of furniture and more than a few toys on the floor.

Bartholomew took a few things, not much of course[8], and began to add them to his bag. He was considering if it would all fit or if he ought to grab another bag from the collection by the sink when Sarah Miller walked in.

"Are you stealing food?"

Bartholomew was still halfway in the fridge. At the sound of her voice, he jumped, and bumped the top of his head on the back of the tray. He rubbed it as he turned around.

At the sight of Sarah, leaning against the kitchen island with her faux-leather notebook and sparkling pen, his brow furrowed. She had a deep, unusually mature voice for a girl her age, and he'd been expecting an adult, not a chubby preteen in overalls and a purple shirt.

"Who the hell are you?" he asked. The warlock had thoroughly vetted Mills Run Heights and made a list of every resident. But he hadn't bothered with anyone under the age of eighteen. Why would he?

"Aurora Moon," Sarah said. "And I already know who you are. Bartholomew Bartlow. Funny name. Did people ever call you Bart Bart?"

"You've a funny name," Bartholomew said, closing the fridge and hefting the over full bag onto his shoulder. "Latin mixed with old English? And whoever heard of a moon at dawn? It's an oxymoron."

"Thank you," she said, making a mental note to look up the word *oxymoron* later. "How did your dog learn to talk?"

Gizmo, whose muzzle was now buried in a set of mashed potatoes, looked up at the mention of himself.

---

8. Just a tray of eggs, a container of milk, a loaf of bread, a bag of oranges, a package of tilapia, a jar of yogurt, a stick of butter, and some pre-cut slices of ham and cheese for Gizmo, who Bartholomew did think of on occasion.

I'm going to murder that idiot, Bartholomew thought. But it didn't matter if this girl had overheard him. She didn't matter. She was a child.

"He can't," Bartholomew said, shrugging his shoulder.

At the same time, Gizmo, who was also trying to cover his tracks, said, "Bark bark."

"Yes, see, just like that!" Sarah snapped her fingers and pointed at the fluffy black dog. "He just said *bark, bark.*"

"No, he didn't.[9]" Bartholomew shoved the pig's ear back into Gizmo's mouth before the demon could make any more stupid decisions, and scooped him into his arm.

With enough free food to last for the week, the warlock walked across the room, twisting between furniture and stepping over children's toys, toward the back door. He squeezed through and left the party, walking along the grassy lawns toward his own house. Everyone else was to the front, and they didn't notice him. It would have been a clean escape.

Except that Sarah followed him.

---

9. Some of you might recognize what Bartholomew was attempting to do as a form of psychological abuse called gaslighting. By lying to Sarah about what she very clearly witnessed, he hoped to make her question her own version of reality and doubt herself forever more. The implications of this might concern you, and you might be wondering how you can possibly root for a man would do such a thing to an eleven-year-old girl. But it is important to note two things in this scenario. First is that Bartholomew's attempts will not work, so you needn't worry about their long-term impact on Sarah's emotional well-being. Second is that as a young child, Bartholomew lost his favorite rubber ducky, which should account for, explain away, and allow you to empathize with much of his poor behavior.

"So, you're retired at thirty-five. You have a talking dog. And you steal food," she said.

"I didn't steal it," Bartholomew snapped. "I acquired it." He hoped she wouldn't ask him what the difference was. The question would have annoyed him greatly, in no small part, because he didn't know the answer.

"Oh you don't have to worry," Sarah said. "I won't tell. I'm an eccentric too. And I'm great at keeping secrets. One time, Mr. Graves lost his umbrella and had a panic attack. He wouldn't come out from under a tree until I got it for him. He made me promise not to tell anyone about his heliophobia, and I never did."

Bartholomew stopped just shy of his own back door. He stared down at Gizmo and saw the same flicker of concern in the demon's eyes.

The familiar, who couldn't see why he was pretending not to talk when Sarah already knew he could, turned to her and asked. "Who's Missa Gways?"

"See, he talked again!" She said, smiling in delight.

"No, he didn't." Bartholomew glowered at the familiar and shifted his arm so that he could clamp Gizmo's muzzle shut with his thumb and forefinger. "Who's Mr. Graves?"

"Oh, he's another eccentric. Like us," Sarah said. "I think we're the only three in Mills Run. He lives in 13B. But he doesn't come out much in the summer, you know, on account of all the sunshine. He's funny though, always drinking wine and dressing like it's the seventeen hundreds."

A sense of foreboding crept up Bartholomew's arms, chilling the back of his neck. But he tried to shake it off. What did some child know? He'd vetted the neighborhood, done his research, found it to be one of the most magically deficient places in the world.

There was no way a vampire was living in Mills Run Heights.

NINE

That night, Bartholomew poured through his notes on the residents of Mills Run Heights. Nowhere in his list was any mention of a Mr. Graves. He'd recorded property 13B as unoccupied.

"How did you learn all of this anyway?" Gizmo asked, reading Bartholomew's notes over his knee.

The warlock sat cross-legged on the cream carpet in his new bedroom, the smaller of the two. He'd hung his suits in the cupboard and made a pillow from the shopping bag he'd taken from the Miller's house. His box of inks and quill rested in his lap.

"Mr. Anderson," Bartholomew said.

"The man who used to own this house?"

"Exactly. He was quite the busy body. Once I discovered this place, I disguised myself as a nurse and snuck into the hospital. He was very chatty. Told me everything about this place." Bartholomew ground his teeth. "But he never mentioned a Mr. Graves."

"Well, I doubt he gets out much. Most vampires don't," Gizmo noted. "You know, on account of the crumbling to dust in the sunlight." At mention of this, both warlock and familiar looked toward Bartholomew's jacket, hanging in the built-in closet. There was a bulge in the interior pocket where The Amulet of the Impaler remained hidden. "You don't suppose—"

"No, I don't," Bartholomew snapped. "Because Otto is handling that side of things. If I cut him out of the deal, he'll definitely rat me out to The Syndicate. And anyway, there might not even be a Mr. Graves." He slammed the book shut. "That kid was probably making it all up. Little pest!"

"I thought she was quite nice," Gizmo said. "Struck me as an interesting sort."

"That's because you have no sense of discernment," Bartholomew grumbled, annoyed that his familiar was once again disagreeing with his objectively correct opinions. "You like everyone." He grabbed the book, stood, and rested it with the few others on the cupboard's shelf. There were only four[1]. He'd done his best to get them to stand upright like they would on a proper bookshelf, but as he added his notebook, they all flopped into a horizontal pile. The sight filled Bartholomew with a sense of frustration.

For almost a century and a half, the warlock had been a collector of books: good, bad, old, new, magical, and mundane. He wasn't terribly particular. The sight of the spines, the smell of the paper, and the sound of the pages as they turned were some of the few things that brought Bartholomew genuine joy. The few people who had visited his apartment had compared it to a public library.

But he'd had to leave all of that behind when he died.

Had he confessed his feelings to Gizmo, the familiar would have comforted him and reassured him that his retirement was a chance to begin his collection anew. It would have been a lovely bonding

---

1. These consisted of Bartholomew's notebook with all the information about Mills Run Heights; an old leather diary that had belonged to his mother; the philosophical writings of the great warlock, Walter Wiselheade, titled "The Wisdom of the Wise"; and a book of poetry by Emily Dickinson.

moment between the two, and Bartholomew would have felt much better afterward.

But a heart-felt conversation would have required the warlock to do a bit of soul searching and recognize the reason behind his emotions. In that moment, all he knew was that he was suddenly terribly annoyed, and he spun around to where Gizmo lay on the ground and snapped at the familiar. "What were you doing talking so much anyway, you foozler? You're going to get us found out!"

"Well she'd already heard," Gizmo objected. He'd left his beloved half-chewed pig's ear in his own room and was now licking the flavor from between the toes of his front paws. "Anyway, she's not going to tell anyone. She's great at keeping secrets."

"Oh really, like she kept quiet about Mr. Graves' heliophobia ?"

"You said she made him up."

"Yes, but—" Bartholomew's hands clenched in frustration. The damned demon had tricked him into arguing against himself. He didn't like feeling like he'd been outsmarted. It was particularly offensive when it was by his own familiar. He stomped his foot, grabbed his jacket from the hanger, and slipped his arms through, still clinging to his box of inks. "Well, come on then."

Gizmo stopped licking his paws and jumped to his feet, following Bartholomew out of the bedroom. "Where are we going?"

"To see if Mr. Graves exists, obviously!"

The two left Number 42A, stomping and trotting as suited their moods. It was approaching midnight, and the streets were dark and silent save for light from a laptop and the voice of a woman saying, "Aiden, are you still awake?" and the muffled, exasperated sounds that followed.

Number 13B was on the opposite side of the development, on the second street after the main entrance. It was a single story, one-bedroom house though it featured the same white walls, red roof, and open-plan as 42A. In accordance with the neighborhood's ordinances, there was no ornamentation on the lawn nor any decoration that might make it stand out from its neighbors.

Except, perhaps, the windows.

From where Bartholomew was standing across the street, the glass appeared to have been colored black with a permanent marker.

"Well, I think we can safely deduce that Miss Moon wasn't lying," Gizmo said.

Bartholomew ground his teeth. "Maybe it's abandoned. We need a closer look."

They crossed the street. Bartholomew lifted Gizmo with one hand, his other still clung to his box of inks. Both pressed their faces to the window.

The glass was dark, but if they squinted they could see thick black shades behind it, an extra blockade against the light.

"Maybe you can slip inside and see if there's a coffin," Bartholomew suggested.

"Me? How?"

"I don't know. Aren't you Gizmorgoth of Darkness? Turn into a shadow or command the door to open."

"We've been together for almost a hundred and forty years, and you think I can just blink and turn into a shadow?" Gizmo pulled his face from the window to stare at the warlock in offense. "Summon fire and darkness and nightmares, sure, but transform myself? Can you not feel how drained I am from changing my shape once? And you think I can just become a shadow?"

"I was speaking metaphorically," Bartholomew said, turning from the window as well and scowling at his familiar. "But you're small. We can break a hole in the glass and sneak you in and—"

A thin, raspy voice interrupted them. "Might I ask why your face is pressed to my window?"

Bartholomew's eyes grew wide. He blamed Gizmo entirely for not noticing that someone was approaching. Why had the familiar taken the form of a yappy dog if he couldn't at least bark in warning when someone was nearby.

Gizmo was too curious to blame anyone. He stretched, balancing his hindquarters on Bartholomew's arm and resting his front paws on the warlock's shoulder so that he could see who was behind them.

Mr. Graves was a man of middling height with skin so white it bordered on transparent. His face was wrinkled and his light hair streaked with gray so that he appeared to be a fit man in his sixties. He wore a high-waisted pair of brown trousers over a white button-down shirt, and a turquoise colonial jacket with puffed sleeves and floral embellishments along the collar. The style had gone out of fashion sometime in the eighteenth century. Although the night was cloudless, he carried a large black umbrella in one hand, which he used as a cane.

That's definitely a vampire, Gizmo thought.

A second later, Bartholomew turned, saw Mr. Graves, and came to an identical conclusion.

Now, if you're hoping for a twist, a reveal that both were wrong, and a lesson about making assumptions about pale men with anachronistic dress, you're about to be disappointed.

Bartholomew and Gizmo were correct.

Frederick Graves[2] was a vampire and had been for almost three hundred years. He had his reasons for living in secret in Mills Run Heights, but for now, it's enough to know that he wasn't keen on being discovered.

---

2. As he currently called himself.

He kept his lips closed as he smiled. His eyes, a pale blue that would have been labeled *cold* if their color was found in a pack of crayons, studied Bartholomew's face.

I know him from somewhere, Frederick thought. He searched through his mind, trying to place Bartholomew. But when you've lived[3] for three hundred years, it takes quite some time to search through all your memories. Frederick soon gave up.

Bartholomew used the vampire's momentary silence to invent an excuse. "Oh, do you live here?" He gestured to the house behind him. "I thought it was abandoned."

As the warlock waved at the wall, his fingers danced over the box in his hand.

Frederick's eyes latched onto it, narrowed, and grew wide. To the average person, the long, thin box, with its dark wood and smooth edges, was an unassuming thing. But Frederick had known warlocks in his day. He identified it at once.[4]

"And do you often stare into abandoned houses?" Frederick asked, hand tightening around his umbrella, ready to raise it and whack Bartholomew if he attempted to reach for his quill or any other rune he might have prepared beforehand.[5]

---

3. Or rather, been undead.

4. He did not, however, recognize Gizmo as a familiar, and his next few thoughts were as follows: "How did a warlock find me?", "Did Spudsy hire The Bearded Syndicate?" and "Why on earth has he got a poodle?"

5. An umbrella would not have been most vampires first choice in this situation, but hypnosis didn't work on warlocks, and Frederick had never figured out how to turn into a bat.

Bartholomew frowned, considering the question. He had no idea that he'd already been recognized as a warlock and was thinking of the best way not to blow his cover. Part of that involved snapping his fingers around Gizmo's mouth before he could speak. He heard the demon give a muffled snort of objection.

"Yes," Bartholomew said, trying to block out the sounds of Gizmo's complaining. "Of course, curiosity is a driver for most humans." *There,* he thought, *that'll stop him from being suspicious.* "Do you often stroll about at night?"

That wasn't the attack that Frederick had expected. The vampire's eyes narrowed and widened as he thought so he appeared a bit like an owl that was trying not to fall asleep. "Yes," he said, not certain what Bartholomew was playing at.

"Seems a bit unusual. Don't think that's a thing most humans do." Bartholomew was hoping to goad Frederick into hypnotizing him. In his experience, vampires tended to get lax when they believed a human under their spell. He might slip up and reveal something of himself.

"You're out walking about at night," Frederick noted.

Under his fingers, Bartholomew felt Gizmo's muzzle tremble as he tried to chuckle. He tightened his grip, pinching the demon's skin and finding something soft and mushy in his fur[6] much to the warlock's horror.

"True, I suppose it's a normal thing for humans to do after all." Bartholomew laughed. It sounded strange, almost as though an old man were coughing out the words *Ha. Ha. Ha.*

---

6. It was a bit of mashed potato from Gizmo's earlier dinner at the Miller's house

Frederick's eyes narrowed once more as he watched the warlock. He began to wonder if Bartholomew in fact had no idea who he was and their encounter was just a terrible coincidence.

"Indeed," Frederick agreed. "A very normal thing for a human like myself to be doing." He too attempted to laugh. It sounded like someone who'd lost their voice to a cold saying *Heh. Heh. Heh.*

Gizmo didn't understand why precisely either man was filling the air with horrible fake laughs, but it seemed to him like it would be much more fun keeping the noise than listening to it. He was quite annoyed with Bartholomew for stopping him from joining in.

The two men continued to laugh, watching one another for a moment. Bartholomew stepped to the side and turned, keeping an eye on the vampire as he backed down the street. "I'll just be heading home then," he said.

"As shall I," Frederick agreed, likewise keeping his eye on the warlock. It didn't escape his notice that Bartholomew was moving deeper into Mills Run Heights instead of leaving it.

Neither looked away until the warlock had turned the corner from sight.

As Frederick misted into his house, and Bartholomew hurried to his[7] a similar thought was going through both their minds.

Mills Run Heights wasn't big enough for a vampire and a warlock. One of them was going to have to go.

---

7. He didn't run, of course. That would have suggested that he was afraid, and Bartholomew was far too talented a warlock to worry about some old vampire in a turquoise coat. He did, however, speed-walk rather quickly while glancing over his shoulder a few times.

TEN

"Well, I can't see why we can't all stay," Gizmo said, chewing on the remaining stub of his pig's ear. He was lying on the carpet in Bartholomew's room, getting dizzy from watching the warlock pace. "If you're very careful, and you don't use much magic, and he's very careful and doesn't go flying around as a bat, maybe no one will notice."

Bartholomew walked in a circle[1] in the center of his room. Red streaks blazed through his eyes and dark bags hung beneath. His curls were wild and frizzy around his head and hints of stubble were appearing once more on his chin. Shadow and sunshine took turns falling across his face as he turned to and from the windows. It was already mid-afternoon, and the warlock had yet to sleep.

Not because he was afraid as Gizmo had so rudely suggested. But because he was thinking.

One warlock in a neighborhood could go unnoticed. He could lay his runes for warning and still be fine. But a warlock crafting magic,

---

1. The second most magical shape. A pentagram is, of course, number one, but it's very difficult to walk in the shape of a five-pointed star unless you've previously drawn an outline on the floor.

and a vampire hypnotizing the residents? It was too much, and he was certain Mr. Graves would feel the same.

He'll be after me now, Bartholomew thought. He could use the last of his inks to secure his house[2]. But what about the rest of the neighborhood? Although the warlock generally preferred his own company and solitude, he despised the feeling of being trapped. He would happily lock himself away and never leave his house. But only if it was his choice!

"I can't keep going through this with you, Gizmo," Bartholomew said, his hands jumping and twisting in the air as though they were speaking and not his lips. "We can't stay here. It'll be too risky."

"But I like it here," Gizmo complained, muzzle sinking to his paws. He'd already started making plans for his bedroom. The demon made his eyes big, peering up at the warlock.

Bartholomew glanced down and for a moment was forced to acknowledge that his familiar had mastered the art of being cute. But demons weren't supposed to be cute! He stopped pacing and threw his hands up in frustration. "Well, what do you suggest then? That we get rid of him? He was here first!"

"No, no. I mean, that would be rude," Gizmo admitted.[3] "But, maybe, if we talked to him…"

---

2. In his time as acquirer, Bartholomew had discovered a variety of protective runes that might stop a vampire from misting through his door.

3. Vampires, warlocks, and most other long-lived species typically believe that the individual who's lived in a location longest should have a say in the area at large. Otherwise, it would be hypocritical of them when they inevitably complain about humans buying up properties near their homes and converting them into shops that sold crotcheted foods and polished rocks.

"He'd attack us or turn us in to The Syndicate," Bartholomew snapped. "You're too naïve, Gizmo." He stomped his foot against the ground, mind made up. "We'll have to go." The warlock adjusted his jacket and stomped out the door.

"What? Right now?" Gizmo asked, leaping after him down the steps. "At least let me say goodbye."

"No not—" Bartholomew stopped before the front door, slipping his feet into a pair of black dress shoes. "Who do you have to say goodbye to?"

"There's my bedroom, and our new friend, and a maple outside that I'm very fond of peeing on for starters."

Bartholomew groaned and rolled his eyes. There were so many ridiculous things about the familiar's statement, he almost didn't know where to begin. No, in fact, he did. "We are not friends with a child," he insisted, heading out the door and walking down the street.

"Well, you haven't got to be if you don't want," Gizmo admitted, wondering where they were going. "But I don't think you can afford to be too choosy."

Bartholomew stopped before the Miller's house and scowled at his familiar before walking up the steps toward their front door. "I have friends."

"Really? Name one besides me."

"We're not friends. You're my familiar. I'm your master. And there's, well, there's Otto and..." Bartholomew's jaw tightened. "I don't have to explain myself to you. You're a dog. Now remember that and don't talk when we get in." He knocked.

A girl with square glasses, frizzy dark hair, and wearing a red dress that made her look more than a bit like an apple opened the door.

"You?" Bartholomew's eyes widened in shock at the sight of Sarah Anne Miller, who if you might recall he believed to be named Aurora

Moon and as such hadn't assumed that she was in any way connected to Dan Miller.[4]

"Hello Ms. Moon," Gizmo greeted her, wagging his tail quite happily.

Bartholomew glared at him.

Sarah, delighted at being called by her currently preferred name, beamed at the two. "Have you come to see me?"

"Certainly not," Bartholomew snapped. "We've come to use the phone. Where are the people who live here?"

"My mum's taken the twins to the park, but my dad's in his office."

As though he'd heard himself mentioned, Dan shouted from upstairs. "Sarah, are you talking to someone?"

Sarah pursed her lips, annoyed with her father for interrupting her conversation. "It's my new friends," she yelled. Her voice was so loud that Bartholomew's hand leaped toward his ears, and Gizmo[5] buried his face in his paws. "They want to use the phone!"

There was a pause. Then Dan shouted back, "Okay! Have fun."[6]

Sarah beckoned them in, leading the way to the kitchen.

---

4. This was compounded by the fact that while both Dan and Lisa Miller were light-eyed blonds of mixed European ancestry, Sarah was Korean.

5. Whose ears were permanently up and therefore more challenging to cover

6. At this point, you might be wondering what kind of father Dan Miller is that he didn't come down to see who his daughter was letting into their house. But Sarah had a tendency of talking to herself and inventing imaginary friends to the point that he was quite certain there was nobody there. And, in what he considered the unlikely scenario that there was in fact someone with her, Dan didn't think he or his daughter could afford to be particular with who she considered a friend.

Gizmo whispered to Bartholomew as they walked in. "Who's Sarah?"

"How should I know," the warlock hissed. "Now, be quiet."

"Here. This is my dad's phone." Sarah reached into a basket of devices and wires that sat on one end of the Miller's counter, just beside the dishwasher. She turned and offered it to Bartholomew. "You can use this. The passcode is zero-eight-zero-nine-one-four."

The warlock tapped the numbers in as she called them, his fingers trembling. He'd never used anything other than an old landline before. He didn't like the fact that there were no buttons.

"Do you want to see my room when you're done?" Sarah asked. "I could show you my collection of yarn."

"No." Bartholomew reached into the pocket of his trousers. It was in there somewhere. "And that's a silly thing to collect." *Aha!* He pulled out a business card and began, after a few moments of fumbling with different apps before he found the correct one, to enter Karen Archer's number.

"I'll come see your yarn," Gizmo offered, wagging his tail politely at Sarah. "Do you crochet?"

"Oh no. That would be far too normal," Sarah said. "I just collect it."

Bartholomew was too distracted to worry about the fact that his familiar was talking again, or stop him when he disappeared up the stairs with the girl. The phone was ringing.

"Hello, you've reached Karen Archer," the realtor's voice was pleasant and cheerful on the other end. "How can I help you?"

"I need to return a house."

There was silence for a moment. He thought he heard her groan, and when Karen responded, her tone had shifted to one of barely masked annoyance. "Is this Mr. Bartlow?"

"Bartholomew Bartlow, that's correct. You oversaw the sale of property 42A in Mills Run Heights. I purchased it from—."

"I remember, Mr. Bartlow." Her tone was curt. "Is this your idea of a joke?"

Bartholomew frowned, his free hand tapped against the Miller's countertop. He waited for Karen to continue. When she didn't, he began to feel frustrated. He didn't have time for this. "Are you going to tell me the joke you want my opinion on or not?" he snapped. "I'd like to get through with the return process. How can I get my money back?... Hello? Are you still there?"

Bartholomew pressed his ear closer to the phone. There was the muttered sound of someone counting to ten.

"Mr. Bartlow," Karen sounded calm once more. "You cannot, as I'm sure you already know,"—frustration cracked through the layer of calm— "*return* a house after the sale has gone through." Bartholomew heard her breathe in deeply, then exhale. "If you'd like to sell it, then perhaps I can assist.[7] But you'll need to get rid of the black mold, the termites, the rats, clean the grout—"

"Oh, I've done all that." Bartholomew waved his hand in dismissal. He'd cleared the runes that gave the house its dilapidated appearance yesterday when he moved in. "So, you'll sell it, how about giving me an advance. I'm thinking, the initial amount I paid, and I'll use that to buy a house in a different suburb. Perhaps you can recommend one that's more..." He searched for the right word. "Dull."

Bartholomew couldn't see Karen Archer, but she was in the middle of preparing a meal of mushed carrots and peas for her toddler. It came in an easy twist and squeeze bottle. As she listened to him, a man

---

7. Karen regretted the offer the moment it left her lips and would soon rescind it, as you'll see.

who'd paid for a house in cash, asking for an advance on a sale that hadn't gone through from her, a realtor drowning in a mortgage, her hand tightened around the plastic until orange mush exploded and flew onto the white curtains above her kitchen sink. At that moment, her husband[8] shouted to let her know that their daughter was awake and getting hungry and that she needed to hurry up before the baby started to cry.

Karen stared at the exploded carrots and forgot all about counting to ten or taking deep breaths.

"Mr. Bartlow, I would not help you sell your house for fifty-percent of the commission," she snapped. "No realtor in their right mind would! You are a nightmare of a client." And then, because she was still a professional, she ended their conversation, "Good luck in your future endeavors!"

It took Bartholomew a few minutes to realize that she'd hung up. "I don't need luck, Ms. Archer. What I need is a new house. Do you understand? Hello? Hello?" He took the phone from his ear and stared at the many apps on Dan's screen.

"Are you really selling the house?" Sarah asked, staring at him from the foot of the stairs. She'd finished showing Gizmo her impressive

---

8. Paul Archer was a plumber. The two had met when Karen was twenty-six, and he was thirty. She'd been seeing her friends start getting engaged and was, foolishly she thought in hindsight, anxious that she was growing too old to still be single. The two had settled into a relationship that dragged on twelve years, during which time Karen waited patiently, then not so patiently for a ring. Eventually, she stopped hinting and started demanding, and Paul gave in. He was no quite content with his wife, and uncertain what he'd been so worried about since it had changed nothing. Karen, on the other hand, was no longer content and believed it had changed everything.

collection of yarn, and the two had come back downstairs to hear the last part of the conversation.

"No," Bartholomew said. His voice took on a sulky tone, something like a petulant old man who was acting like a toddler, and he slumped against the counter, arms crossed. "Karen Archer is a very difficult woman. I don't think she fully understands the situation we're in."[9] He looked at Gizmo. "We have no money. We can't buy another house."

Gizmo's eyes grew wide. He ran across the living room floor, hopping over a wooden train and a rabbit plushie, to reach the warlock. "So what does that mean? Will I not have my own room anymore?"

"Neither of us will have their own rooms. We won't even have a roof. We'll have to live in the woods and acquire food from campers," Bartholomew snapped.[10] His lips twisted, and then his dark brows rose. A slash of a smile lifted his mouth. "Unless... we aren't the ones who leave." He looked at Gizmo.

The familiar understood the warlock's meaning at once, and his tail stopped wagging. He stared at the wooden floor, weighing their options.

On the one hand, Mr. Graves had been there first. He had every right to stay in Mills Run, and it didn't seem quite fair to force him from his home.

---

9. Seeing that Karen knew nothing about warlocks, vampires, or talking demons in the shape of Pomeranian-poodle mixes, this was certainly true.

10. It should be noted that there were almost certainly other options available, and had the warlock paused and thought for a few days, he could have arrived at a better solution. However, in his current state, Bartholomew wanted an excuse to be angry at the universe, so he imagined the worst scenario he could think of.

On the other, Gizmo really wanted his own bedroom.

Sometimes, the ends justify the means, he rationalized. And aloud he said, "Let's get some garlic."

ELEVEN

I f you're running low on blue and indigo inks, garlic is a cheap and effective way to repel vampires. Mostly because, with a sufficient amount of garlic, you can repel everyone.

This was not a problem to Bartholomew. The smell, however, was.

He stood in the middle of his kitchen. One hand pinching his nose while the other used the back of a spoon[1] to crush a clove of garlic[2] against a white plastic bowl.[3] A few feet before him, sitting in the center of the empty living room, were Gizmo and Sarah.[4] There was a cup of peeled cloves and a spool of white and green yarn beside them.

---

1. Which he'd acquired from Dan Miller's house.

2. Likewise acquired.

3. You get the gist.

4. Who was only there because she threatened to tell her parents about the many things that Bartholomew had now acquired from their house if she wasn't allowed to come along too. And Gizmo had refuted any of the warlock's threats that he would transform her into a rat, with *"But how would you do that? You don't know the rune for rat. And it's almost impossible to transform a living being!"*

"First, you thread it," Sarah said, holding up her needle as she demonstrated for Gizmo, who watched intently despite the fact that he lacked the opposable thumbs to ever repeat the process. "And then, you push a hole in the garlic, like so— oops!" The clove slipped from her hand and rolled over the floor.

Gizmo leaped up and bounded after it, overcome with the sudden desire to chase and catch the small moving object. In the kitchen, Bartholomew rolled his eyes.

Sarah smiled guiltily as the familiar dropped the clove back onto her lap. "Works better with popcorn," she said.[5]

Bartholomew scoffed. He couldn't think of anything quite as ridiculous as popcorn on a string. What purpose would that serve? The scent of butter never kept anyone out. In fact, it could easily have had the opposite effect, and you might end up with a house full of brownies.[6]

Gizmo, on the other hand, felt his mouth start to salivate. He thought a long string of popcorn sounded delightful, especially if there was someone flicking it around for him to chase. It wouldn't have lasted long enough to attract brownies.

"Never mind a garland," Sarah said, staring down at her supplies. "Maybe we could get some glue and make it into a Christmas wreath instead." The idea struck her as even better than her first. There was nothing quite as eccentric as Christmas decorations in the middle of summer.

---

5. Though the garlic may have proved less challenging had she not been trying to string it together using a plastic crotchet needle and heavy duty yarn.

6. This refers to the hobgoblin type of bronwies, who are well known for their love of all things dairy.

"We don't need a wreath or a garland or anything else," Bartholomew snapped. His voice was unusually high and nasally for he was still pinching his nose. He stepped away from the counter, carrying his bowl of garlic paste in one hand. "All we need is the smell."

Sarah wrapped her arms around her elbows, and her shoulders slumped forward, so she looked like a tomato curled on the floor. "I was only trying to help."

Gizmo rested his chin on her knee in support. "I liked your popcorn on a string idea. Let's do that."

Bartholomew was forced to release his nose in order to smear the paste onto the door The scent of garlic made his lips curl. He hated that he might have to suffer indefinitely. The thought of being trapped in a house that reeked of garlic, hiding from a vampire, and living with an unwanted horde of brownies was too much.

"Definitely not!" the warlock stomped his foot and scowled at the two people behind, each more useless than the other. "The only thing we should be doing is thinking of ways to get rid of a vampire."

"Well that's easy," Sarah said. If she'd known that was what the garlic was for, she could've saved them all a lot of time. Part of being an eccentric meant that when other girls were dreaming about unicorns and fairies, she was busy researching horror movie monsters. "You drive a stake through their heart, or chop off their head, or burn them in sunlight, or drown them in holy water, or starve them of blood."

Bartholomew stopped painting the door. He turned to stare at her, garlic still on his finger.

Even Gizmo lifted his head from Sarah's knee, and his brows rose.

The two exchanged a look. Bartholomew was a bit impressed, and Gizmo a bit disturbed, though neither would have cared to admit it.

Sarah, who had no idea that they were talking about Mr. Graves,[7] had just offered a number of ways that they could commit murder.

"We can't kill him," Gizmo said. Acquiring things was all well and good, and he wasn't above a bit of light torture when the situation warranted it, but even a demon had to draw the line somewhere.

"Well, I mean..." Bartholomew floundered for a response. The embarrassing truth was that the warlock, despite working for The Bearded Syndicate for over a century, had never killed anyone. The thought of doing so now made him quite squeamish. But he didn't want to admit that in front of a girl who could so casually and confidently plot murder. To his relief, he thought of an excuse that didn't make him sound weak. "We can't! If he died, it would attract all sorts of attention to Mills Run. The wrong people might come snooping around."

"Exactly," Gizmo agreed, more than a bit relieved that he wasn't going to be contractually required to assist the warlock with murder. "The best-case scenario would be getting him to leave of his own accord."

Perhaps we could find old castles for sale in Romania and slip them under his door, the familiar thought. *Or maybe a nice dungeon somewhere in Bulgaria.*

The warlock was thinking of something else entirely. Blackmail!

Bartholomew smeared the last of the garlic around the edge of the door, set the bowl down, and turned to Sarah. He stared at her, rubbing his hands together like a very hungry man who'd just seen a piece of steak.

Perhaps there was a way for her to be useful after all.

---

7. Who she actually quite liked seeing as he was a fellow eccentric.

"Ms. Moon," Bartholomew put on his most flattering voice[8] and gave her his most charming smile.[9] "Tell me, what do you know about Mr. Graves?"

Sarah, who somehow deduced that the warlock wanted information and wasn't plotting a way to trap her in a web and slice into her with a knife and fork, saw an opportunity to use this to her own advantage. She returned the smile. "I'll tell you, but only if we're friends."

"Of course," Bartholomew said, but he crossed his fingers behind his back.

---

8. Which was low and sinister, and much like one might imagine a spider would sound when talking to a fly

9. Which involved the left half of his mouth spreading in a line upward to his cheek while the right half remained frozen and was

TWELVE

S arah was able to tell Bartholomew a great deal about Mr. Graves, not all of it relevant.

"And then last winter I made a family of snowmen in my front yard, and he lent me proper top hats to put on all of them, you know— real, authentic ones like what you draw a snowman wearing," she said.[1]

Bartholomew's jaw clenched.[2] His fingernails sank into his palms, and he pounded his fists to his forehead, trying desperately not to scream. In his estimation, Sarah had been prattling on about nothing for the past two hours.[3] Any begrudging acclaim he'd given the young girl for her willingness to stab a vampire through the heart, had vanished.

---

1. Sarah considered this of great importance. She'd always wanted to put a top hat on a snowman but her father owned exactly none. The fact that Mr. Graves owned several cemented him as a person of great significance.

2. The warlock, who did own a top hat, considered the vampire's wardrobe irrelevant.

3. It was in fact, thirty minutes.

"My dad said that was really nice of him, but my mum said it was out of character because Mr. Graves normally doesn't talk to anyone, but I said that wasn't true because he does in the winter."

Bartholomew was no longer listening. His hands hovered by his ears. He considered taking the last bulb of garlic and shoving it in Sarah's mouth.

"But then my mum said that wasn't true because he was miserable the day before too because he looked into my brothers' pram, and one of them, I think it was Nicky, reached up and grabbed Mr. Graves' handkerchief from his pocket, and a little pin fell out, and he got really angry." Sarah ran out of breath and was forced to pause for a moment before she launched back into her story. "But then I said to Mum that if Mr. Graves was really so miserable, he wouldn't have come over to look at the twins anyway, and she said—"

"Enough!" Bartholomew could take no more. "I wanted to know if you'd seen him sneaking off somewhere at night or meeting with strange people, not if he'd built snowmen!"

"No, he didn't build them, I did," Sarah said, concerned that he had missed the entire point of her story. Admittedly, however, she'd lost it herself too, and for a good twenty minutes had mostly been speaking out of the sheer delight of having an adult listen to her.

The only person who caught what Sarah had just said was Gizmo. He'd been lying on the floor, chin against his paws, desperately wishing he had another pig's ear or at least a piece of cheese to bury his nose in and drown out the scent of the garlic. But, he had been listening. The demon had heard every word Sarah said, and at the mention of a pin, his ears grew more alert, his head lifted and tilted to the side.

"I don't care who built the snowmen!" Bartholomew's blood was starting to boil. He rose to his feet and glared at the small tomato-like girl on the floor. He had the urge to lift his leg and squash her. "Or who owns how many top hats. You're the most useless informant! No wonder they don't hire children as ratters![4] Get out. Go home. Shoo!" He waved his arms at her as though she were a possum that had wandered into his house.

The warlock intended to be intimidating and terrifying. Perhaps, if he'd still had his dark pointed beard and menacing slicked back hair, he would have been.

But with his thick curls and smooth cheeks, gangly limbs and twitchy movements, he looked more like a lanky ape attempting to perform an interpretive dance.

Sarah giggled, but there was a hint of fear rising in her.

Not because of the warlock[5] but because he'd mentioned her home. Sarah hadn't told her father she was leaving, which wouldn't have mattered, except that her mother might be home by now. She tended to get very angry when her daughter wandered off, though Sarah couldn't see why.

I'm always fine, she thought.

But just the same Sarah hopped to her feet. "Thanks for having me over, Mr. Bartlow, but I'd better leave before my parents get worried. We should make garlic wreaths together soon." And to Bartholomew's confusion, she stood on the tips of her toes and jumped to kiss his cheek in farewell. Then, she patted the top of Gizmo's head and hurried through the door.

---

4. The Ratting Department was one of the many divisions of The Bearded Syndicate. Their tasks included: eavesdropping, snooping, and general busy-bodying.

5. Sarah had a curious taste in people, and for reasons no one would ever quite understand, found Bartholomew delightful.

What the hell just happened? Bartholomew thought, momentarily stunned into silence. Finally, after she'd disappeared through the door, he shook his head and turned to his familiar. "That is precisely why children shouldn't be allowed out of their rooms until they've matured. Have you ever heard anyone talk for so long and say absolutely nothing?"

"Bit of a paradox," Gizmo noted, stretching unknowingly into a yoga position called upward dog. "But I think our new friend told us a lot."

"Friend! Pah!" Bartholomew snorted and kicked the ball of yarn where Sarah had forgotten it on the floor. "All she did was drone on about top hats."

Gizmo's eyes watched the yarn unfurl with only mild curiosity. He was glad he wasn't a cat, or he might have been inclined to do something silly. "But she also gave us our first clue," he said. "And told us about popcorn strings. Do you think we could make one? And maybe add some bacon and cheese?"

Bartholomew stared at the demon, now rising from his stretch. "What was that?"

"Well, I just think that bacon and cheese would pair quite well with popcorn."

"Not about that. About the clue."

"Yes, well I suppose it's not much," Gizmo said, wrinkling his nose as the mushed garlic wafted toward him from the door. He hoped the scent wouldn't reach to his room. "But if he's got a pin, that's a start, wouldn't you say?"

"Yes, indeed." Bartholomew froze, lips pulling tight. He wracked his brain, trying to think what relevance a pin had to anything. His knowledge of vampires was limited to the best ways to break into their coffins and acquire old treasure. However, he couldn't bear to admit that his familiar knew something he didn't. "Very significant and I know precisely why. Obviously. But why do you think it's interesting?"

"Because of an old tradition," Gizmo explained, braving the reek of garlic to cross toward the fridge. "There were a few hundred years where wealthy vampires considered it terribly gauche to bite their victims. It became fashionable for them to craft pins and prick them with those instead." The demon stared at the closed fridge, batted it with his front paw, and turned his big brown eyes to Bartholomew.

The warlock opened the door before his familiar could start whining. "That seems terribly inefficient for feeding," he noted. "But how does it help us?"

"Because wealthy vampires don't just purchase pins from thrift stores. They have them hand-crafted." Gizmo rose onto his hind legs and grabbed a slice of cheese from the bottom shelf. Tail wagging, he trotted toward the stairs.

Bartholomew's fingers rubbed the stubble on his chin, thinking as he stared into the fridge. He was starting to understand. Frederick Graves was almost certainly not the vampire's original name. This pin might be a clue as to who he really was and, by extension, what he was doing in a place like Mills Run Heights.

And once I know that, I'll know how to blackmail him into leaving, Bartholomew thought. *I just need to see what the pin looks like.*

But the thought of breaking into the vampire's house or stalking him at night made the warlock's stomach flip. He wouldn't say that he was afraid,[6] but he was low on inks and trying not to use any runes. It simply wouldn't be safe for him to try and identify the pin.

---

6. Though other people certainly would have.

However, he could think of two individuals that would be more than suited for the task.

Bartholomew's lips slanted in a smile. His eyes went to the bottom of the stairs where the demon was ripping the plastic off his slice of cheese.

"Gizmo," he said. "How would you and your new friend like to go on an adventure tonight?"

THIRTEEN

Day was stubborn in the summer. The sun stayed in the sky until almost nine before finally sinking behind the horizon.

Bartholomew stayed in his bedroom, where it was safe. He kept his quill pinched between his thumb and finger, drawing runes in the air. His inks were at the ready in case something went wrong.

"You'll come and save me if I'm not back in a few hours," Gizmo said. He was in the room with the warlock for the moment, but was getting ready to leave.

"Of course, of course," Bartholomew lied, not quite meeting his familiar's gaze.

Gizmo was not much reassured, and his eyes narrowed as he went toward the door. "I'm still not sure why you can't come with me."

"I've told you, I've important things to do," Bartholomew said, and he meant it. Assuming Gizmo completed his task without being captured and locked in a coffin for the rest of eternity, the warlock would have a very significant decision to make. He needed time to sit and think. "Anyway, you're taking the girl. She'll be the decoy. If something goes wrong, let him eat her and run back here."

With that parting advice, Bartholomew opened the door, pushed his familiar out with the side of his shoe, and quickly closed and locked it back.[1]

Gizmo sighed, trotted down the stairs, and over to Number 46A, where Sarah was waiting for him.

Had the eleven-year-old asked her parents' permission to wander Mills Run Heights after dark with only a talking dog for company, they would most certainly have said no. Though the neighborhood was perfectly safe,[2] every parent suffers with a low level paranoia that convinces them that the world is full of criminals and kidnappers all waiting for an excuse to steal their child. The moon has the curious effect of amplifying these fears by a factor of ten.

So Sarah didn't ask her parents' permission. Instead, she took her collection of yarn, built it into a log under her blankets, and wrote a nice little note by her pillow, just in case her parents noticed.

It read: *Don't worry. With a friend. Gone to see pin and give popcorn. Will tell Mr. Graves you say hello.*

Had Lisa or Dan Miller found this note, they most certainly would have worried.[3] Their daughter had no friends as far as they knew, and

---

1. Though a lock was unlikely to do much good against a vampire.

2. Except of course for the vampire, warlock, and fluffy black demon that were now all living there.

3. Though they would have at least understood why their daughter had snuck buttery bag of popcorn up to her room when she'd announced she was going to bed.

they'd have ended up arguing over what precisely *see pin* meant in this context.[4]

Luckily, Sarah's parents never found her note.

She slipped on her sneakers, grabbed something from her shelf, and tiptoed down the stairs and out the door.[5] Gizmo waited for her outside, tail wagging.

"Hello, Ms. Moon," he greeted her. "Ready to see Mr. Graves."

"Oh yes," Sarah said. She was quite looking forward to it. It was very eccentric, she thought, to pay someone a visit in the middle of the night. And when Gizmo had appeared at her door a few hours prior and invited her to come with him, she'd been positively delighted. Though she was still a bit confused about some of his rules. "I made something for you."

She held out her hand revealing the item within. It was, if you asked Sarah, a friendship bracelet. The trend was popular among girls at her school, and they braided them from colorful bits of thread. But Sarah didn't want to copy the normal, boring way that everyone else was making them. She'd come up with her own. Her initial plan was to

---

4. Dan would have assumed she'd meant to write *sleep in*, while Lisa's mind would have spun it into a euphemism for drugs, connecting pins to needles. Both would have found the other's assumption understandably preposterous and the fight would have sounded a bit like this: "Sarah's eleven. How could she be doing drugs?" "Exactly! She's eleven. She's not going to mix up *sleep in* and *see pin*." This would have been repeated in a loop while they drove around the neighborhood for the next hour.

5. Her parents, who were pleasantly surprised that their daughter had chosen to go to bed early that night, were in their own room taking advantage of the opportunity, so they didn't hear the steps creak beneath Sarah's feet.

thread the yarn through the popcorn, but when that failed, she'd gone for the glue instead.

The result was a tangled mess of wool with stale pieces of popcorn falling off of it.

Most people would have raised their eyebrows in confusion when Sarah presented it. They would have needed to ask what it was.

Gizmo took it from her hands with his mouth and swallowed it in a single large gulp: yarn and glue and all.

"Delicious," he said, and his tail spun like the blades of a helicopter for a moment before he took off the down the street, leading the way to Mr. Graves' house. "Now remember, when we get there, you do the talking. I don't want him to notice me, or he might not show you his pin."

Sarah nodded. She didn't quite understand, but she was delighted to have a talking dog as a friend and happy to help in any way she could.

There were a few people still outside, taking advantage of the cool night to tend to their approved flowers[6], sip wine on their lawn chairs, and stroll along the pavement. One or two waved to Sarah.[7]

Mr. Graves' house waited for them, its dark windows ominous.

Gizmo hid behind Sarah's ankles, trying not to be seen as she knocked on the red door.

No response came.

She tried again.

---

6. Which consisted of a short list of only five that Mr. Anderson had deemed appropriate for the aesthetic and environmental health of the neighborhood.

7. Who pretended not to notice and pulled her hair like a curtain around her face in an attempt to stop from being recognized. She didn't want anyone calling her parents.

There was a loud sigh from within.

Frederick Graves was currently in his kitchen, soaking a bag of dried type-A blood flakes in a cup of hot water to prepare his usual tea. He'd woken only a few minutes ago after a difficult day's sleep.[8] Since seeing Bartholomew, the warlock had been very much on his mind. The vampire had been searching his memories to figure out who he was. But it was a long, arduous process. Frederick hadn't made it to the end of his second century yet when he heard the knocking. He very much intended to ignore it.

But then there was a loud shriek, like a deep-voiced banshee, "Mr. Graves! Mr. Graves! Are you there? It's Sarah Miller!"

Frederick was familiar with the peculiar little girl who lived down the street. He considered her a minor nuisance, but harmless enough. She'd helped him once when his umbrella flew out of his hands, and he hadn't forgotten it.[9]

What does she want? The vampire wondered and walked to the front door, white socks making no noise against the carpet. He tied the string of his fuzzy pink bathrobe so that it wouldn't come loose and reveal his white and gray striped pajamas beneath. He opened the door.

Standing on Frederick's front step was Sarah, dressed in a large purple t-shirt and denim shorts. At her feet was the same little black dog he'd spotted with the warlock.

Gizmo noticed the vampire staring at him.

"Woof woof," the demon said.

---

8. He'd gotten only ten hours sleep in total, instead of his usual twelve

9. Though to Frederick's knowledge, Sarah had. After all, he'd used his powers of hypnosis to make her forget, and so far, had seen no reason to question the efficacy of his abilities.

What a curious bark, Frederick thought. But fluffy black dogs were of little concern to him.[10] He turned to Sarah. "Can I help you?"

"Yes. I've come for a visit."

Frederick glanced over his shoulder and into his living area. It couldn't be seen from the doorway, but among the dark furniture was a large black coffin, tucked into the corner. "I'm afraid I'm terribly busy at the moment."[11] He moved to close the door.

"Wait!" Sarah's hand grabbed the edge. She tried to think of something that might change the old man's mind. "Can I borrow some sugar?"

This might have raised the eyebrows of someone born in the past two centuries. Frederick, however, accepted this explanation with a curt nod. "Have you a cup?"

"Er—" Sarah glanced at Gizmo, who shrugged his shoulders as best he was able. "No, I don't. Can I borrow one of those too?"

Frederick sighed. He closed the door, twisted the lock, and went to search his kitchen. During this time, a whispered conversation took place between Sarah and Gizmo, about handkerchiefs and pins and sneezes, but he heard none of it. When he returned, they were silent, and Frederick was holding an old-fashioned glass mug with crystals of sugar glittering like snow on the top.

---

10. At least for now. In the future, they would preoccupy a good deal of Frederick's thoughts.

11. Which was not a lie. Frederick had a great deal of thinking to do, much like Bartholomew, who was at his house doing the same.

"Here." He passed the glass to Sarah. "See and return it when you're done." His eyes narrowed, and his raspy voice grew stern, stressing this point. It was very important to him that he not lose his mug.[12]

"Oh yes, of course, sure thing, Mr. Graves," Sarah said, taking the sugar.

"Ehem." There was a strange coughing noise from the dog at her feet. Gizmo nudged her with ankle with his hip.

"I know, I know," Sarah muttered. She inhaled deeply. "Oh no, oh no. I can't hold it back," she said, eyes closing and mouth opening wide. "Ah-ah-ah-choooo!"[13] Sarah dropped the glass mug, covering her mouth and nose so that it wasn't obvious that no snot had come out. She pretended to sniff. "Oh, yuck, oh no. Could I borrow your handkerchief, Mr. Graves?"

"No!" Frederick wasn't responding to her. He was staring at his poor mug, suddenly anxious. It had landed on the black carpet within his home, sugar crystals mixing in the fabric. Getting them all out, even with a vacuum, would be no small feat.

But the mug had been lucky. Sarah was short, even for her age, so it hadn't dropped from very high and the carpet broke its fall. Only the glass handle snapped off.

It made Frederick somewhat more forgiving. "Here! Take it and go, please." He pulled a green handkerchief from the pocket of his bathrobe and passed it to Sarah.

---

12. Not because it was of any significant value, but because he was down to only two, and most vampires find shopping for home furnishings difficult. Most stores that might sell silverware aren't open at night, and most vampires are too old to recognize the convenience of online shopping.

13. It was a rather over-acted performance in Gizmo's opinion, and he regretted very much not faking the sneeze himself.

She took it and wiped her face with a sense of despair. No pin had fallen from its folds.

"I've a lot of cleaning to do now," Frederick muttered. "But at least this glass can still be used." He bent at his hips and leaned forward to recover his mug. As he did, his striped pajama pants rose higher on his leg. Something silver flashed on his sock.

Gizmo, who was right at ankle height, was in exactly the right location to see what it was: a pin. The silver had been fashioned in the shape of a swan.

Their mission, as Sarah would learn on their way back, had been a success. And after Gizmo bid the little girl farewell, he trotted back to Bartholomew feeling particularly proud.

Though there was still one problem.

Gizmo had no idea which vampire was known to own a silver swan pin, nor would Bartholomew.

This was the precise dilemma that the warlock had been busy contemplating while his familiar potentially risked his life.

There were few people who cared enough about vampiric heritage that they would keep records of pins. Bartholomew could think of only three.

Constance Payne, the record keeper for The Bearded Syndicate, was a miserable witch with a quick tongue and slow brain. She'd had a grudge against Bartholomew since he'd acquired an old book that she'd tried to keep secret. If she learned that he was still alive, she'd hand him over to The Syndicate without a flicker of remorse

Lum Lumbkin was a troll who lived under a bridge in the city. He liked to keep records of anything shiny on the off chance that he could one day add it to his own collection of stolen goods for sale. Lum didn't like The Syndicate, who took a rather large percentage of his profits. But Bartholomew owed him money, and trolls weren't big believers in credit. If Lum learned the warlock wasn't dead, he might take it upon himself to rectify that.

Which left only one option: Raffiel the Fallen.

It would be even worse if he learned the truth. He wouldn't want to kill Bartholomew or turn him in to The Syndicate.

Raffiel would want to keep in touch.

FOURTEEN

To the west of the city, at the top a very large tree, there lived the preeminent historian of all things magic: Raffiel the Fallen. He was, or had been depending on whose perspective you asked, an angel. As such, Gizmo had little interest in meeting him.[1] He assumed, like most people did, that Raffiel was as unlikeable and unscrupulous as the average angel.[2] Bartholomew, who had his reasons for allowing

---

1. "It's not that I'm prejudiced or anything," he'd explained to Bartholomew. "But angels are a pretentious lot, you know. They look down their noses at us demons just because they think their realm is better than ours." Which of course, it was. There was a reason that even the great Gizmorgoth of Darkness had chosen to leave the underworld in exchange for eternal servitude. But that wasn't his point.

2. The negative opinion of angels that is widespread among the magical community is not entirely justified. It can best be compared to walking into a room full of sanctimonious vegans, parents who don't believe in the word "no", and people whose entire identity is *gym*, and using them to judge all of humanity. You see, although angels can fly between their realm and ours, few ever bother. Their home is said to be beautiful, with the music of harps and scent of fresh baked bread constantly present. The ones who come to Earth, have been cast out for one reason or another, though they seldom care to admit it.

his familiar to continue with this false assumption, went to the tree alone the following night.

It was just after three in the morning when he arrived at the tree. Bartholomew was miserable and grumpy. His dwindling funds had forced him to travel by bus, and the trip had taken twice as long as he'd anticipated. When the service stopped running, he'd had to walk the last mile on the road alone, and then another two in the forest where Raffiel lived. Now, there were twigs in his hair and mud on his shoes, and the scent of the woods clung to his jacket.

"Ugh." Bartholomew's nose wrinkled in distaste as he brushed pine needles from his sleeves. He wished he did know a teleportation rune. The thought of trekking back through the forest and to the nearest bus stop filled him with dread.

But first came the part the warlock loved, the part he'd once been employed to do, the part he was best at.

Bartholomew Whit— no, Bartlow was going to acquire a book.

He stared up at the large house high in the tree, cracked his knuckles, pulled out his quill, and got to work.

With blue ink, he drew runes to detect any alarms or traps that laid in wait of intruders.[3] Once he was certain it was safe, he switched colors. Plants had never agreed with Bartholomew, but few decades back, he'd discovered the symbol for *handhold*. It worked well enough when used on a sturdy tree like this one.

The warlock had little brown ink left to spare. He clung to the bottle in one hand as he climbed, holding his quill between his teeth and searching for natural grooves in the trunk. It was lucky his limbs

---

3. He found none because there were none. Raffiel had never even considered someone might attempt to rob him in the middle of the night. But he would have been quite tickled to know that anyone cared that much about his work.

were so long, or he might have run out of ink halfway and found himself stuck, fifteen feet in the air, legs swinging from a branch.

As it was, by the time Bartholomew reached the wooden platform that served as the tree house's porch, his bottle of brown ink was empty.

Otto had better come through he thought, as he wiped the tip of his quill clean. Brown ink was crucial for shapeshifting, be it of objects or words. The warlock had used most of his supply changing the name and image on all of his documentation. If things went bad in Mills Run and he was discovered, Bartholomew would have a difficult time changing his identity again.

But there was no reason for the warlock to start worrying about any of that. Things would go well because he was going to see to it that they did. He just had to get rid of that pesky vampire.

Bartholomew dipped his quill into the indigo. With it, he drew three runes. One, on the doorknob, translated to *open*.[4] The others went on the bottom of his shoes.

His footsteps were soft as he snuck inside.

Although there was a section near the back that had been designed for living, the tree house was more of a library than it was a home. The space was packed with long rows of shelves, interspersed with wooden desks, and hanging lamps. Everywhere was packed with books.

The warlock closed his eyes and inhaled, breathing in the scent of the pages. It made him miss his own collection, and envy grumbled in the pit of his stomach. He quashed it with his usual disdain.

This isn't a real book collection, Bartholomew reminded himself as he crept along a row. *They've all got the same author.*

---

4. This was, in fact, unnecessary. Had Bartholomew tried the door, he would have found it already unlocked.

This was true. Any writing in the room had been penned by Raffiel the Fallen himself. The preeminent historian had dedicated himself to recording the life of every magical individual.[5]

I just need to find where he keeps the information on vampires.

Bartholomew's eyes scanned the different names. He recognized warlocks, witches, goblins, trolls, fairies, pixies, until finally, he stumbled across the vampires. Their shelf was full of black and red notebooks with names like Lazarus De Vile and Svetline Morningstar and Ignacio Morganti the Third.

The warlock wasn't sure where to start.

I'll figure it out. They must be in some sort of order. He recalled Frederick Graves' turquoise coat. He guessed that had been the fashion about four hundred years ago and reached for a burgundy text on a shelf near the top, intending to look for a date.

What Bartholomew found was a great deal of dust.

It puffed off the pages of the notebook and cascaded onto the unsuspecting warlock. His nose started to itch.

And before he could stop himself, Bartholomew erupted in a very real sneeze.[6]

Oh no.

In all his years as an acquirer, the warlock had never made such a grave mistake. Death had made him sloppy.

There were footsteps from the other side of the room.

---

5. At least, as much as he knew. After his fall, Raffiel had no longer been able to observe our realm at a distance, and magical individuals are highly secretive. Not one was willing to share intimate details of the past twenty years of their life.

6. Had Gizmo heard it, he might have reconsidered his thoughts on Sarah's acting, for Bartholomew's sneeze was equally dramatic.

Bartholomew needed to leave.

He turned in the direction of the door, but he hadn't made it far when he saw the glimmer of a candle, flickering behind his back.

"Bart!" A voice, soft and beautiful, melodic as a harp, enough to make a young girl's heart melt and a young boy stop in awe to listen, called to the warlock. "My dear friend! Is that you? I thought you were dead!"

Bartholomew's jaw clenched. He wished Gizmo was there so he could somehow blame this entire mess on the familiar. But the warlock was alone. He'd have to fix this himself.

FIFTEEN

G rinding his teeth, Bartholomew turned. "Hello, Raf."

The angel appeared to be a blue-eyed, blond-haired youth[1] with a light sprinkling of freckles over his nose and cheeks. His lips, plump and pink, spread in a bright smile like what every renaissance painter wished they could have depicted on a naked cherub. It reeked of innocence and stank of sweetness. "It is you! Only beardless— and look at your curls! I can't believe it. I was so upset when I saw that your plane had crashed. I cried for the next week.[2] To see you here, alive and well, is all I could have wished." He approached with his arms out-stretched.

Bartholomew sensed an impending hug and quickly stepped back. "No, Raf, you misunderstand," he said, mind spinning for an excuse. "I am dead."

Raffiel froze. The beautiful smile fell from his face and his expression changed into one of endearing curiosity.

---

1. Some might have guessed as young as eighteen, others as old as twenty-five. In reality, Raffiel had been aware of his existence for over five thousand years.

2. He was the only one.

Bartholomew had no idea where he'd intended to take this lie, but he was committed to it now, so he held out his hands and continued, "I'm a ghost."

"Really? You look so solid." Raffiel lowered his lantern, resting it on a nearby desk. He tapped his chin and studied the warlock. Slowly, he started to nod. "Yes, I suppose that does explain your complexion."

"Exactly, it— wait, what?"

"You're so pallid," Raffiel said. "And your skin looks cold and clammy, like a sheet of ice."

"Well, that's not quite true," Bartholomew objected, crossing his arms.

"No, it is. The lingering hand of death is still on you, but it's erased the years. You look almost like a child now you're clean shaven."

Bartholomew scowled. He considered this comparison unnecessarily rude. Through gritted teeth, he muttered, "It's the curls."

"So what are you doing here? Have you come to haunt my library?" Raffiel's face lit up suddenly. He'd always wanted a ghost. All proper libraries had one. The angel laughed with joy at the thought. It sounded like music, some horridly soothing notes on a flute. "I should love to have you as my ghost, Bart! It does get lonely here, writing on my own all day. Having my best friend[3] as a permanent companion would be a dream."

"No that's certainly not..." Bartholomew paused. The thought of dying and returning as a library ghost was appealing. But not here! Not

---

3. You are likely asking why an angel as nice as Raffiel the Fallen would ever have a miserable warlock for a best friend. The long answer involves a goat, a feather, and an inedible pie. The short answer is that, during Raffiel's twenty odd years on Earth, he had been treated like a pariah. Bartholomew was the only one who'd ever visited and returned.

with Raffiel talking all the time. The angel was too nice, the human equivalent of a bag of candy. In small doses it seemed sweet, but too much would turn your stomach and rot your teeth.[4] "I'm here on a mission, Raf. I have to get information about a vampire in order to..."

Bartholomew floundered for a moment, trying to think what reason a ghost would have to do anything.

"Ascend!" He snapped his fingers.

Raffiel's eyebrows lowered. Ghosts were incorporeal. They weren't supposed to be able to snap their fingers.

But Bartholomew was feeling too pleased with his invented story to notice his mistake. "I'm stuck in purgatory, Raf. Yes, that's what's happened. And in order to get out, I need to learn the identity of a vampire. Do you know which one owns a silver swan pin?"

"I do," Raffiel said, forgetting, for the moment, his concerns about the tangibility of ghosts. "But I shouldn't think you'd wish to know who he is."

Bartholomew's jaw clenched. His fingers tapped against the table.

Funny, Raffiel thought, *shouldn't they slip right through the wood?*

"I've just told you that I *do* want to know," the warlock said, voice low and cranky. His patience, already thin, was likely to tear soon, and the angel's presence was making Bartholomew consider knocking over the lantern and setting the whole tree ablaze. "That's the whole reason that I'm here."

"But don't you think you're safer in purgatory?" Raffiel asked, too polite to say more.

---

4. Only when people spent too much time with Raffiel, his exhausting kindness and positive attitude made them want to steal lollipops from babies and give people compliments on unflattering haircuts. Anything that would provide some sort of negative balance to the angel's goodwill.

But Bartholomew was starting to understand. His teeth ground together, jaw clicking to either side. "My soul is going to ascend if I get this information, Raf. Not sink into depths of the underworld!"

"Oh, good, good, that's...[5] What pin was it that you said the vampire had?" Raffiel moved toward the shelf, his fingers flicking over the titles.

Bartholomew's lips pulled into a tight line. He was considering arguing more with the angel about the fate of his soul,[6] but perhaps now wasn't the time. "A silver swan."

"Ah, yes. Here it is." Raffiel pulled out a black notebook. There was a rather crudely sketched outline of a swan done in white paint. "Erasmus Alabaster the third. Born 1639 in Bath, England. Son of—"

"Yes, yes, I get the picture." Bartholomew didn't have time to listen to over three-hundred-and-fifty-years of biographical history. Whatever had brought the vampire to Mills Run would have been more recent. Bartholomew would skim Raffiel's writings for whatever it was and plot his blackmail from there.

The warlock snatched the book from the angel's hands. As he did, his fingers brushed Raffiel's skin.

---

5. He wanted to say *shocking* or *unlikely* or *a concerning sign that heaven might have been letting its standards slip*. But none of that would have been very polite, and Raffiel would have hated to upset his friend.

6. Not that the warlock was delusional enough to believe that he was owed eternal happiness and everlasting life in a celestial paradise, but eternal torture in the pits of hell seemed extreme. What would he even be punished for? His only crimes were deserved backstabbing, necessary lying, fair cheating, a sprinkling of blackmail, gaslighting a child and a few adults, and acquiring other people's belongings without their consent.

They don't feel cold or clammy at all, the angel thought. And, though Raffiel was the trusting sort, he finally began to grow suspicious.

Bartholomew hurried to open the book. The moment he did, his expression turned to one of utter fury. He threw the book. It almost hit the lantern, but luckily, the warlock missed, and the large tome landed harmlessly on the desk.

"What am I supposed to do with that?" Bartholomew's hands attempted to strangle the air for a few seconds before pointing at the book, which had fallen open somewhere in the center, revealing tea-stained white pages. There was nothing written on them. "It's empty!"

"Because I haven't gotten to writing about anyone born in the 1600s yet," Raffiel explained. "I'm only now at about 3,000 BC."

"Ugh!" Bartholomew groaned and slapped his fist against his forehead. What a waste of time this had been. Unless... he grabbed Raffiel's collar, shaking the angel in desperation. "You must know something useful about Mr. Graves— I mean, Erasmus Alabaster. What's the most recent thing you remember about him from before you fell?"

"He purchased a very nice pink parasol from an estate sale that he passed—"

"No, I mean the most significant thing you remember. Something that might be—" Bartholomew cut himself off. He'd been about to say *useful for blackmailing*. But Raffiel was unlikely to help if he knew the information would be used for something nefarious.[7] "Important, to help him on his spiritual journey of making amends."

---

7. The angel always suspected that any assistance he gave the warlock *might* have been unfairly used, but there was a difference between suspecting and knowing. The first allowed Raffiel to sleep at night.

Raffiel frowned. He was beginning to suspect that the warlock before him was very much alive. But the angel was an optimist. He decided to trust that Bart had a good reason for lying and was trying to help a poor old vampire.[8]

"Erasmus lost his fortune through a number of bad investments and got involved with some shady people," Raffiel admitted, rubbing his head as he recalled the story that he'd witnessed while still in his realm.[9] "He ended up stealing a pot of gold from Spudsy O'Cabbage and going into hiding. No one's heard from him in five— no I suppose it's twenty-five years now. If his soul is looking for peace, perhaps he could apologize?"

"To a leprechaun?" Bartholomew couldn't think of a creature with a worse temper. Leprechauns were small, feisty beings with some of the most powerful magic in existence. Cross one and you would be lucky to come out of the ordeal *only* dead. And there was nothing they treasured more than their pots of gold. A smile slashed across the warlock's chin. "Yes, Raf, that's an excellent idea. I think I'll suggest it to him."

And if he doesn't like how that sounds, then he'll just have to leave Mills Run Heights.

Bartholomew rubbed his hands together, and a low, ominous cackle rose from his lips.

Raffiel smiled and waited politely until the warlock had finished. "Would you like some tea?" He asked. "I could tell you more about

---

8. The chances were about 1 in 10,000. But for Raffiel, that was enough.

9. Knowing precisely which memory he needed to access meant that he was able to recall it much faster than Frederick Graves, who was still trying to figure out where he'd seen Bartholomew's face.

the histories in here. I'm writing a thrilling one now about a goblin called Twik who died in three thousand and twenty B.C. who—"

"Ah, no. I'm afraid I must go. The afterlife is calling."

"Oh, that's a shame." Raffiel sighed. "But I'll see you out." They crossed the long row of books, the angel holding his lantern at the ready. He stopped before a window and undid the latch. "I suppose you flew in, seeing as you're a spirit and all."

"Uh..." Bartholomew peered out the window. It was a very long way down to the grass below.

"Unless of course, you're not dead," Raffiel suggested. He didn't want to accuse his friend of lying, but also wanted to give the warlock the opportunity to tell the truth.

"Don't be silly. Of course, I am," Bartholomew insisted. A lump rose in his throat. He didn't know any runes that would allow him to fly, and even if he did, he doubted he'd have the right ink. The warlock cleared his throat, hiding his unease, and turned from the window.

He could see in Raffiel's eyes that the angel knew the truth. The correct thing to do would have been to admit it.

Bartholomew's lips curled in defiance. With a tone that dared the angel to challenge him, the warlock announced, "But ghosts still use ladders."

SIXTEEN

By the end of their discussion, the angel had insisted on walking Bartholomew back to the road, and the warlock had decided to take advantage of his friend's kindness. He convinced Raffiel to pay for a ride home for him. Ghosts, according to the warlock, neither enjoyed walking nor had money to spare.

Bartholomew was exhausted and eager to return to his subdivision, but he didn't dare go straight to Mills Run Heights. Raffiel, who was paying for a private car and driver, waited cheerfully until it arrived. The warlock suspected that his friend was attempting to learn his destination.[1]

Very sneaky, Bartholomew thought, admiring the angel's slyness. But, he wasn't going to fall for it. There was somewhere else he needed to visit anyway. So when the driver arrived, Bartholomew announced

---

1. His suspicion was misplaced. Had Bartholomew chosen to whisper the destination to the driver, and then double the real price, the angel would still have happily paid. The real reason Raffiel was lingering was to give his friend as many opportunities as possible to tell him the truth, for he felt certain the warlock was being tormented by having to lie. This was also an incorrect assumption.

with a smug sense of satisfaction, "Beech Point Nature Reserve, please."[2]

There was some grumbling from the driver over the distance, but a large wad of cash from Raffiel proved sufficient.[3]

The reserve was on the opposite side of the city to the forest where the angel lived. It was mid-morning by the time Bartholomew arrived. He trudged toward the tree, drawing confused looks from the few hikers he passed, none of whom were expecting to see a man in a suit strutting through the woods. A few shouted, smiled, or waved in greeting. The warlock grunted in response.

He drew more than a few looks from the animals too, but Bartholomew didn't notice them. Otherwise, he would have seen the squirrels and realized something was off. There were three of them, tottering on a branch like drunks on a tightrope. One was changing color, another's limbs were growing and shrinking so that it was consistently out of proportion, and the third stared into the woods with stars in his eyes. Bobbing on the leaves beside them, like plain Christmas decorations, were two empty glass bottles.

---

2. Only part of Bartholomew's glee was the result of feeling like he'd outsmarted the angel. The other was that he knew how far the reserve was from the angel's house, and it was an absolute relief to be able to travel the distance on someone else's tab.

3. You might now be wondering where exactly an angel who lived alone in a forest, writing history books that no one cared about, would have gotten cash. Raffiel often wondered the same thing. The wind caught lost bills, picked them up, and carried them through his windows. He assumed this was the result of choosing a fortunate location for his house, but it had significantly more to do with many of the angels still in their realm lending a helping hand.

Bartholomew arrived at his tree, hoping to find a fresh supply of inks waiting within. Instead, there was only another note. It was not as friendly this time.[4]

The warlock's scowl grew deeper and darker as he scanned the letter. *You get more money? I'm being grossly undercompensated as is...* Some more unnecessary ranting led to an exaggeration of Otto's role... *More dangerous than expected... The Syndicate on the lookout...* And so on, and so on. But what about Bartholomew's inks? There was no mention of them except for right at the very end. *I've sent the two bottles I had to spare. But I can't afford to supply you indefinitely. If you're unable to purchase inks, you'd best learn to brew them yourself!*

"Brew them myself," Bartholomew muttered the final line under his breath. "What does he take me for, a witch?"

And where was the ink that Otto promised?[5]

The warlock squeezed his hand into the trunk. His long fingers searched within. There was nothing.

"Damned liar!" Bartholomew muttered, scowling.

And it was at this very moment that misfortune befell him, though he wouldn't know the full extent of it for some time.

Bartholomew's hand was stuck. He yanked and tugged, cursing and grumbling for the next few minutes. By the time he managed to get it free, there was an angry red bruise around his wrist, and his mood was fouler than usual.

---

4. Iit would be unfair to judge Otto for this. He was copying the tone of the warlock's own letter, which had demanded fresh inks and money be sent in order to "ensure the safety of the amulet."

5. You have likely already deduced the answer, though poor Bartholomew never learn that his inks had been stolen by a trio of squirrels who'd drank a few drops and spilled most of the rest.

At no point during the ordeal did he notice someone in a dark black hood, who stood among the shadows of the trees. But the watcher saw Bartholomew and, despite the lack of beard and mop of curls, recognized him.

A sinister plot began to take shape.

Not that Bartholomew knew it.

By the time he'd broken free, there was no more shadowy, hooded figure to notice, and the only plot on the warlock's mind was his own.

He returned to Mills Run by bus, purchasing a postcard and a pen from the kiosk at the reserve before he left. The warlock composed a message on route, and when he returned to his neighborhood, he stopped by Mr. Graves' house and slipped it beneath the vampire's door.

The message read as follows:

Invitation for Mr. Graves. Meeting at Mills Run pool, midnight exactly. Blackmail to be discussed.

Seventeen

The Mills Run Heights Community Center was located on a large lot in the middle of the subdivision. It consisted of several buildings, which included public restrooms, an exercise room, and a hall for public functions. The center also featured the only HOA-approved white picket fence, which protected a sizeable swimming pool and thin stretches of lawn that had been cut off from the parkettes beyond. Bartholomew, who cared little for swimming, exercise, or interacting with others, had given the Community Center little thought prior. But a neutral location[1] was crucial for a negotiation.

Not that the warlock intended to do much bargaining.

Bartholomew sat on the edge of one of the pool's lounge chairs. He kept his back straight and his hands folded on his lap. But it was difficult to know what to do with his legs. The chairs were low and his limbs were long. If he stretched, his shoes would drop into the pool, if he bent his knees they might knock his chin. Neither made for an intimidating pose.

---

1. Though preferably one where the warlock still had the upper hand.

The time was currently 12:07 AM. Bartholomew was growing worried. Perhaps specifying blackmail in his note had been a tad too direct. But that was no excuse for the vampire to snub the invitation.

Preemptively annoyed by the slight and unable to arrange himself in a comfortable manner, the warlock turned his scowl toward his familiar, lying on the chair beside him.

Gizmo's head was on his paws, ears up[2] and tail alert.

"If you were a cat, you could lie on my lap," Bartholomew snapped at the demon. "That's the most obvious way to look intimidating." The warlock had images of old villains from fifties movies, who spun around in leather chairs while stroking grumpy-faced white cats.

"I still could," Gizmo offered. He had no objections to being a lap dog. "I'm not any bigger than a cat."

"Don't be an idiot. There's nothing threatening about a man with a yorkie."

"Well, maybe there isn't, but I don't see what that has to do with me. I'm a pomapoo."

"A what?" Bartholomew had never heard a more ridiculous word. He forgot about looking intimidating for the moment. His legs folded, crossing at the knee in the manner of a very demure giraffe, and he glared at his familiar.

By this point, it was 12:09 AM.

Before Gizmo could explain, the motion lights near the picket fence flicked on. Both Bartholomew and his familiar turned in time to see Mr. Graves slip through the white gate. A moment later, the vampire, unaware that he'd already been spotted, dropped a homemade smoke bomb onto the thin strip of mowed lawn. There was a burst of gray mist.

---

2. They always were.

With a flourish of his turquoise coat, Mr. Graves emerged from the smoke and stepped onto the concrete pool deck.

Gizmo clapped his paws against the edge of the chair. Though he wasn't sure why a vampire would bother with smoke bombs instead of swooping in as a bat, he still found the display impressive.

Bartholomew rolled his eyes. Mostly he thought the entrance silly, but he felt immediately jealous to hear Gizmo applauding, and there was a small part of him regretting that he hadn't prepared his own superior display. And he still hadn't found a way to sit menacingly on a pool chair.

Frederick paused for a moment, surprised to see the little black dog once again present. However, the vampire wasn't one to shun applause. He inclined his head in a small bow and swept forward, "Thank you, thank you."

Bartholomew scowled. He didn't appreciate Frederick's calm confidence. The vampire was supposed to be on edge, anxious, worried about who'd summoned him to the pool that night.

The warlock cleared his throat. He was the one doing the blackmailing. He was the one in charge. It was time he took control of the situation.

"I suppose you were wondering who invited you here tonight," Bartholomew's voice was deep and clear as though there was a weight to every word he uttered. "It was I!" He attempted to rise to his feet in a single motion, lithe and fluid, like a panther. But the chair was very low. The warlock's ass rose only a few inches up before his legs failed him and he dropped back down.

Beside him, he could hear Gizmo holding back a snicker.

Traitor, Bartholomew thought, and vowed to move the cheese to the top shelf of the fridge when they returned.

Frederick's eyes flicked over the warlock, who was pushing himself to his feet in a manner that reminded no one of a panther.

"Indeed," the vampire said, spinning his umbrella in his own attempt to add a bit of theatrics to his words. His fingers fumbled the handle, and it dropped to the concrete. Frederick leaned back and slipped his hand into his pocket as though this was what he'd intended all along. "I was expecting you."[3]

Bartholomew, who'd now managed to stand, clenched his jaw, and his eyes narrowed at the vampire, standing on the opposite side of the pool.[4] Frederick Graves didn't seem to understand how mysterious invitations with vaguely threatening messages worked.

"No," the warlock corrected him. "I'm the one who was expecting you."

"But were you?" Frederick raised his arms in a display of showmanship. He was referring to his delayed dramatic entrance. Very few people expected a vampire to show up late in a cloud of smoke.

"Yes, obviously!" Bartholomew didn't understand what mind games the vampire was trying to play. "I slipped the letter under your door. I invited you here. I'm the one doing the blackmailing."

Frederick frowned. His fingers pressed together in a steeple beneath his chin. Now he was wondering if Bartholomew understood how blackmail worked. "No, no, you're the one who's going to be blackmailed. Isn't that what you wanted to discuss, Mr. Whitlock?"

---

3. The only other person Frederick could think might slip a strange note under his door was Sarah Anne Miller, and Bartholomew's slanted scrawl in no way resembled an eleven-year-old girl's handwriting.

4. Though it should be noted that Frederick was a good few feet from the pool's edge. He disliked water, even when it was stagnant.

At the sound of his former name, Bartholomew froze. He opened his mouth, ready to deny this fact, but Mr. Graves was no naïve angel. There was a cold certainty in his eyes, and his lips curled in a smile that said he thought he'd won. There was no lie Bartholomew could invent that the vampire would believe. His blackmail plan was swiftly falling apart. But how?

The warlock's eyes flicked to Gizmo, and the two exchanged a look. Both assumed they were thinking the same thing.[5]

"You called me by name that night, didn't you?" Bartholomew said, scowling at the familiar. "Gizmo, you foozler! This is your fault."[6]

"What night?" Gizmo asked, perplexed as to what the warlock was talking about.[7]

Frederick was quiet for the next few moments as Bartholomew attempted to pass the blame to his familiar. The vampire had no intention of revealing how he'd actually deduced the warlock's identity. Few people would have connected the clean-shaven, curly headed youth with the slick-haired, pointy-bearded man who'd died on a

---

5. They were not. Bartholomew was thinking *he must have overheard us talking outside his window,* while Gizmo was wondering what kind of fortune-telling would be required for someone to think to send an invitation to their blackmailer before they'd actually started the process.

6. In fact, as the warlock was quite aware, he was the one who'd called Gizmo by name that night. But he was already furious about what his slip-up had cost them. He didn't have the emotional bandwidth to feel guilty for it too. The familiar needed to share some of the burden.

7. Though neither Bartholomew nor Gizmo noticed, Frederick's eyebrows rose in astonishment at hearing the small, fluffy black dog talk. Despite the many clues, it had not occurred to him until this moment that a great demon and warlock's familiar might take the shape of a toy-breed poodle mix.

plane. Frederick had only pieced it together because he'd had a vested curiosity in the story.

But he didn't want Bartholomew (or Gizmo) to realize that.

While the warlock and his familiar argued, Frederick went over the speech he'd rehearsed in the mirror before leaving. He repeated a short tongue twister to loosen his lips.[8] Then he patted his chest and coughed.

"Now, my terms are simple," he announced. His voice rose above the warlock's grumbles, silencing Bartholomew, but it remained unfortunately raspy. No amount of thespian voice exercises could undo centuries of sleeping in a coffin. "I will not inform The Bearded Syndicate of your deceit, providing that you comply with two simple requests. Chief among them, you must leave Mills Run Heights. It is your own business where your journey next takes you, so I shall not ask. My only curiosity is for the cargo that you possessed when—"

"No, no, no," Bartholomew's voice boomed across the pool, interrupting Frederick's speech. "I'm not going anywhere. You're not the only one capable of blackmail, Erasmus Alabaster the Third."

The vampire's ears tingled at the old, familiar name. It had been decades since anyone called him that.

A crooked smile curved Bartholomew's lips as he saw the surprise on Frederick's face. *Finally, I'm in charge of this conversation.*

"And my terms are thus, either you leave Mills Run Heights or I inform your old friend Mr. O'Cabbage where you've been hiding all these years." Bartholomew was also very interested in the leprechaun's pot that Frederick had stolen, but when it came to blackmail, he found it best to start simple and gradually ramp up the demands.

---

8. "Red leather, yellow leather, red leather, yellow leather…"

A cold sweat started to form on Frederick's brow. He pulled a white lace handkerchief from the top pocket of his shirt and dabbed his face. It hadn't occurred to him that Bartholomew could have learned the truth of his past.

The warlock's smile grew more slanted, and his dark eyes gleamed at the sight of the now anxious vampire before him. He reveled in the sense of outsmarting his opponent.

Until Gizmo went and ruined it by stating the obvious.

"That doesn't really make sense though does it?" the demon said, curling so that he could scratch his ear with his back paw. His forehead twitched with the movement. "I mean, you'll both end up having to leave, and that just doesn't seem utilitarian."

Bartholomew's teeth ground together. He had a vivid fantasy of wringing his familiar's neck. "I beg your pardon?"

"It's the philosophical idea that we should aim to maximize happiness for the greatest number of people," Gizmo explained. He hadn't missed the unsubtle sarcasm and poorly masked frustration in the warlock's tone, but that was so common with Bartholomew that the demon seldom paid it much mind. "But it seems to me, that both of you leaving would be the opposite of that. And both of you staying wouldn't work either. You'll each rat the other out, and no one will be very happy with that outcome."[9]

"Well, obviously, Gizmo." Bartholomew's hands tugged at his curls. "We already know one of us has to leave. That's the whole point of this meeting."

---

9. There were in fact several people that would have been thrilled by this outcome. Among them were Spudsy O'Cabbage, the leaders of The Bearded Syndicate, Constance Payne, Lum Lumbkin, and a host of other individuals that either Bartholomew or Frederick had wronged.

"Yes," Frederick agreed from across the pool, bending at last to retrieve his umbrella. He was less concerned about his performance now that he understood the situation better. "But if neither of us can blackmail the other into fleeing, then the question remains as to who?"

Eighteen

N o agreement could be reached.

Frederick argued that Mills Run was rightfully his territory since he'd arrived first. Gizmo returned to his rather recent utilitarian philosophy and pointed out that he and Bartholomew should be allowed to stay since there were two of them. The warlock, for once, agreed vehemently with his familiar.

Hints of pink tiptoed into the edges of the sky and their discussion drew to a necessary close. Frederick raised his umbrella, sheltered in its shade as he retreated to his house.

Bartholomew, alone[1] at the pool with the toasty swaddle of morning, two sleepless nights, and no more need to look intimidating, collapsed onto the chair. His eyes drooped shut, and his head slid onto his shoulder. *I'll just stay her and think for another moment.*

Gizmo thought a nap seemed a good idea. He jumped onto the chair with the warlock and pushed his muzzle into the crook of Bartholomew's elbow.

---

1. Save for Gizmo, who the warlock was no longer counting as a person since voting was finished.

So they slept, an image fit for a magazine, providing someone was very skilled with photoshop. The warlock's limbs jutted at awkward angles, like the outline of a cartoon cadaver. Gizmo's teeth gnashed in his dream,[2] and his lips curled back, giving him the expression of a very angry rodent. A thin waterfall of saliva cascaded from the corner of Bartholomew's mouth, creating a lake of drool on the top of his familiar's head.

That was how they were just before nine, when Dan Miller arrived at the community center.

Dan wore dark jeans and a white button down shirt with long sleeves. It took every ounce of his self-control not roll them up and undo the top few buttons so he could open the collar. Sweat gathered in the small of his back.

He stopped for a second, taking a breath in the shade of a maple near the corner of the functions' hall. There was a folder in his arms, full of papers. Among them were his bright orange campaign flyers. He took one and fanned himself with it.

Only one more week of this nonsense, he thought. The dress codes inflicted on anyone wishing to attend a homeowners association meeting were the first thing Dan intended to change once he became president.

A walkway between the functions' hall and exercise room led to the pool. From the corner of his eye, Dan could see the white picket fence. Behind it, there was a dark shape lying on one of the chairs.

Dan's first thought was that someone had forgotten a towel or a bag. It should have been perfectly safe. There was almost no crime in

2. Where he was a great demon once again, chasing down his enemies and burying them in a pit of darkness.

Mills Run. But Dan was one of those strange individuals who got a kick out of helping people unnecessarily.

He checked his watch. Still a few minutes before nine.

I've got time. Let me grab it and see if I can return it to its owner.

Smiling at the thought of doing a good deed, Dan jogged toward the white fence. His eyebrows rose as he realized what it was. A good many questions tripped over themselves in his mind, starting to form only to be quickly replaced by another, until he landed on the most significant one. *When did he—What was he—Has anyone—Why is he wearing a suit?*

Another neighbor might have given a judgmental scoff and walked off quietly with several incorrect assumptions to share with friends over too many glasses of wine. But Dan Miller had gone to the pool with the intention of helping.

"Hello, Bart!" He shouted, waving over the white picket fence.

The sound of Dan's voice was a gnat in Bartholomew's ear. He recognized the sound, but that didn't mean he appreciated it.

The warlock swatted his fist in the direction of his neighbor.

Dan chuckled. "Wild night last night?"

It was around this moment that Bartholomew became conscious enough to realize that he was lying in a pool chair in the middle of Mills Run. He shot up, wiping the back of his hand over his mouth, and throwing Gizmo onto the floor.

The demon awoke in time to land on his paws. He shook his head and flecks of saliva splattered onto the concrete pool deck. "Why am I wet?"

"Because you drooled all over yourself," Bartholomew hissed. "Now hush."

On the opposite side of the picket fence, Dan thought he heard an unfamiliar voice and looked around, searching for the source. He lacked his daughter's vivid imagination, so it never occurred to him that the speaker might have been a dog.[3]

Bartholomew pushed himself upright, managing to muster a little more grace than he had the previous night. He straightened his blue silk tie, attempting to maintain a modicum of dignity, and raised his hand in a gesture that was half wave, half shoo. The warlock couldn't quite bring himself to meet Dan's eyes. A small part of Bartholomew was just self-aware enough to be embarrassed for drooling in public. A larger part, with less self-awareness but adroit skills of self-deception, insisted that his only real shame had been cuddling his familiar.

Gizmo must have crawled into my lap, drooled on my chin, and put my arm over him just so that I'd look like a fool when I was discovered.

Yes, that was certainly it!

For some unfathomable reason, Dan was still standing at the picket fence with his mouth agape like some sort of fish.[4]

"Well, good day," Bartholomew said and turned toward the gate. It was, in his opinion, an obvious indication that their interaction was finished. Indeed, he hoped it suggested that it ought never to have started.

Unfortunately, Dan's understanding of warlock non-verbal cues was lacking.

"Hey, man, don't worry!" Dan laughed and climbed over the picket fence, jogging along the pool deck. He clapped his hand against Bartholomew's back.

---

3. And it definitely didn't cross his mind that it might be a demon, come to earth to be a warlock's familiar.

4. At least that was Bartholomew's impression. Gizmo, who was also there, would simply have said that Dan was smiling.

The warlock jumped, his eyes growing wide. He hadn't expected Dan to run up and assault him. Bartholomew tried to twist free, but his neighbor had a vice grip on his shoulder.

"You have nothing to be embarrassed about. Both Norm and I have passed out on those chairs after a few too many drinks." Then, just to ensure Bartholomew didn't get the wrong impression, he quickly added, "Luckily, our wives were there to wake us up."

Bartholomew's eyes narrowed. How dare his neighbor suggest he was embarrassed! He was an incredible warlock. Dan was... well his name was Dan and quite frankly that said everything anyone needed to know.

And now he has the audacity to compare his drunken misadventures with my clandestine scheming!

It was an insult like no other.

Unaware of the grave offense he'd just given, Dan kept talking, "Otherwise, we might've slept till morning too. And boy, I would hate to hear Ida if she saw that. I'm sure there's some obscure rule in the bylaws that prohibits it." In a high-pitched, squeaky voice that was meant to mimic an old woman, he said, "That's a five thousand dollar fine for sleeping in a pool chair! Didn't you read the homeowner covenants?"

Gizmo's head tilted to the side. He was sitting by Bartholomew's feet, listening to the exchange. Most of it was, quite literally, over his head. Who was Ida? Where were these bylaws? And what were covenants?

His eye glanced the orange flyer in Dan's folder.

"Oh," the familiar said. "Does this have to do with your Who-Ah?"

Dan's brow lowered. He looked around searching for the sound of the voice. "Who just asked that?"

Bartholomew knocked his shoe against Gizmo's muzzle before the familiar could respond. "That was me. I did."

"Oh." Dan paused. The voice had been sunny and cheerful, nothing like the warlock's old-man-on-a-ham-radio baritone. And Bartholomew's lips hadn't moved. Dan was certain of it.

The warlock's hand twitched to the quill in his pocket.

But he needn't have been concerned. Dan shrugged and brushed off his confusion. There was no one else around. Obviously, the voice had been his neighbor. Bartholomew must have been very eager to learn more about the HOA.

Dan was delighted to tell him. "Exactly! The Homeowners Association," he said, clapping Bartholomew on the back once more. "They're the ones who make the rules. I mentioned to you that a lot of them are quite..."—he paused to search for a polite term—"...*antiquated* ideas. But Mr. Anderson wasn't the only one to leave this year, so the old guard is pretty much all gone. I'm think it's time to get some young, fresh perspectives in there. Really shake things up."

Gizmo yawned halfway through the explanation. This who-ah, or whatever it was called, didn't sound like it was at all relevant to their lives. *Fresh. Young.* Bartholomew was more of an old and stale type of fellow. This wasn't the sort of thing that would be of interest to him.

Gizmo was very wrong.[5]

There was the dangerous flicker of an idea brewing in the warlock's dark eyes. "So this Homeowners Association are the rulers of the neighborhood?"

---

5. You must forgive Gizmo for this. Usually, he was quite astute in predicting Bartholomew's responses. But the familiar was tired, hungry, and very distracted by thoughts of cheese.

Dan scratched the back of his head. He'd never thought of it in quite those terms. "Sort of. I mean, most serious changes come to a vote, but given the low turnout, I suppose."

The corner of Bartholomew's lip twitched upward. His fingers opened and closed on his palms like sports fans in a stadium performing the wave.

Gizmo watched. He knew that look. It seldom meant anything good.

Dan[6] was just pleased to have anyone young express an interest in The Association. His friends had all declined his previous invitations, but he was feeling optimistic.

"There's a meeting now," he said. "It's open to everyone. Would you be interested?"

"Oh yes." The sinister slash of a smile spread across the warlock's face. "Yes, I would."

---

6. Who did not know Bartholomew's looks.

NINETEEN

The Mills Run functions' hall consisted mainly of a single, large rectangular room. The size and space of it would have made Bartholomew most uncomfortable were it not for the copious amounts of furniture packed within. For none of the residents had been able to agree on the precise purpose of the building.

At the entry was a fireplace surrounded by plush floral-print couches full of patterned pillows and crocheted blankets. Two large antique lamps with cream shades and gold tassels guarded the corners. It appeared much like the den of an old lady.[1]

From there, the room transformed into a recreation area. There was a shelf of board games, a billiards table, and another more curious[2] counter on which tiny skewered men faced off over a green felt top.

Beyond that was an assortment of mismatched plastic chairs and tables, precariously stacked in the middle. They were sandwiched between a bar on one side, wiped clean and granite glistening, and a

---

1. Mostly because it had been decorated by one.

2. To the warlock, at least, who was unfamiliar with most games from the last century.

kitchen counter, which was buried beneath appliances. The scent of coffee rose from a pot. A small fridge hummed beneath.

But it was the final quarter of the room that drew Bartholomew's attention. The walls were lined with wooden bookshelves, full of fading histories, stained romances, and glossy nonfiction titles that had never been opened for more than a few seconds. The warlock's eyes widened, consumed by the sight.

He almost didn't notice the long oak table that the books surrounded, nor its ten wicker chairs, nor the little old woman sitting at the head.

However, she certainly noticed him, strolling into *her* meeting three minutes late.

Ida Meadows was a bundle of contradictions wrapped in a small, floral-coated parcel. A former elementary school teacher, she'd never been fond of children. A lifelong spinster, she had opinions on the shortcomings of every wife and mother. And, though in her estimation most of her neighbors were disrespectful nuisances who she wanted little to do with, Ida made it her mission to know and judge the intimate details of their lives.

"Ahem. Ahem." Ida cleared her throat and lifted her chin until it was parallel to the floor. She peered at the two men through a pair of cat eye glasses that pinched the tip of her nose, tapping a metal ruler against a thin gold watch. "You're late, Daniel."[3]

Dan sighed and rubbed his temples as he sat down at a chair. *This is why none of my friends will come to these meetings*, he thought. The

---

3. To clear up any confusion, Daniel was not, nor had it ever been, Dan Miller's full name. He'd explained this fact to Ida multiple times and even shown her his ID card hoping to clear up the issue. It had done little to help, and Dan had eventually given up.

Association members were pedants and sticklers, or at least they had been. It was only Ida and Dan left now.

"This is my friend," Dan said, forcing a smile, as he introduced Bartholomew. "He's just moved into Mr. Anderson's place and is interested in joining the association."

Ida sniffed, chin still high as she turned to the warlock. Her initial instinct was to dislike and mistrust anyone below the age of sixty. They were all flighty and disorganized, their brains stifled by too much time matching colorful candies on screens. None of them had them the life experience to understand how the world really worked.

She was eager to dismiss Bartholomew. But there was something about him that caught her attention and paused her judgement: his three piece suit. Even having slept in it the night before, the dark fabric remained unwrinkled and it was evident that the blue silk tie matched the jacket's lining.

Well now, Ida thought to herself, *it's not often you find a young man who still takes pride in his appearance.*

"Bartholomew Bartlow, madam." The warlock took Ida's fingers, bowed, and pressed his lips to the back of her palm.[4] "An honor to make your acquaintance."

"Oh, my, yes!" Once again Ida was caught off guard. This was the level of respect she was due. But people seldom offered it. "Yours as well Mr. Bartlow. I'm Ida Meadows, treasurer of The Homeowners Association and current acting President. Please, do take a seat. It's nice to have a respectable young man here in Mills Run. Most of the others are under the mistaken impression that denim counts as appro-

---

4. This was not how Bartholomew typically greeted women, but his understanding of HOAs was rudimentary at best, and he was under the opinion that Ida was a woman of great power and importance.

priate business attire." She shot an annoyed glare in Dan's direction. "Now, onto the matters of the day—"

"The election," Dan said, interrupting her and pulling out his folder. "I've organized everything. We have volunteers to man the booth and..."

While he spoke, Bartholomew settled into the wicker chair to Ida's right. Gizmo followed and jumped onto the seat beside him.

"Excuse me," Ida said, interrupting Dan and turning a rather affronted look to the dog that was now sitting at their table. "Is this your animal, Mr. Bartlow?"

"Woof, woof," Gizmo said, wagging his tail.

The warlock glared at his familiar. Of course, the demon would choose now to embarrass him, right when they were meeting of the ruler of Mills Run Heights. They were going to need to have a long conversation about appropriate dog behavior.

"My profuse apologies, madam." Bartholomew snatched Gizmo from the chair and dropped the offended familiar to the floor. He wrangled the demon's small, furry black frame still between his shoes so that he couldn't jump up onto the furniture again. "Gizmo belonged to my late mother. I'm doing my best to train him, but truthfully, I've always been more inclined to cats."

"Have you now?" Ida's high opinion of Bartholomew was at once restored. "I've three at home: Sprinkles, Skimbleshanks, and Mr. Fluff. You must come for tea and meet them one afternoon."

"I should be honored."

Dan watched this exchange with some confusion. He assumed that Bartholomew was simply being polite, but he'd never heard Ida extend a kind word to anyone below the age of sixty. Now, she was gazing at their new neighbor with a strange, doe-eyed expression.[5] Dan couldn't quite say why, but it made him feel very uncomfortable.

He cleared his throat and looked back at his papers. "So as I was saying, the election—"

"Yes. Yes. You've sorted it all." Ida waved her hand in annoyance. "The real matter of the day is Veronica Thompson."

Bartholomew leaned forward, intrigued at once. He had never heard of this woman.

Dan frowned. "You mean the nine-year-old girl who lives in 61B?"

"Precisely. She jumped into the pool and splashed water onto the side," Ida said, pointing her ruler at Dan as though he were the guilty party who'd abetted her in this crime. "That is a violation of Pool Rule 14, subsection B. Residents' rights to a relaxing pool environment cannot be infringed by—"

"Yeah, okay. But she's nine years old. What do you want us to do?"

"This is her third violation. Warning letters are no longer enough. Her family should be slapped with a fine."

"Because their nine-year-old acted like a regular child?" Dan's voice rose a fraction louder than intended. He sighed and covered his eyes with his palm. He wanted to think the best of everyone, he truly did, but Ida presented a challenge at times.

The crackling tension brought a natural pause to the conversation.

Bartholomew seized the moment. He leaned forward, expression serious as he looked at Ida. "You seem well-versed in the rules of this neighborhood, Madam. I wonder, are there any prohibitions as to the tinting of windows?"

---

5. It was not unlike how many a woman has stared at a romantic movie lead when he ripped his shirt off or emerged from the ocean or suddenly confessed his love.

Gizmo, who'd been pouting on the floor, struggling to focus on anything but the grumbling in his stomach, lifted his head. His ears rose higher. He finally understood what they were doing in the functions' hall.

Ida smiled, and for a moment there was a hint that she'd once been a girl and not a thin-lipped, wrinkle-necked lady of seventy-three. Flattered to finally have someone appreciate her talents, she tapped her ruler to her cheek. Tinted windows seemed like the sort of thing that ought to have been against the rules. Mr. Anderson had been diligent in ensuring uniformity. Yet, she couldn't think of anything in the bylaws that mentioned windows.

"I don't believe there are," she answered, lips puckering in disapproval. "An oversight on the part of our former President."[6]

"So you agree that something should be added to the rules to prohibit such a thing," Bartholomew pressed.

Ida considered it. "Yes, I think we should."

A wicked sense of delight made the warlock's fingers flutter across the table. "So you'll fix it," he suggested, eyes burning with excitement as he stared at Ida. "You'll change the rules and outlaw tinted windows?"

"Won't be enough," Gizmo muttered from under the table.

Bartholomew squeezed the demon tighter between his ankles and glared down at him.

Luckily, however, neither of the two humans in the room with them heard. For at the same time that the familiar spoke, so did Dan.

---

6. On this, Ida was mistaken. The lack of rules relating to windows had not been an oversight on the part of Mr. Anderson. The former HOA president had made a purposeful decision to never think about windows, mostly as a result of vampiric hypnosis.

"Whoa!" he said, confused by the turn this was all taking. He'd had no idea that his new friend had such strong opinions on windows. "That's not how this process works at all. First of all, Ida is *acting* president. She runs the meetings, but we can't make any real decisions until there's someone officially in the position. But even then, this is a democracy. The president can't make unilateral changes. His[7] job is to oversee the upkeep of the neighborhood and listen to the concerns of the committee. If he thinks something should change, he has to present it to the community at large. All residents get the chance to vote on new bylaws."[8]

Bartholomew was only half listening. For during Dan's explanation, another conversation was occurring, unnoticed by either of the HOA members.

The warlock's head was tilted down. He glared at the demon between his feet and mimed stapling Gizmo's mouth shut.

Unfortunately, Bartholomew wasn't talented enough at charades for the familiar to understand the gesture.

"Won't work," Gizmo said, sticking his tongue out at the warlock.[9]

"Shut up," Bartholomew hissed, shifting his hand so that it blocked his face from view. It wouldn't do if either human noticed him muttering to a dog. "It will."

---

7. Dan wasn't being sexist by assuming that the president was a man. He was, however, being presumptuous and already thinking of the position as his.

8. Though this was technically true, Dan omitted the fact that most people didn't bother. As such, votes on bylaws were almost always limited to HOA members.

9. This did not have the effect that the familiar desired, mostly due to the fact that, in his current dog form, Gizmo's tongue lolled from his mouth quite frequently.

Gizmo shook his head.

Bartholomew's jaw clenched. His familiar was being purposefully difficult. This plan was brilliant.

Dan finished talking and Bartholomew looked up again.

Beneath the table, Gizmo barked, "Curtains. Curtains."

Ida frowned. She turned to Bartholomew. "What about curtains?"

Bartholomew squeezed Gizmo before he could think of responding. "I know what about curtains," he muttered, glowering at the demon. The tinted windows were only one measure of Frederick's precaution. The vampire might be unhappy to lose them, but they didn't guarantee his defeat. He had another layer of defense: the heavy black curtains beyond.

They had, perhaps, temporarily slipped Bartholomew's mind. But only because he was so focused on dealing with the tinted glass. Once he'd solved the first problem, he'd have remembered the curtains and addressed the issue then. He didn't need his familiar to point out the obvious!

But now, Gizmo had mentioned the curtains, and both Ida and Dan were looking at Bartholomew, waiting for an explanation.

The warlock had to invent one quick.

"Some curtains are very problematic," he said, holding out his hand. This statement earned a nervous chuckle from Dan[10] and a raised eyebrow from Ida.[11] Bartholomew didn't let either of their reactions bother him. He was busy inventing a case against curtains.

---

10. Who hoped, but was not entirely convinced, that Bartholomew was making a joke.

11. Who had a pair of loose floral curtains in her own home, but was always open to bit of judgmental hypocrisy. She could be persuaded that someone else's curtains were somehow wrong.

"They don't let in the sun if they're too thick. That's very dangerous. People in the neighborhood could catch rickets."

The warlock paused, trying to gauge the effect of his argument on his listeners. Both remained skeptical.

"They're a fire hazard."

Still no hint of sympathy.

"They enable all kinds of suspicious activity."

Dan laughed, truly hoping this was a joke. But Ida's other eyebrow rose. Bartholomew had her attention.

"What kind of suspicious activity?' she asked.

Bartholomew had her now, and he knew it. The corner of his lip twitched. "Any kind. Drugs. Gambling. Animal abuse. There's no real need for curtains if you've nothing to hide. I mean, why should an upstanding citizen have a problem with someone pressing their face to a window and seeing in their house? Allowing the wrong kind of curtains will attract the wrong sorts of people."

"Or just people who like to walk around in their underwear," Dan suggested with a slight uncomfortable laugh.

But Ida wasn't listening to him. Her mind was doing cartwheels, trying to recall which of her neighbors had thick curtains. All of them had broken the bylaws at some point, which made them criminals in her eyes. What else might they be hiding?

"Yes, Mr. Bartlow," she said, chin bobbing like fishing bait as she nodded. "I quite agree. Wrong kind of curtains, wrong sorts of people. The rules should be amended."

Dan pushed his chair back and stood. This joke, though he was growing increasingly anxious that it was not one at all, had gone too far. He held up his hands. "Look, I'm not against letting people vote on tinted windows. Even I can admit that Mr. Graves' house looks a little out of place because of them. But there's no problem with people having curtains. It would be silly for me to even bother putting that to the community."

"Well, that's not your decision to make yet. Is it, Daniel?" Ida rapped her ruler against the table, less than an inch shy of Dan's hand. "You're not the president."

"But I will be," Dan pointed out, flinching away the metal ruler. "I'm running unopposed."

At this Bartholomew's eyebrows rose. Even Gizmo, grumbling to himself about the unfairness of the entire situation,[12] silenced at these words. He had a feeling he knew where this was going.

The warlock's hands pressed together. There was a dangerous gleam in his eye. Why hadn't this occurred to him before? The most powerful position in the entire neighborhood was up for grabs. If Bartholomew secured it, he could oust the vampire.

"You shall not be unopposed, Dan Miller." The warlock stood too, a smile rising on half of his face. "I too will run for this illustrious position. And *when* I become President of the Homeowners Association, curtains will be banished from Mills Run Heights."

---

12. "Relegated to the floor without even a cushion or a pig's ear to chew. Don't animals have any rights? There isn't even anyone in most of the chairs."

TWENTY

The announcement that Bartholomew Bartlow, a resident for less than a week, was now running for president on a campaign to ban curtains, might have shocked the Mills Run Heights community *if* anyone cared much about The Homeowners Association. In general, it was viewed as an antiquated gathering of retirees with too much time and too little empathy. Although most residents had received a sternly worded note from the HOA committee for some minor infraction, it was worth little more than an eye roll. They had children and spouses and jobs. Bylaws and covenants ranked low on their list of concerns, if indeed, they registered at all.

There were, of course, a few individuals who cared about the warlock's late entry into the presidential race.

Gizmo, obviously, was required to care by virtue of being Bartholomew's familiar. Because he considered them friends, the demon also volunteered for the position of campaign manager and had his application swiftly rejected. But Gizmo ignored Bartholomew and gave himself the title all the same. He knew someone would need to help the warlock and make up for his severe lack of interpersonal skills.

Dan Miller and his friends had varied opinions on the issue. Running on a campaign to abolish curtains seemed a bit of a joke. Some thought it was a great laugh, and others were annoyed that he'd placed himself in opposition to someone who'd welcomed him to the neighborhood. Dan himself felt relieved. He'd been a bit embarrassed to be the only candidate. This way at least, when he won, he thought it would feel more deserved and less like a default title.

There was also a small group of meddlesome individuals who were intrigued by Bartholomew's proposal. Chief among them was Ida Meadows. She'd become quite enamored of her dashing young neighbor who comported himself with the dignity of an old-fashioned gentleman.

But there was one person in Mills Run Heights who cared above all others.

Frederick Graves was in his kitchen, brewing his usual sundown blood-bag tea, when a knock came at his door.

Not again, he thought, assuming that it was Sarah. *I'll run out of cups if she keeps this up.*

The vampire was in no mood to deal with a child. He'd met with Bartholomew the previous night and then spent the next thirteen hours asleep in his coffin. Who knew what the warlock might have planned during that time? Frederick needed to plot quick and catch up.

But ideas were scarce. He could set fire to Bartholomew's property, but anything large-scale like that would attract more attention than it was worth. He could hypnotize the neighborhood into ousting the warlock, but anytime he'd tried to control a mob in the past it had gotten quite out of hand.[1] He could slip mean notes under

---

1. This was partly because Frederick had never been able to hypnotize more than one person in a single day since using his ability gave him a horrible headache. It would take him almost a year to gain control of the entire neighborhood, and the effects of hypnosis had a tendency to fade.

Bartholomew's doorstep, undermine his self-esteem. Frederick fancied himself a bit of a wordsmith and was certain he could come up with some truly devastating insults. But even he wasn't sure how that would force the warlock to leave.

The knock came again, followed by a voice. It wasn't Sarah but her father, calling into the house. "Hello! Mr. Graves, you there?"

Frederick frowned. He went toward the door, grabbing his turquoise coat from the closet and slipping it on while maneuvering his cup of blood tea. The vampire was a bit concerned that something serious had occurred. He couldn't imagine why else Dan Miller would be knocking this late at night.

"What's happened?" Frederick asked as he pulled open the door.

Dan stood on the front step. He'd switched his formal button-down for a plain blue t-shirt and matching baseball cap. His hands were full of bright orange campaign posters.

"Hope I didn't startle you, Mr. Graves," Dan said, smiling. "Only I know you're a bit of a night owl, so I didn't think you'd mind my knocking so late. I just wanted to remind you about my campaign platform."

He paused, noticing the cup of liquid in the vampire's hand. It was a dark red. A little tag hung from the side: *type A+*.

I didn't know they graded teas, Dan thought. He'd always preferred coffee himself, but his wife, Lisa, had spent most of last year talking about how wonderful England sounded, and he'd bought her a box of British teas for Christmas. She'd seemed unimpressed. Had he accidentally given her a *C-minus* box?

"Yes, yes, fun for Dan," Frederick muttered, mixing up the slogan. He took a flyer for the sake of politeness, though there was already one stuck on the fridge in his house. The vampire tracked the HOA more closely than most of the Mills Run residents. "Why are you bothering to campaign when you're the only candidate?"

Dan frowned. He glanced over his shoulder to the blue mailbox at the front of Frederick's walkway. The flag was down. "Didn't you read the notice that came today? There's been a new addition to the race—Bartholomew Bartlow."

The vampire's eyes grew wide.

"Here, I think I have a copy of the notice in my pocket. You're not the first one who missed it." Dan pulled a slip of white paper from his jeans. The announcement had been typed in Arial, size 12 font, double spaced, and stamped with the official seal of the Homeowners Association. He passed it to the vampire.

Frederick's lips curled back in a snarl as he read the announcement.

Dan tried not to stare. Mr. Graves certainly did have some pointy teeth.

"I assume I can count on your vote," Dan continued, averting his gaze to his own flyers so that he had something to distract him from his neighbor's unsettlingly sharp cuspids.

"That depends," Frederick said, his thumb and forefinger stroking the point of his chin. A brilliant idea was beginning to form in his mind. The warlock wasn't the only one who could manipulate the HOA to his advantage. "How do you feel about dogs?"

"Oh, I quite like them," Dan started to say, but the words died on his lips.

He'd made the mistake of looking at his neighbor. Before him, Frederick's eyes spun like cold, white pinwheels. They were at once terrifying and mesmerizing. Dan found it impossible to look away.

TWENTY-ONE

T he next morning, there were new orange flyers stuck under windshield wipers, shoved into mailboxes, and stapled to telephone poles. Dan Miller remained smiling in the center. However, his slogan had changed. He was no longer campaigning to ease the neighborhood rules. In large block letters, the flyers' declared: *DAN AGAINST DOGS.*

The few who read the announcements before crumpling them and tossing them in a bin, were of three minds about the sudden shift. The dog-owners among them were aghast and vehemently against the proposal to ban their pets from the community.[1] But a few—older, grumpier, and with more sensitive ears—were in favor.[2] Others, mainly Dan's friends, assumed it was a joke.[3]

Within Bartholomew's house, he and his familiar remained blissfully unaware of the flyers until late afternoon. They'd spent most of

---

1. "We'll have to burn the curtains your mother gave us in protest," Chloe Robinson of 58B said to her husband with a rather forced sigh. "As much as I've always loved how the bright magenta flowers clash with the cool neutrals in the living room, it's them or Bandit."

the morning debating the warlock's campaign. Bartholomew, overestimating the appeal of his platform thanks to Ida's enthusiasm, felt his argument stood on its merits alone. Give him the chance to speak to the feeble-minded residents of Mills Run, and he'd convince them to make him supreme ruler and oust Frederick without issue.

Gizmo had less faith in the warlock's rhetorical capabilities. If they wanted to win this election, Bartholomew would need to go door-to-door, win the love of the residents, just like Dan was doing. But the warlock wasn't ready for that just yet.

"No, no, no," the familiar said, resting his chin on the kitchen floor and covering his eyes with his paws. Bartholomew prepared a couple of sandwiches for their dinner. They'd spent most of the day locked inside, role playing different scenarios that might occur during the campaign. "You can't threaten to burn their house down if they don't agree with you."

"I didn't," the warlock objected, slathering some acquired mustard over the bread. "All I said was that failure to comply with my regime would mean watching their house and everything they love burn and crumble to ash.[4] What part of that could possibly be misconstrued as a threat?"

All of it was the nonconstructive but nonetheless accurate answer that Gizmo would have given, were it not for a loud shout from outside.

"Bartholomew! Gizmo! Something's happened!" Sarah banged on the door.

The warlock groaned, rested his mustard knife on the plate, and reluctantly went to peep his head out. "What?"

---

4. It seemed abundantly clear to Bartholomew that this was due to the fire hazard caused by curtains.

"It's my dad," she said, rushing inside. Her large purple shirt and denim shorts made her appear like a plum perched on a blueberry. There was a bright orange flyer in her hand. She shoved it forward, holding it out for them to read. "I told him he has to change his policy or I'll never forgive him, but he won't listen."

Bartholomew and Gizmo scanned the flyer. The warlock's chest grew tight. The familiar breathed a sigh of relief.

"Thank goodness!" Gizmo declared, collapsing onto his side with a laugh. "I was thinking you'd never be able to compete with someone as naturally charismatic as Dan. But he's killed his own chances with this. Why would anyone want to get rid of dogs?"

"Oh, gee, I don't know," Bartholomew said, voice dripping with sarcasm as he scowled at the fluffy black demon whose tongue was lolling on his floor. "You attract fleas, you shed, you lift your leg on all the maple trees."

He counted the reasons on his fingers, fear turning in his stomach and boiling into rage. Dan's original campaign was *fun*. It was non-sensical, meaningless, easy to defeat. But this was a policy the warlock might have supported if his circumstances were different.

"This was why I told you to become a cat," Bartholomew snapped. His fingers clenched into fists. He took a swing at the garlic-scented air.

"Oh come on," Gizmo said, pouting. "You don't think anyone will actually support this ridiculous measure?"

Bartholomew certainly did, but he couldn't be certain. His lips pressed together for a moment in thought. Then he said, "I think I know who we can ask."

———————◆○◆———————

Ida Meadows lived in house 53A, one street north of Bartholomew. It was a single story, one bedroom model with the same open plan living area. She'd decorated it in blue and pink florals, which might have tricked someone into believing that they were in a garden. If they'd lost all sense of smell.

Bartholomew was convinced that cats were clean and tidy until he entered Ida's home. An aroma of cat pee, litter, and saliva rolled into him like a fur ball. He hadn't known it was possible to long for the scent of garlic that still dominated his doorway.

Ida's annoyed frown turned to a smile as she saw Bartholomew. She smoothed the pink pleats of her long skirt. "Goodness, Mr. Bartlow, I wasn't expecting company."

"I know, Ms. Meadows, and I do apologize for the intrusion, but I needed some advice from someone who knows this neighborhood."

The compliment was enough to make Ida blush and welcome the warlock in. It wasn't quite sufficient to stop her from noticing the fluffy black dog and small plum-shaped child that followed.

Ida's thin, wrinkled hand whipped from the puffed sleeve of her white blouse. It was no less daunting for lack of its ruler. She blocked Sarah's path. "You know you're not welcome in my house, Ms. Miller. There's breakables. And keep that one with you."

She pointed to Gizmo, who'd trotted past her hand and was now attempting not to retch while he inhaled. Green eyes glared at him from beneath the couch. He crouched down, ready to face this new opponent, only to feel a pair of hands wrap around his torso.

Ida lifted Gizmo as though he were the one with the smell, holding him at arm's length. She flung him toward Sarah, and the two were then unceremoniously evicted. From the doorstep, they heard the door lock behind them.

"Terribly rude," Gizmo noted, shaking out his fur as Sarah rested him on the lawn. He didn't appreciate Ida grabbing him like he was some inanimate object.[5] "Why won't she let you in?"

"Just doesn't like kids, I guess."[6]

"Or dogs." Gizmo snorted his disproval, shaking his head. But the thought made his confidence waver. What if Dan Miller's new campaign wasn't as hopeless as the demon had assumed? The familiar might have his work cut out for him after all. He turned to Sarah. "How many other dogs are there in Mills Run? We're going to need an itemized list if we're going to manage Bartholomew's presidential campaign."

And the two got to work on the grass at once. Behind them, the sun sank in the sky.

Within Ida's house, Bartholomew perched at the edge of a round pink pillow that did little to keep the fraying wicker from poking at his back. The dining room chair rocked beneath his weight, legs

---

5. It was tantamount to assault in the demon's opinion. The only reason that he couldn't persecute was because the infrastructures of Earth were inherently species-ist.

6. This was true, but not the specific reason that Ida had banned them from her house. The former schoolteacher was afraid of her belongings being damaged as a child had once broken a beloved vase of hers. However, learning this truth would not have comforted Sarah. For the incident had occurred decades ago, long past the statute of limitation for being upset about such a thing. And the child in question bore little resemblance to Sarah seeing that he was a boy, five years old, and Ida's nephew.

threatening to give out at any moment. He refused to breathe through his nose.

"Milk and sugar in your coffee, Mr. Bartlow?" Ida asked, taking a floral print tea pot from the stovetop.

Now that Gizmo and Sarah were outside, two of her three cats had come out of hiding. A tabby walked across the counter, tail brushing against the appliances and leaving a clump of hair in the toaster. A gray cat, who might once have been furry, rubbed its balding head against Bartholomew's ankle, as needy for attention as any dog.

"Black,"[7] the warlock said, scratching behind the gray cat's ear. "Thank you for your hospitality, Ms. Meadows. I promise, I shall not keep you long." He intended to be true to his word, in no small part due to the smell.

"Please, call me Ida," she said, waving her hand and smiling in a manner that would have made her label a different woman as a coquette. "And you're welcome anytime. Though I'd ask you to leave your friends behind." She gave him a stern look over her glasses as she carried their coffees to the table. "Curious company you keep, Mr. Bartlow."

It took the warlock a minute to realize that she was referring to Gizmo and Sarah. "Those two fools? Please, madam, they are not my friends. Gizmo is my pet and my penance.[8] Aurora's parents are

---

7. Not everyone who drinks their coffee black is a psychopath. But it is generally accepted that all psychopaths drink their coffee black. Whether this is relevant information in the case of Bartholomew is up to the reader's discretion.

8. Bartholomew didn't consider this statement to be a lie.

a dreadful influence, and I'm afraid she's seen my capabilities and latched onto me.[9] You've seen Dan Miller's new campaign?"

Ida frowned. She had no idea who *Aurora* was, but she was relieved that Bartholomew hadn't tried to defend the whining, scratching and shedding creature that he'd brought to her house or his dog.

"Yes, I did," Ida admitted, taking a seat at the head of her dining table, right beside the warlock. She always checked her mailbox first thing when she arose. Sometimes she checked her neighbors' too. "Quite a shift of message. This might be a closer race than I anticipated."

Bartholomew's fingers tightened on his coffee. His lips grew thin. This was exactly what he'd been afraid of. "Please, tell me plainly then. Have I lost your vote, Ida?"

The old woman lifted her chin, posing for a moment, enjoying having Bartholomew's attention on her. She tapped her finger to her thin, pink-painted lips as though she were only now considering.[10]

"Not mine," she said at last. "This is just Daniel trying to get a rise out of his new competitor. He'd never ban dogs. He's too weak to ban anything. But I know that because I know him. A lot of other people might fall for it."

Bartholomew sighed. He rubbed one of his temples with a finger. He hated to think that Gizmo might have been right. "So if I have any

---

9. Even Bartholomew wasn't good enough at lying to himself to think this was true.

10. This wasn't true. Ida already knew her answer. She'd determined that earlier this morning and already discussed it with everyone in a ten-mile radius who hadn't been fast enough to hide indoors at the sight of the former schoolteacher marching down the street, waving an orange flyer while her eyes hawked for their next victim.

hope of winning, I shall have to campaign door-to-door and interact with all my neighbors, even the foolish ones who'll misinterpret perfectly good advice as threats and insults."

Ida's heart, covered in cobwebs and weighted with dust for most of the past few decades, fluttered back to life. She stared at the handsome young man before her, with his dark eyes and dark curls, hand rubbing the head of her beloved Mr. Fluff. Despite the large gap in their ages, they were kindred spirits.

The old woman was struck by a sudden desire, one she hadn't felt before, not even in her decades teaching. Ida wanted to help.

"Don't you worry, Mr. Bartlow—it won't come to that," she promised, pushing her chair back. With short, quick strides, Ida crossed the room to an old antique wooden cabinet that had been decorated with white crochet. She removed a small notebook with purple flowers from one of the drawers and brought it back to the table. "Now, let's see here."

She licked her thumb and flipped through the pages. Tiny, cursive letters smushed together so that it was almost impossible to distinguish the individual words. Ida was a meticulous keeper of thoughts and observations.[11]

Contained among the idle comments about her neighbors' comings and goings were detailed notes on all of the Homeowners Association meetings. Every individual who'd ever attended had been added to Ida's notebook along with her own theories about how they'd voted.

Bartholomew's dark eyes grew hungry and dangerous as he scoured the pages. His lips slanted upward; his hands rubbed together in glee.

---

11. Others might call it gossip or, in an oft-heard phrase, "none of Ida's damn business".

Thanks to Ida's notebook, there was no need for pointless interactions with residents who'd never cast a vote in their years at Mills Run. The warlock could determine precisely who he needed to target in order to win his campaign.

With this information, it would be impossible for Dan Miller to defeat him. The poor fool would need some sort of supernatural intervention.

Now that, Bartholomew thought, holding back a chuckle, *would be so ludicrous, I'd almost like to see it.*

TWENTY-TWO

I da's notes created a blueprint for Bartholomew over the next few
days.

Only thirty-two residents had ever voted at a Homeowners Association meeting. Of those, seven no longer lived in Mills Run, one
was Dan, and another Ida herself. That left Bartholomew with twen-
ty-three potential henchmen,[1] most over the age of sixty-five. Thankfully, this was one demographic where being a stuffy, close-minded
curmudgeon with antiquated ideas could prove useful.

There was no need for Bartholomew to knock on doors, press his
lips to saliva-covered babies or run his fingers through flea-infested
fur. Instead, he infiltrated the Mills Run Heights Retiree Club, who
met thrice weekly in the Functions Hall. Officially, these were for
events and occasions such as bridge, dominoes, book club. However,
most meetings devolved into complaints about today's youth, nos-
talgic yearning for the old days, and a battle of woes as each individual attempted to outdo the others with their list of aches and pains.
Bartholomew had never been one for idle chit-chat, but belabored
belly-aching was perfectly acceptable in his book. He bided his time,

---

1. The warlock's term for them, despite Gizmo's frequent reminders that *sup-
porters* would be a more apt description.

listening with as much sympathy as he could feign, before seizing the soap box to rant and rave about the dangers of curtains.

Not everyone was amenable to his arguments, but enough were that Bartholomew had soon amassed a group of loyal underlings twelve retirees strong. If they held for the next three days prior to the election, there was a chance that the warlock would have a slim majority.

But it wasn't guaranteed. The other eleven voters were under Dan's sway[2], and he continued his door-to-door campaign. His jovial smile and relaxed attitude made him popular among his peers. So long as he didn't talk much about his new platform,[3] he was likely to inspire more than a few first-time voters.

If Bartholomew wanted to win, he'd have to do the same.

The warlock lacked the charisma, likeability, and general sense of decency to appeal to younger voters. So, as Bartholomew's campaign manager, Gizmo took the matter into his own paws.

He and Sarah hadn't been idle on the lawn while the warlock first met with Ida. Together, the two had formulated their own plan to ensure Bartholomew's victory in the election. When the warlock disappeared to woo his band of bitter retirees, his unofficial campaign

---

2. One had a son with dog allergies that she swore were deadly despite the fact that he'd hugged his neighbor's golden retriever and remained very much alive; three were convinced that the mud that squelched on their lawn whenever it rained was secretly full of dog poop; two were tired of listening to their neighbor talk about her purebred show poodle and hoped she'd move away if the rules changed; four were retirees, who'd either developed grudges against Bartholomew or delighted in being contrarian. The last was Dan's wife, Lisa.

3. At which point Sarah reported that his eyes grew "weird" and his voice became "like an evil robot."

manager and even less official assistant, worked tirelessly on his behalf and without his consent.

Sarah and Gizmo visited every house with a dog in Mills Run, putting on quite the show: a sweet eleven-year-old girl holding a wide-eyed toy poodle mix, begging people to look into their hearts, to think of the children and the pets and the future, to be the change they wanted to see. It was a fine speech, in both her and Gizmo's opinion, for they'd written it themselves, borrowing generously from television and radio advertisements.

For those on the receiving end of Sarah's speech, it was rather unnerving, mostly because whenever she faltered, they swore they heard a man whisper the cue. Only no one of them could figure out where the mysterious prompter was hiding. A few worried that she was being forced to speak against her will, but all accepted the hand-drawn flyers she gave them. Most failed to recognize the oval with black swirls as a drawing of their new neighbor's face, but they understood the bubble-letter message written in purple sparkly pen beneath:

My Dad Dan Hates Dogs! Vote for Bartholomew Instead![4]

If at least a few could be persuaded, Gizmo was optimistic about their chances.

"Joe won't vote for my dad," Sarah said, as they walked back from the Baker's house. "Victor told me that his dad said my dad had gone crazy, and then he said that I'd probably given it to him because the kids at school say my weirdness is contagious, and I told him..."

Gizmo only understood so much of Sarah's story, but the important thing was that they'd secured another voter for Bartholomew.

---

4. The warlock's name was actually written on Barthollowmew on the first few flyers before Gizmo noticed.

That made the suffering he'd just endured at the hands of the Bakers' boxers worth it.

The demon shook his fur. Boxer slobber dripped onto the pavement. The sun had sunk below the horizon, casting Mills Run into shadow. It would be Sarah's bedtime soon. Her parents might notice that she'd left if she wasn't back by then, and they would not be pleased. Which wasn't fair since Sarah wasn't technically breaking any rules. She was allowed to explore the neighborhood once she was with an adult. Gizmo said that he was more ancient than humanity's existence, which was pretty darn old as far as the eleven-year-old could tell, and her parents had never specified that the adult needed to be a human.

"We're up to almost eighteen then," Gizmo guessed[5] as they neared the Miller's house. His tongue fell from his mouth in a smile; his tail began to spin like a helicopter propeller spitting boxer drool. "That might be enough for Bartholomew to win. All thanks to us."

The two basked in a moment of delight and self-satisfaction.

Until something strange caught Gizmo's eye as they turned onto the parkette. A dark figure wearing a turquoise jacket and holding a large black umbrella crossed in the shadows of the trees toward the Millers' home.

The demon stopped.

Sarah almost tripped over him and splattered like a lemon on the sidewalk. But she managed to remain upright as she stumbled forward.

"Hey, why did you—"

---

5. He was perhaps being a tad optimistic about the number of residents he and Sarah had persuaded to vote.

"Ms. Moon," Gizmo said, interrupting her with uncharacteristic curtness. A number of things were starting to click into place for him. "You said your father's eyes look weird sometimes now. Can you be a bit more descriptive?"

Sarah chewed on the end of her hair as she considered. Before summer, she'd learned all about figurative language. "His eyes grow as big as sau—frisbees[6] . And glassy[7] as a glass bottle. And he stares above your head like a man lost in a... glass bottle."

"Has your father always had an inexplicable and irrational[8] dislike for dogs?"

"Nope! He used to want a golden retriever, but mom says we have to wait until my brothers are at least three to add any more chaos."

Gizmo kept an eye on the approaching Mr. Graves as he listened. There was no question where the vampire was heading.

"You sneak around the back, Ms. Moon," the demon said, hopping to life and sprinting toward the community center's white picket fence. "I've got to find Bart!"

---

6. She almost said saucers, but that would have been a cliché. And, truth be told, Sarah didn't entirely know what saucers were if they weren't of the flying variety.

7. Unfortunately, this description at once seemed apt, and Sarah overcommitted to the word *glass*.

8. As any dislike for dogs was in Gizmo's opinion.

TWENTY-THREE

While Gizmo was trying to figure out how to get into the functions' hall where Bartholomew was currently pretending to care about crotchet, Frederick Graves knocked on the Millers' front door.

Pockets of fading sunlight lay scattered around the neighborhood like bear traps, threatening to, perhaps not cook Frederick alive, but at least toast his skin. He clung to the handle of his large black umbrella with both hands. It wasn't his habit to be out so early, but he hadn't been able to sleep. He'd awoken long before sunrise with a nagging sense of peace and relaxation. The light throb behind his eyes had vanished—a clear sign that the effects of hypnosis would soon be wearing off.

Frederick had risen from his coffin, lit a candle, and paced among the dark, gothic furniture that decorated his living room. Normally, the austere grandiosity of his Queen Anne couch, the dramatic light from the fire, and the vaguely foreboding presence of the stuffed barn owl[1] who lived beside his coffin, were enough to soothe Frederick's racing mind,[2] but not this evening. He needed to ensure that Dan Miller remained firmly under his thumb.

So the vampire had donned his fine beige shorts, turquoise coat, and black umbrella, and slipped into the fading sun to make the hazardous trek. Now, he stood on the threshold.

Frederick's ability to mist through doorways would have allowed him to enter the Millers' home with ease. But it was considered terribly uncouth among vampires[3] to barge into a house without an invitation. So instead, Frederick knocked.

Lisa Miller answered, swinging the door open. Her hair was pulled into a frazzled nest near the top of her head. Her blue shirt was covered in stains and minted with a rag that had once been white but was now covered in snot. She shuffled a ruddy-cheeked, runny-nosed toddler in one arm.[4]

Drat, Frederick thought.

Aloud, he cleared his throat, trying to rid himself of some of his rasp, and tilted in a shallow bow. "Good evening, madam. I've come to speak with your husband. Might I come in?"

Lisa wiped the toddler's nose with the snot-rag over her shoulder. Her eyes narrowed at the vampire. "Why?"

Frederick hesitated. He hadn't expected that question. When he'd been a lad, women hadn't been so curious about their husbands'

---

2. Not by quietening it necessarily, but by providing a suitable atmosphere for it to continue.

3. And most decent people.

4. It was Johnny, though Frederick neither knew nor cared which twin it was. He was more concerned with keeping a safe distance for there was a yellow-green bubble growing in one of the toddler's nostrils.

private affairs. But the world just wasn't what it had been in the late seventeenth century.

The vampire racked his brain for a reason a neighbor might show up on a doorstep without warning.

"To borrow a cup of sugar?"

Lisa stared at Frederick for a moment. There were a number of things she might have said in response. However, as anyone who's ever had the misfortune of taking care of a toddler for more than ten minutes will already know, Lisa was exhausted. Arguing with an old man in a turquoise jacket over cups of sugar was far beyond her current bandwidth.

So, with a sigh, she turned and shouted into the house, "Dan, you need to come to the door! It's Mr. Graves!"

Bartholomew never ran.[5] It was unbecoming of a warlock of his talent. It might make him seem afraid, which was preposterous. He was, however, concerned, and speed walking across the center's paved paths was perfectly dignified.

His arms pivoted at his sides, the bottom half of a broken windmill. His feet rose and fell with sufficient speed that most people would have thought[6] that he was jogging.

---

5. Except in extreme circumstances when his acquiring had gotten him into trouble.

6. Incorrectly, of course, for this was not the case.

"This is a relief, isn't it?"[7] Gizmo said, leaping at the warlock's heels in order to keep up.

Bartholomew frowned. He failed to see how.

"*If*," he made a point of stressing the word with a sneer for the familiar, "you're right, and it would be a first, then it's an absolute dis—"

The warlock cut himself off as he spotted the Miller's front door. It was diagonally across the road from the community center, but buildings and trees had blocked his view. Now, he could see Dan at the front door, speaking with Frederick on the step.

Bartholomew and Gizmo reached the end of the Miller's walkway just in time to witness the final few seconds of a vampiric hypnosis.

Dan's eyes were indeed glassy as Sarah had described and wide, perhaps not as large as frisbees, but something more akin to white bottlecaps. The blue irises within spun like pinwheels. He blinked, and they returned to normal. Dan's brow furrowed for a moment in confusion. With a nod, he retreated into his house.

"Told you so," Gizmo said, tail thumping against Bartholomew's calf.

The warlock's jaw tightened. This was very bad. On top of which, he didn't like the smug sense of certainty in the familiar's voice.

"You said he *had* hypnotized him. Not that he was *going* to," Bartholomew snapped, wringing his hands around an imaginary neck a few feet over the demon's head. "You could have stopped him instead

---

7. For the demon, it was. Gizmorgoth of Darkness delighted in crushing his enemies and drowning them in the agony of their defeat. But Dan Miller was so dreadfully human and unoffensive, there would be nothing fun about destroying him. It was a relief to learn that he wasn't an enemy at all, but just an unwitting pawn.

of running to me, taken some initiative and done something useful for a change. This is entirely your fault now!"

"But—" Before Gizmo could object,[8] Frederick turned.

The vampire pressed two fingers to his forehead. The effort of hypnotizing someone[9] had brought on a dull pain between his eyes. He wanted very much to return to his coffin and sleep in until the neighborhood was pitch dark.

But his eyes landed on Bartholomew and Gizmo.

Oh dear, Frederick thought, *this could be a problem.*

Aloud he said, "Ah, good evening, gentlemen!"

The vampire descended the stairs with a theatrical flourish of his umbrella. Given the pain in his head and early hours of the night, he hoped to avoid any discussions of plotting or scheming or blackmail. They hadn't scheduled a meeting, and it would've been poor taste to discuss business in the middle of the Miller's drive. After all, being enemies was no reason to be uncivilized. So, with a thin, polite smile, the vampire attempted to make small talk. "Fine weather, isn't it?"

Bartholomew ground his teeth and glared at the vampire. He wasn't much good at small talk. "Why are you hypnotizing Dan Miller? You'd best stay away from him."

Frederick gave an annoyed sniff. *So much for civility!*

The vampire kept his umbrella open before him as a shield. He didn't trust warlocks, particularly not ones who'd been so closely affiliated with The Bearded Syndicate, and his eyes watched

---

8. He was going to expound on the philosophical danger of placing blame when any number of small actions might snowball to a large one. This likely would have included asking Bartholomew if he would blame a butterfly for an avalanche, to which the warlock would have given him a definitive *yes*.

9. Particularly someone who didn't wish to be hypnotized.

Bartholomew's fluttering hands, concerned they might disappear into his jacket and return with a rune-engraved wooden stake. Frederick longed for his coffin, but retreating too quick might make it seem like he was fleeing. He didn't want the warlock thinking he had the upper hand!

"Your concern for Mr. Miller is most touching. I wasn't aware that you were so fond of him," he said. Frederick fully intended it as a devastating insult.

And so it was interpreted by Bartholomew.[10]

His jaw tightened, and his eyes narrowed. He was a great and powerful warlock! The insinuation that he would care about some insignificant human like Dan Miller was absurd.

"My only concern is for the integrity of the democratic process," Bartholomew said, jaw still clenched as he spoke. "It's in poor taste to interfere with so dignified an institution."

Frederick's lips pulled into a thin, tight line. He didn't appreciate the warlock questioning his sense of decorum. "Indeed, I saw that you'd thrown your hat in to be president. A ban on curtains, is it? How quaint." His lips tilted upward in a smile. He had to have devastated the warlock with that barb.

He had.

Quaint? Bartholomew's thoughts seethed. *It was a brilliant maneuver of cunning and guile!*

"Better than a ban on dogs," Gizmo said with an annoyed huff. He had no idea that the two were engaged in a war of words and couldn't understand why they were being so polite. "No one is going to vote for that, you know."

---

10. Though Gizmo, standing at the warlock's feet, had no idea that the first arrow had been shot in a battle of words.

Frederick's outward expression of polite superiority didn't falter, but the familiar's words made his stomach turn. His head suddenly felt even more in pain than before.

He's right, the vampire thought. *I need a foolproof plan to ensure my victory.*

"Precisely. Your defeat is imminent," Bartholomew agreed with Gizmo aloud, mostly so that Frederick didn't judge him as a warlock that couldn't control his own familiar.

Within, however, Bartholomew's stomach turned and his heart twisted. Gizmo, was of course, in his opinion, incredibly wrong. Not only did that platform make complete sense to the warlock, but he hadn't considered that Frederick would interfere in his brilliant scheme! The vampire had powers of hypnosis. He could command the entire neighborhood to vote as he wished.[11]

Frederick wracked his now anxious brain for a devastating final insult. When one didn't come, he resorted to classic kindergarten rules.

"No, your defeat is imminent," he rasped, and mostly to hide the fact that he was backing away, he let out a high, hissing laugh.

The warlock mistook this as a show of confidence and nonchalance, so joined in with his own deep, bellowing guffaws.

Gizmo watched the two of them, laughing and backing away from one another.[12] He hadn't a clue what was going on.

---

11. At least, Bartholomew thought that he could.

12. As did Lisa Miller who heard the strange sounds and peeped out their windows to see Mr. Graves and Mr. Bartlow engaged in what seemed to be some bizarre performance art.

Nor did he until they were safely in their garlic-scented house, when Bartholomew finally turned to him. There was a dangerous glint in the warlock's dark eyes, the kind that meant he was up to something.

"We have to win Gizmo," he said. "And that means, we have to cheat."

TWENTY-FOUR

B artholomew had just one problem when it came to cheating. It wasn't a moral qualm obviously, or even a lack of know-how.[1] It was a dearth of inks.

On the days that he wasn't preoccupied with rallying retirees to his anti-curtain cause, the warlock had made the long bus journey to visit the reserve, hoping to find a message from Otto. But the only thing Bartholomew ever found in the tree were the scribbled notes he'd left there himself, still folded into triangles, unread and uncollected by his co-conspirator.

The day after their discussion with the vampire, Bartholomew and Gizmo made their final trip to the reserve,[2] hoping that a message had finally come through.

---

1. For Bartholomew knew exactly how he could win the election and circumvent Frederick's hypnotic mind-control of the voters. The idea came to him quickly as a result of the many papers and identification cards he'd had to alter to fake his own death. If he used brown ink to write the rune for his name, and pink to set a timer on the magic, he could create an enchantment that would cause Dan's name to shift into the warlock's own on each ballot after it had been cast.

2. At least for the scope of this story.

"Maybe Otto's right, and you'll have to start making your own inks," the demon suggested, stopping to growl at a woodpecker who was peering at them from his tree. It flew off, and the loss of its weight shifted the branch, causing droplets to splatter to the ground.

A speck of mud bounced from a puddle onto the warlock's shoe. Bartholomew stopped, scowling at the stain. But the insouciant fleck of wet dirt remained untroubled, unmoved and undistinguisable from the rest of the stains, making it a rather unsatisfactory target for his ire.

The warlock turned his glare to his familiar.

"Would you leave the wildlife be. You've ruined my shoes." He pointed to his feet.

Gizmo looked at the black dress shoes. The day's earlier rain had turned the nature reserve into a minefield of mud puddles. For a former acquirer who'd navigated plenty of magical booby-traps, Bartholomew had done a remarkably terrible job at avoiding them.

But perhaps that is my fault, the demon thought.

"You're right," Gizmo said, with a thoughtful shake of his head. And for a moment, Bartholomew was so delighted by these words that he forgot to be annoyed. Then, the familiar continued, "I ought to know you're not capable of navigating dangerous terrain without my help."

Bartholomew's hands curled into fists. His teeth ground against one another with a strength that would have concerned many a dentist. There was no need for Gizmo to chase away any more woodland creatures. They were sufficiently spooked by the sound of the warlock pulverizing his enamels as he stomped through the reserve.

Bartholomew was silently ruing the day he'd first met Gizmo. *Take me on as your familiar, he said. Having a great demon to do your bidding will strike envy into the hearts of all. Useless foozler! Ought to have told me he'd be an eternal obstreperous thorn in my side who won't just accept that he's to blame for everything that goes wrong.*

The warlock was so worked up that he forgot to look down and ended up stepping in another two mud puddles before they reached the tree.

"Anything interesting inside?" Gizmo asked, sitting on top of a raised root. He was careful to keep his tail up and away from the ground.[3]

Bartholomew, who was still ranting at the familiar in his head, was a bit behind on the conversation. "And another problem with you," he said, pointing his finger in accusation at the familiar. "Is that you can't even make useful suggestions. Brew my own inks? How? In what cauldron? With what recipes? Do you know the secret ingredient in brown ink?"

"I imagine we could figure it out, or ask—"

"There's no one we can ask. I'm dead, and you've oozed back into the underworld. Damned incompetent familiar," he muttered the last bit under his breath as he slipped his hand into the tree.

Only the small, folded papers of his previous notes shuffled around his fingers.

"Squids!" Bartholomew slapped his hand against the oak. The tree, who didn't accept being a target for misplaced rage with nearly as much grace as Gizmo, poked a splinter into his palm. With a hiss, the warlock pulled away. "Ouch!"

---

3. Unlike the warlock, there was no mud on the familiar. Gizmo had bounced over the puddles and avoided any wet patches on their stroll. The whole thing had been quite fun for him and reminiscent of his time in the underworld. "The floor is lava" has long been a popular game among demons. Which one had the brilliant idea to introduce it to human children remains a mystery.

"Nothing from Otto then, I take it?" the familiar asked politely as he watched his supposed master shaking his fist at the oak.

"Obviously not!" Bartholomew slammed his knuckles against the trunk without thinking and received another splinter. He scowled as he sucked it from his pinky. The warlock was (quite rightly) beginning to think the tree was doing this on purpose.

"Oh dear." Gizmo lowered his head and let out a small, sad whimper. "You don't suppose something's happened, do you?"

"Yes, something's happened. This oak is attacking me." Bartholomew's eyes narrowed at the tree, ready to dodge a swing from one of the branches.

"I meant if something's happened to Otto," the demon said, though he did begin retreating from the root, just in case the tree decided not to distinguish between warlock and familiar. "The Syndicate might have had an eye out for someone trying to fence the amulet."

A bolt of terror made Bartholomew straighten and turn away from the oak.[4] "Gizmo, I think I'd die if the Syndicate caught Otto."

Seeing the warlock struck by what he assumed was a rare moment of kindness, the familiar's heart softened and his big brown eyes grew wide. "Otto knew what he was getting into, Bart. You can't blame yourself if something goes wrong."

The warlock frowned. "Of course I wouldn't. It would be Otto's fault entirely. Why on Earth would you think I'd blame myself for his idiocy?"

"But you just said you'd die if—"

---

4. The tree considered taking the opportunity to strike him with one of its branches at this moment, but the oak had some empathy, and the look of panic on the warlock's face made it reconsider.

"Because I very likely would! If the Syndicate catches Otto, do you really think the Questioners won't get the truth out of that slimeball? He'll rat me out in a second! And if they find out we're not really dead, they'll kill us!"[5]

Gizmo mulled over the matter for a moment. He'd always liked Otto. Despite working as a fence, he was a jovial fellow and one of Bartholomew's closest friends. But that last wasn't saying much. If betrayal became beneficial, Otto had a temperamental compass guiding his moral convictions and a talent for self-preservation.

"That does pose a problem," the demon admitted.

"Exactly! And the jerk didn't even have the decency to send me more ink before he betrayed me. He's left us defenseless!"

Bartholomew raised his arm to slap the tree again before thinking better of it. He stomped the earth instead and was repaid for his consideration by a shower of mud on the hems of his pants. The warlock scowled at the ground, his fingers clenching and scraping at the air. With nothing to take out his anger on, he began to pace.

"Everything's against me. Otto. The tree. The mud. The Syndicate."

"Now hold on," Gizmo said, trotting beside the warlock as he stomped in angry circles around the oak. "You're getting ahead of yourself. I was only supposing something bad might've happened. We don't even know! Maybe Otto's just had a cold the past few days or he's gone on a business trip. He might have found a buyer for the amulet!"

---

5. You might notice Bartholomew's use of the pronoun *we* to include Gizmo. This should not be misinterpreted as a genuine concern for his familiar, who in fact was almost unkillable. It was rather his attempt at subtle manipulation to ensure that Gizmo became appropriately paranoid.

"Perhaps," Bartholomew said, but his pessimism promised him that the worst had definitely occurred. "Still, we can't sit around ink-less and hopeful like a pair of fools. If the Syndicate are searching for us, we need to know."

"Should we write Otto a letter asking if he's betrayed us then?" Gizmo suggested. "Then we could analyze his handwriting to see if it looks like he's lying."

Bartholomew stopped pacing for a moment. "Do you know how to analyze handwriting, Gizmo?"

"No, but Ms. Moon has a book."

"We're not going to a five-year-old for help!" Bartholomew snapped. Honestly, how Gizmo had ever earned the classification of a *great* demon was a complete befuddlement. "There's only one way we're going to be able to learn the truth."

"Crystal ball? Seer? A fourth conspirator?"

"Third conspirator," Bartholomew muttered the correction, his teeth beginning to grind once more. Those were all ridiculous suggestions. Couldn't Gizmo see that relying on Otto had already been a mistake? They weren't going to compound the issue by continuing to trust people! "And no, you moron. We're not doing any of those things. If we want to figure out the truth, we'll have to sneak into the city and find it on our own."

TWENTY-FIVE

B artholomew spread his inks on the kitchen island before him: half a bottle of indigo, a splash of blue, and a few drops of pink. He'd used the last of his white that morning, creating healing strips for the cuts on his chin. The warlock had yet to master the art of shaving.

He rolled his quill between his fingers, running through all the runes he'd memorized. Some were well known: *past, present, future.* Some would have made other regarded warlocks quake with envy: *enchantment, destruction, restoration.* Some were so absurd as to appear useless unless the correct situation presented itself: *gingham, handhold, potato chip.*

The answer had to be in there somewhere. There was a combination that would work. Bartholomew just needed to be creative.

He looked again at his limited supply of inks. Indigo weakened; blue detected; pink had temporal properties.

But brown was the only ink that changed shapes.

"Gah!" Bartholomew tossed his quill across the still empty living space.

Gizmo dashed from the warlock's feet to fetch it.

"I could craft a blocking rune that would stop anyone from detecting my magic, but there's no way to change my appearance."

"Maybe no one will recognize you without the beard," Gizmo suggested before picking up the quill in his mouth and trotting back over. He dropped the dark feather at the warlock's feet, hoping[1] for a pat on the head or at least another toss.

Bartholomew scowled at the familiar as he snatched his quill from the floor.

"No, never mind," Gizmo said, falling onto his stomach with a sigh and continuing to gaze hopefully at the feather. "One scowl, and you'll give yourself away, and I don't imagine you could go even a few hours without doing so."

"I could last an entire week without scowling," Bartholomew argued, the scowl etching itself deeper into his face. "But I daresay most other warlocks will recognize my eyes."

"They are noticeably shifty, and they do have that sort of evil gleam."

Bartholomew's jaw clenched. The familiar was being purposefully perfidious. "It's a glint of power and strength."

"Is it? Huh? Don't suppose I've ever thought of it like that. But maybe it is. How far do you think you could throw that quill given all your strength?"

Bartholomew's eyes narrowed. He didn't like how the familiar was staring at his quill. He stopped flicking it between his knuckles and slipped it into his pocket. "It's not that kind of strength, you numbskull."

Well, it's not a magical kind either, or you'd know how to disguise us, Gizmo thought, but he was too polite to say it out loud. He didn't believe it anyway. Bartholomew's talent wasn't at fault here. Even the

---

1. But as always, not expecting.

most powerful warlock couldn't work miracles without the proper inks.

Without another scathing response from his familiar, Bartholomew had no clear outlet for his frustration. He sighed and slumped down, his back falling against the white cabinets of kitchen island until he was on the hardwood floor beside Gizmo.

"Cheer up," the familiar said, inching forward so that his head was as close to the warlock's hand as it could be before Bartholomew grew annoyed and accused Gizmo of trying to use him as a pillow. "We can still sneak in."

"With no disguises?" The warlock spied the demon's wet nose shifting closer to his fingers and pulled his hand away. "That's madness!"

Gizmo quite agreed. But with their magic limited, neither familiar nor warlock could think of any possible way to disguise themselves.

But they were about to be saved by an unexpected source.

"Gizmo, are you in there?" Sarah's low, too-adult-for-her-age voice shouted from the door. Her fists pounded against the wood. "We're supposed to go campaigning today."

Bartholomew glared at his familiar. "What is she talking about?"

"Oh, who can ever be sure with children," Gizmo said with an uncomfortable laugh. He wasn't hiding his and Sarah's campaigning efforts per se, but given Bartholomew's current mood, it seemed safest to avoid the topic.[2] The familiar hopped up and went toward the door.

"Tell her to go away," Bartholomew muttered.

---

2. Given that Bartholomew's moods were seldom good, Gizmo was likely to take this stance for the foreseeable future.

"I can't tell her anything.[3] I can't open the door."

"You could shout."

"But what if someone on the road heard my voice. I thought you said I needed to be careful."

Bartholomew's jaw clenched, and his fingers attempted to squeeze the oxygen from the air. Gizmo's selective following of orders was going to drive him to insanity one of these days.

Sarah's face pressed itself against the window. Her cheeks were pink and her shirt was green, so that she appeared a bit like an upside down cherry tomato wearing a pair of square framed glasses. Her eyes landed on Bartholomew, still sitting on the kitchen floor.

The warlock glowered at her. He was going for intimidating, so terrifying that a little girl would run screaming.

Sarah smiled and began to wave. "Mr. Bartlow, are you coming with us? Look at the flyers I made for you!" She pressed a drawing against the glass. The warlock could only assume it was a scoop of caramel ice-cream with very large black sprinkles sitting on top of an upside-down cone. He didn't see what it had to do with him.

"Go away!" he shouted.

Sarah didn't appear to hear him.

With a groan, Bartholomew pushed himself from the floor, stomped to his door, and swung it open.

"I said, go away. We're very busy."

Sarah heard everything the warlock said, but she'd gotten very good at ignoring orders from adults over the past year. She bounced to

---

3. This was a lie for the obvious reason that Bartholomew was about to point out, but Gizmo liked Sarah very much and would much prefer to leave any curt dismissals to the warlock.

the top of the steps and slipped her foot through the door before Bartholomew could slam it and hurried into the empty house.

The warlock spun around, trying to determine the best way to get rid of this current pest. Evidently, the scent of garlic worked on vampires not eleven-year-old girls.

Sarah was like a small red-faced, green-shirted, yellow-shoed tornado whirring through the room. She spun in a circle.

"Hi Gizmo!" She spotted the demon's head peeping at her from behind the door and gave him a large smile before continuing her whirl. "Ooh! Are you painting something?" Her feet slapped against the floor as she ran toward the kitchen. Before Bartholomew could register what was happening, the eleven-year-old was inspecting his inks.

Although the warlock and his familiar didn't know it at the time, this would become a core memory for Sarah.

Her fingers closed around the indigo ink, and she felt a strange buzz against her skin, like lightning pulsing through the bottle. She lifted it and held it up to the sunlight, her eyes growing wide. Sarah had never seen anything so vibrant, so brilliant. There was something eccentric about whatever was inside. She could just tell.

"It's not like any paint I've ever seen," she whispered.

"That's because it's not paint!" Bartholomew snatched the bottle from her hand, hiding it in his pocket before she could break it. "Now go home, sit in your room, and don't come out until you're at least twenty-one."

Sarah laughed. Her eyes had gone at once to the other two bottles of ink that the warlock was now packing in their wooden box. "What is it?"

Throughout this exchange, Gizmo crept forward and hid behind Bartholomew's ankles. The familiar considered himself to be in a difficult situation. Sarah obviously expected them to continue their door-to-door campaigning today, and he hated to disappoint her, but Bartholomew, whether he would admit it or not, needed Gizmo more at this current moment.

The demon cleared his throat and lifted a paw to his muzzle. "Ms. Moon, I am dreadfully sorry, but I'm afraid Bart is right about us being busy. We've something important to work on."

"What is it?" Sarah asked, hoping that it had something to do with the inks. "I can help!"

Bartholomew sneered. "Oh really? How? Are you a master of disguises?"

Sarah pursed her lips. "No, but I have a dress-up box in my room."

Bartholomew froze, his back growing suddenly straight. He'd never spent time around children, and *dress-up box* sounded suspiciously magical.

"A what?" he spun, hand reaching out and grabbing Sarah by the collar of her shirt.

For once, the eleven-year-old was actually a bit nervous. "You know, a box full of wigs and costumes and some of my mom's old clothes."

"Oh." Bartholomew released her. He had just enough decency to feel a hint of guilt for grabbing her unjustly, but far too much pride to apologize. "Well, that's nothing then. That's useless."

But an idea had begun to form in Gizmo's mind. "Is it?" he asked, staring up at the warlock with a large, pink-tongued smile. "Or has Ms. Moon just solved all our problems?"

"No."

Gizmo's tail started to wag. "But maybe—"

"No, absolutely not!"

Sarah straightened her shirt. Now that Bartholomew had released her, she was beginning to find the whole scenario quite thrilling once more.

Nothing about my life will be ordinary now that I'm friends with other eccentrics, she thought.

Before her, Bartholomew and Gizmo exchanged looks. Finally, the warlock's jaw clenched, and he turned to Sarah with a glower.

"Fine," he said. "Take us to this dress up box."

TWENTY-SIX

The next morning, on the bus that carried vehicle-deficit north-ern suburbanites into the city, there was a most unusual pas-senger. A tall blonde woman in a short blue dress sat near the front. Curly black hairs sprouted from her long legs. She wore bright pink lipstick and smooth winged eyeliner around a pair of dark, deep-set eyes. There was a stroller beside her.

A middle-aged accountant on her way to work stopped to peer at the baby within only to discover a small, fluffy black dog, wearing a pink onesie and holding a pacifier in its mouth.

"Goo goo," it said.

The accountant nearly fainted. She stumbled toward the back of the bus, pressed her hand to her forehead searching for a fever, and spent the rest of the ride with one eye on the stroller.

About halfway through the journey, she saw the little black nose peep out from the fabric at the side. Luckily, she was too far away to hear the dog whisper, "Bart? Are we there yet?"

The unusual blonde woman's jaw clenched. Her dark eyes nar-rowed at the dog in the stroller.

She was, as you have no doubt deduced, not a woman at all but a warlock, disguised in an eleven-year-old's synthetic toy wig, an old blue maternity dress, and a pair of unisex loafers that had been acquired from Dan Miller's closet.

"Don't talk," Bartholomew hissed, speaking from the corner of his mouth so that none of the other passengers would notice that he was talking to a dog in a stroller. "How many times do I have to tell you that dogs can't talk?"

"I'm not a dog," Gizmo objected. "I'm a baby." He grabbed the pacifier with his mouth and displayed it proudly.

Bartholomew ground his teeth. There was no reason for his familiar to be disguised. None of the syndicate would guess that the great Gizmorgoth of Darkness had shed his crow feathers and become a useless ball of fluff. And the demon's disguise was ridiculous. As the warlock had spent almost an hour trying to explain with no avail, nobody was going to mistake a dog for a human baby. But continuing the argument now that they were already on the bus would drive Bartholomew mad.

"Those don't talk either," he muttered and pushed the entirety of the pacifier into Gizmo's mouth.

The familiar coughed it onto the cushion beneath him. *How rude,* he thought, but he remained quiet until the bus stopped and Bartholomew, disguised as an unusual blonde woman, lifted the stroller, and stepped into downtown.[1]

---

1. At which point, Gizmo broke his silence with a loud, "About time!" His outburst earned him a sharp glare from Bartholomew and, unknown to him, caused the accountant to make an emergency appointment with her psychologist.

All cities are much the same. The buildings are tall, various shades of dull, with glass windows and tiny balconies. The roads are narrow, and if they're not, then they appear to be thanks to the sheer quantity of traffic. The people hustle and bustle with their heads down, clinging to their purses and cell phones, somehow on the constant watch for an attack yet managing to ignore everyone else around them.

No one noticed the blonde woman pushing a dog in a pink-onesie down the street, and certainly, no one thought to warn her when she turned down a dark and unfriendly alley.

Otto's apartment was on the top floor of a crumbling building with broken windows and spray-painted depictions of male genitalia. An ominous aura clung to its once red bricks, advising anyone with good sense to turn and run.

Bartholomew and Gizmo certainly had sense. But there is very little *good* about most warlocks or their familiars.

There was a shoddy electric lock on the door at the bottom. An indigo rune that read *lock* was enough to send it spluttering to death.

Bartholomew pushed the door open and went toward the elevator. Once they were within, Gizmo jumped from the stroller. The excess fabric of the pink onesie dragged along the floor.

"We'll probably find Otto sitting at his desk, inspecting some stolen statue with his magnifying glass, and feel terribly silly," the demon said, giving an awkward laugh as he watched the numbers on the elevator display rise. But despite his usual optimism, even Gizmo doubted his words.

There was a ding as they reached the top floor. They crossed a narrow, dimly-lit hall to a brown door at the far end. The same rune that had allowed them into the building caused it to swing open.

Beyond was the cramped living space of a single-bedroom apartment. A small plastic dining table squashed into the kitchen, just before the oven, and a brown leather loveseat pressed against the far wall. Beside it was a gleaming desk made of fine mahogany wood. The matching chair before it had fallen onto its side.

Bartholomew and Gizmo noticed this at almost the same time. The two exchanged a look. For once, they were correct to believe that they were thinking the same thing.

That's not a good sign.

"Otto?" Gizmo's voice sounded almost timid. He went to enter the apartment, but Bartholomew's acquired gray loafer stopped him.

"Wait," the warlock said. He peered into the room, dark eyes glinting. Over a century robbing tombs and breaking into secret caverns might not have given Bartholomew the skills required to dodge muddy puddles in a forest, but they'd honed his natural inclination toward mistrust.

The warlock wiped the last fleck of indigo ink from his quill[2] and pulled the bottle of blue from its box within the stroller. With a series of quick, practiced flourishes, he dipped the nib in the new color and whisked the inks back into his pocket.

"Bit much, don't you think?" Gizmo said, observing the warlock. "It's just Otto's apartment."

Bartholomew scowled at the demon. "I do think, which is precisely why we're checking."

He slipped his hand through the doorway and traced the word for enchantment in blue ink along the wall. Both held their breath and counted to five.

Nothing happened.

---

2. This was common practice when changing colors, and Bartholomew was too proud to attempt to salvage a few measly drops.

"See?" Gizmo started to say, just as a large cage fell from the ceiling and crashed to the floor.

Both jumped back.

"Aha! I knew it!" Bartholomew's pink painted lips slanted upward in victory as he turned to his familiar. "Now will you stop questioning me? I'm the one in charge for a reason." He flipped the synthetic blonde hair over his shoulder and strode into the apartment. No was quite as adept at gloating as the warlock.

Gizmo took it in stride. *Even Bartholomew is bound to be right sometimes. It's rare enough that he might as well get to bask in it.*

Though there was a small part of the familiar that regretted not rubbing it in the warlock's face when they'd been forced to accept Sarah's help.

The demon stepped around the cage more gingerly, stopping to sniff the metal wires near the bottom. His sense of smell had increased quite substantially in his new form, and he could detect a mixture of inks.[3]

"Do you suppose this was set by Otto or for him?" Gizmo asked.

"Yes," Bartholomew responded, which did not at all answer the question.[4] He'd made his way toward the desk with its fallen chair. It was an obvious place to start an investigation into whatever might have happened. But that wasn't what had attracted the warlock.

Otto's desk was covered in rare and curious artifacts. A collection of fine quills in a gold tub boasted peacock, macaw, and ostrich feath-

---

3. Indigo and pink to be precise, but there was a third at play too, one that Gizmo couldn't smell.

4. The warlock would be damned before he admitted anything to his familiar, especially his own ignorance.

ers. Trinkets and baubles of gold and silver glittered within an open ceramic jewelry box. Brilliant gemstones winked beside them.

Bartholomew's hands fluttered toward them. But his fingers avoided the obvious display of wealth. If there was anything likely to booby trapped, that would be it. However, he couldn't resist the three bottles of ink, shimmering on the desk: pink, indigo, and orange.

"Still nothing that will help us win the election," he muttered. But he picked them up and didn't put them down until he'd returned to the stroller in the corridor.[5]

Gizmo raced through the small apartment, sniffing the floor. There was no one hiding behind the shower curtain or beneath the bed or even in the dusty closet.

"Wherever Otto is, it's not here," the familiar announced, trotting back into the cramped living room. He stopped by the still fallen chair near the warlock's feet. "Any idea what might've—oh, what's that?"

Gizmo sniffed a piece of white paper trapped beneath the chair's leg.

Bartholomew bent down, lifted the fallen furniture, and retrieved the note. Together, they read:

Listen Bart, this is going to be my last note. I'm out. Fencing the amulet is too dangerous. Don't try. Hold onto it! Or you might approach the wrong buyer like I did

There was no period at the end.

Just like Otto to ignore the importance of punctuation, Bartholomew thought.

Gizmo's thoughts led him a different direction, and the fur rose on his spine. What had happened that stopped Otto from finishing?

---

5. He would have slipped them into a pocket, but as he'd discovered, much to his distress, the dress didn't have any.

TWENTY-SEVEN

The Pilfering Cheese was an underground pub about four blocks shy of Otto's apartment complex. It was full of dark tables, bartenders of questionable species, and regular patrons whose pockets had a curious habit of growing heavier instead of lighter as the night went on. The Cheese paid its dues to The Syndicate as required though there was some speculation that the owner, Ed Beaselton,[1] fudged numbers in order to pocket more than his unfair share.

Warlocks were welcomed but not wanted at the pub. Bartholomew, who had no desire to be around crowds of people, had been more than happy to avoid the establishment. He'd only gone once when Otto had first approached him about a potentially lucrative idea.

Now, he made his second visit, disguised as an unusual blonde woman in a blue dress pushing a stroller that had been packed with blankets, clothes, inks, quills, and a few choice jewels. Somewhere among the recently acquired goods was Gizmo.

The loud sounds of chatter and laughter made Bartholomew shudder. He had no interest in visiting The Pilfering Cheese, but it had been Otto's favorite establishment. If anyone knew what had hap-

---

1. Who was either a very large goblin or very small troll, but was certainly not an ogre as some had attempted to claim.

pened to the missing fence, they would be here. So, making great efforts not to scowl, the warlock stepped inside.

He was hit at once by the scents of overripe fruit and rotting logs. That was a hint to the establishment's patrons: goblins and trolls.[2]

Bartholomew's eyes landed on a large orange lump tearing into a leg of mutton in the corner. The lump was Lum Lumbkin.

The troll looked up at that exact moment and caught the warlock staring.

"Oh no," Bartholomew muttered. He slipped into the closest booth, pulling the stroller close, ready to use it (and Gizmo by extension) as a shield in case Lum tried to attack.

"What's happened?" The demon's nose poked out from beneath a red checkered blanket to lift the cover of the stroller.

"Lum Lumbkin is here," Bartholomew hissed.

Gizmo's ears twitched within the stroller. "The troll you owe money to?"

"No, Bartholomew Whitlock owed him money, but since he's dead, he can't very well repay it, can he. I'm—" the warlock cut himself off as he saw Lum rise from his table. "Squids! He's coming this way. Don't speak, Gizmo. Remember, you're supposed to be a..." Bartholomew trailed off as Lum's large orange form halted before him.

Oh no. If he recognizes me, I'm dead.

Bartholomew didn't dare smile for fear the troll recognized the expression. Instead, he tried to make his eyes as wide as possible and pretend that his heart wasn't racing in his chest. In a feminine falsetto, the warlock said, "Hello."

---

2. While it is true that their sweat is similar to these descriptors, most goblins and trolls are quite clean and perfectly capable of using deodorant. The crowd that The Pilfering Cheese attracted was simply an unhygienic lot

"Hi, there." Lum smoothed his few strands of dark red hair with the palm of his hand. He peeled back his lips to reveal a row of sharp bottom teeth and wagged his eyebrows as he rested a large mug of ale on the table. He slipped into the seat across from the warlock.

Bartholomew's heart leaped into his throat. He assumed the display was intended to be vaguely threatening and was waiting for the troll to grab him by the neck and fling him across the pub at any moment.

Lum, in contrast, thought his methods of seduction were working quite well.[3] He leaned over the table, eyebrows still rising and falling. "You're a brave one, coming into a place like this."[4]

Beads of sweat glistened around the edge of Bartholomew's wig. He patted his forehead with his hand. *He's onto me,* the warlock thought, and his fingers fluttered under the table toward the stroller where his quill and inks were hidden. He didn't know the rune for *troll* to weaken Lum using indigo, but that wasn't necessary. Bartholomew had orange ink now, that was destructive by nature.

Lum reached forward and grabbed the warlock's hand before it could reach his weapon.

"You've lovely, soft hands," the troll noted. "Very feminine."

Bartholomew scowled. It would have given him away at once if Lum could see it.

"What's your name, gorgeous?"

The warlock's brow furrowed. His scowl shifted to a frown. *Does he really think I'm a woman?* Bartholomew wasn't sure if to be offended or relieved.

---

3. Trolls have poor eyesight and rely primarily on their sense of smell to distinguish individuals. In an establishment like The Pilfering Cheese, Lum was practically blind.

4. He was referring to the fact very few women ever visited The Pilfering Cheese.

A voice from the stroller, copying the warlock's falsetto from earlier, answered on his behalf, "I'm Cindy."

Bartholomew glared at Gizmo's muzzle, peeking from the stroller. He didn't understand why his familiar couldn't follow basic instructions.[5]

"Let me buy you a beer, Cindy," Lum said, gesturing to the waiter before Bartholomew could object. The ogre turned, offering his new companion what he intended to be a charming grin. "What brings you here?"

Bartholomew frowned. Ogres were a naturally jowly species, Lum even more than most. His charming grin had all the qualities of a snarl. It did little to make the warlock feel at ease. Sharing a drink with a troll who wanted to kill him was a terrible plan.

But Lum was a central element of the city's seedy underbelly. Bartholomew needed information, and he wasn't likely to find a better source.

"I'm looking for a friend of mine," the warlock said, trying to match the pitch Gizmo had just used. "Maybe you know him. His name is Otto Ewing."

The snarl, that was in fact intended to be a charming grin, slid from Lum's face.

"I'm sorry to be the one to tell you doll, but Otto is—" He slid a round sausage-shaped finger across his throat, then lifted his mug and took a sip of his ale. "At least that's the word on the street. They say The Syndicate finally caught up to him."

Bartholomew froze. He wasn't sure what he'd expected Lum to say, but it certainly wasn't that.

---

5. Gizmo didn't know why the warlock couldn't think of a fake name at a reasonable speed.

Most people would have experienced a sense of shock, or grief, or guilt at learning that their closest confidant (barring their familiar) had been killed due to the ruse. Bartholomew might have felt something similar, albeit quashed and faint due to years of ignoring his own emotions, *if* he believed for a second that Otto was actually dead.

That's impossible. He'd make a deal, rat me out to The Syndicate and save his own skin.

The thought of Otto performing an act of self-sacrifice was unconscionable.

"Are you sure he's not in hiding somewhere?" Bartholomew, speaking in the ever-changing voice of Cindy, asked.

"Who's it you're looking for, love?" Ulmer Grule, a thin green-skinned goblin waiter with the face of a rat, arrived at their table with a metal tray in his hand.[6] Unlike Lum, Ulmer's eyes were keen. He was quite aware that Bartholomew was a male wearing a dress. But Ulmer fancied himself a financially-incentivized progressive ally, which was to say that he didn't care about the gender identity of any patron so long as they put money in his pockets.

Lum answered before Bartholomew could, slamming his mug onto the table. The troll was a bit light-headed from booze, and he'd mistaken Ulmer's question for flirting. He grabbed the warlock's hand and held it up as though it were a trophy. "This here's Cindy. I'm buying her a drink. What do you want, doll?"

Bartholomew wiggled his hand free of the troll's grip. With a grimace, he wiped the sweat onto the brown plastic seat. He'd never been much of a drinker—a splash of wine or sherry on occasion, but not much more.

---

6. He never used the tray, but he thought it was a rather fine accessory for a waiter.

What's something a woman would order?

"Strawberry lemonade with a splash of vodka," he said as Cindy. "Go easy on the simple syrup. I'm watching my diet."

Ulmer's eyes narrowed at the unusual customer. "I'll get you a beer."

Lum's grimacing smile returned as he watched the waiter retreat. He took another sip of his ale and tried to make out the features of the woman before him. The troll couldn't see, but he still wanted any potential mates to be attractive as a point of pride. He also wasn't keen on warlock leftovers.

"What did you say your relationship was with Otto again?"

"He's my... cousin." Bartholomew tapped his fingers along the edge of the table. "Are you absolutely certain he's not just with the questioners?"

"Who's this?" Ulmer asked again, returning with the beer.

"Otto Ewing's her cousin," Lum said, wanting to make the relationship between them perfectly clear before rumors spread about him trying to hit on widows. "I was just telling her that The Syndicate killed him."

"Oh he's dead, all right," Ulmer said, resting the beer before Bartholomew. "But it wasn't The Syndicate. Saw the whole thing myself through the window. Happened just outside the bar, late night a few days ago. Otto'd been drinking, said he didn't want to go home, but Dev said he couldn't stay here and kicked him out, and then, next thing you know there's a shot, like a real gunshot. Hits Otto's body and splat! Down he drops, dead as a corpse."[7]

"What happened to the body?" Cindy's voice asked from the stroller.

---

7. A remarkably undescriptive simile.

Bartholomew lifted his hand to his mouth, trying to hide the fact that he wasn't speaking.

Lum was too blind to notice, Ulmer too preoccupied by his own tale.

"Well, we couldn't leave it in front the bar, could we? Bad for business. So Dev and I dumped him in the river. Suppose it's still down there somewhere if you've the right runes to dredge it up." Ulmer gave an apologetic shrug.

Bartholomew flicked his fingers in dismissal. He didn't care where Otto's body was, and he hadn't a clue why Gizmo had asked. There was only one question that mattered now. "But who was it that killed him?"

"Couldn't say, love. I'm afraid I didn't see. But I know it weren't The Syndicate. Them sorts of warlocks don't use guns."

Bartholomew took a sip of beer and almost spat it out. Ulmer was right. The Bearded Syndicate were too clever and too dignified to revert to a barbaric human-made device. Someone else had killed Otto.

Was it the buyer he found for the amulet? Gizmo wondered in the stroller. This was a mystery he felt they owed it to Otto to solve.

Bartholomew, however, had no interest in sticking around to search for clues.

"Thank you, boys, but I need to use the restroom," the warlock said, leaping from his seat. He made a high-pitched tittering noise that he intended as a giggle, grabbed the stroller, and hurried back onto the street.

Otto was dead. Without him, Bartholomew had no way to sell the amulet, no means of funding his retirement, and no source of future supplies.

As far as he could tell, the details of what happened didn't matter. Either way, he was screwed. The identity of the killer made no difference to his own current life.

On this last point, Bartholomew was gravely mistaken.

TWENTY-EIGHT

The day after their ill-advised visit to the city, Bartholomew lay face down on his newly acquired blanket in the center of the small, carpeted space that was the warlock's room. Gizmo pawed at his socks.

"Well, if you're not going to solve Otto's murder—" the familiar said.

"I'm not."

Gizmo huffed to make it clear what he thought of that decision, but there was no sense starting a fight about it now. There would be time to work on building Bartholomew's sense of loyalty[1] in the future. Eternity was a long time.

But theirs was about to get very unpleasant if they didn't find a way to save their home.

"You still have to get up. The retirees club is gardening today. You have to get all the votes you can."

"What's the point?" Bartholomew said, turning his face to scowl at his familiar. "I hate plants and mud and anything outdoors, and even if I somehow managed to convince everyone that curtains are a larger

---

1. And curiosity, which was the real drive behind Gizmo's desire to solve Otto's murder.

nuisance than dogs,[2] it won't matter. Graves will hypnotize them into voting for him, and we'll be forced out. All because you didn't become a cat."

"You've said that before, but I really think that Mr. Graves would have targeted whichever animal I was."

"Yes, obviously, but no one would vote against cats."

Well, they would if they were hypnotized, Gizmo thought, but he decided against pointing out the obvious flaw in Bartholomew's logic.

"Come on. We haven't lost yet," the demon said. "There's still a chance."

"*I* haven't lost yet," Bartholomew corrected him, narrowing his eyes at his familiar. "And how?"

"You're a powerful, talented warlock, aren't you?" Gizmo rested his chin on his paws, making his eyes wide and affectionate. He'd been with Bartholomew long enough to know how to handle the situation. Whenever the warlock grew sour and attempted to slink into a mood, he could only be dragged out by his ego. "Surely, you're not going to let yourself be bested by a vampire, not when you have a quill and fresh inks at your disposal. I'd have thought you could have come up with something. But I suppose that's why everyone warned me not to bind myself to you."

Bartholomew pushed himself upright and spun so that he was sitting cross-legged, glowering down at his familiar. "Nobody warned you against choosing me."

---

2. An easy task, in Gizmo's opinion.

"A great demon with a talentless young warlock? You'll be the laughingstock of the underworld, they said."[3]

Bartholomew's jaw clenched so hard that his gums could feel the tension. "You're the one making me a laughingstock," he growled between his clamped teeth. "You think I can't find a way to best an old, dust-covered vampire? Of course I'm going to win this election!"

"That's the spirit!" Gizmo barked. "So what's the plan?"

Bartholomew slumped forward, chin falling to his palm. "We take a moment to think."

After a few hours of thinking and scribbling thoughts into a notebook, the warlock and his familiar came up with three serviceable ideas.

Plan A: Bartholomew could discover a new rune. If he knew how to write *hypnosis* or *vampire*, they would be in a position of instantaneous strength. *Sunshine* or *curtain* might work too. But uncovering a long-forgotten word in a long-forgotten script was a painstaking process.

Plan B: The warlock could take advantage of his newly acquired ink. Orange was not a color Bartholomew enjoyed working with. It was volatile, with a tendency to destroy either too much or too little,

---

3. This was, for the most part, true. But the other demons had called Bartholomew *difficult, volatile, miserable* and a host of other words, none of which had been *talentless*.

but seldom the precise amount needed. However, there was a way, in theory, to use it to defeat Frederick.[4]

Plan C: Bartholomew continued campaigning, played fair and hoped that Frederick would too.

That last idea was written in a much larger, shakier font, a bit like if a toddler had scribbled with a crayon and it was only a trick of the eye that made it look reminiscent of words.[5] Bartholomew didn't believe it should have counted at all.

However, as the sun descended on their final day before the election, a small part of the warlock began to hope that Gizmo was right.

Plan A had failed. Hours of grinding, grumbling, and guessing had proven futile. Bartholomew had stumbled upon no new runes.

The dangerous plan B seemed as hopeless. Preoccupied with plan A, Bartholomew had made the mistake of entrusting most of the early work to his familiar. With Sarah's assistance, Gizmo had baked a batch of cheese flavored cupcakes.

"We need people to eat them, you foozler!" Bartholomew cried when the two proudly brought them to him.

"I'm sure they will," Gizmo assured him, licking crumbs from his mouth. "These are delicious. I've already had several."

The warlock tugged at his curls. But there was no sense fighting his familiar about cupcake flavors. These were already baked.

---

4. Bartholomew theorized that, by writing the rune for *memory* in orange and hiding it within some sort of food, it might be possible to erase any effects of hypnosis in those who took a bite. But he'd never tried this before, and even his ego wasn't so grand that he fancied this option.

5. This was, in fact, what it looked like when a sentient dog attempted to write by holding a pen between his teeth.

Bartholomew drew the runes on top the first tray of cupcakes with a heavy hand, so that there was almost as much ink as there was flour. A single bite would be potent enough to break the effects of hypnosis. This was crucial because there was no chance of anyone who tasted the cupcake taking a second.

In order to hide the ink, Sarah slathered a thick layer of brown-icing over the top. It had a curious smell.

The warlock was almost afraid to ask. "Any chance that's chocolate?"

"Oh no," Sarah assured him. "That would be such a boring flavor. We used beef jerky."

Bartholomew groaned and covered his eyes with his palms. Convincing people to take even one bite of a cupcake was going to be harder than he'd realized.

"Cheer up. There's still plan C," Gizmo said, sensing the warlock's distress. The familiar lay on the kitchen counter, licking the spoon that Sarah had used to mix the frosting.

Bartholomew had the overwhelming urge to take the spoon and fling it across the room. But Gizmo might mistake the act of fury for a game of fetch, defeating the purpose.

Instead, the warlock began to pace around the kitchen island, watching the light vanish from the sky. Every inch the sun retreated brought him closer to his inevitable demise. He was certain that Frederick would be out that night, hypnotizing as many people as he could before the election.

"Plan B could still work.[6] These are kind of good," Sarah said, though it didn't sound like she believed it.

---

6. As far as Sarah knew, Plan B was to give out cupcakes to voters prior to the election as a last-minute reminder to vote for Bartholomew.

Bartholomew and Gizmo both turned to the girl at once. She'd taken two bites of one of the cupcakes.

"What are you doing? That's dangerous!"[7] The warlock swiped it from her hand. His eyebrows rose, and he considered her for a moment. "How do you feel?"

"So happy. I loved it." Sarah's stomach turned as she forced a smile. She did not, however, attempt to recover the cheese cupcake that Bartholomew held high over his head. There was something about the panic in his eyes that she recognized from other adults. "Don't worry. That wasn't one of the special ones that you added grown-up juice to." She winked at the euphemism, amused that her new friends had called it by such a silly name. Sarah wasn't a baby. She knew what alcohol was.

"Yes, well, see that you don't." Bartholomew eyed her with a bit of apprehension and dropped the un-inked cupcake to the counter.

Gizmo gobbled it up at once.

The warlock lifted the tray of enchanted desserts and rested it on the top of the fridge, away from the eleven-year-old's reach. "These are only for very special voters."

"Who?" Sarah asked.

"The ones whose eyes go all funny when they go into the voting booth."

"But how will you know? You're not allowed to look at people when they're voting."

---

7. You might be surprised that Bartholomew would care about Sarah's safety. You're not alone. He would be equally perplexed when he later recalled this moment and convince himself that his only real concern had been for his wasted ink.

"Because I'll ask them beforehand," Bartholomew snapped. He ought to have asked Ida for help instead. The eleven-year-old was starting to question him almost as much as Gizmo.

Right on cue, the familiar stopped licking the beef-jerky frosting from the counter to look up and say, "I don't know, Bart. Ms. Moon has a point. What if you don't manage to talk to everyone? It could be bad if we gave someone who wasn't hypnotized a cupcake, don't you think?"

Sarah's ears perked up at the word *hypnotized*. It was the first time either had said such a thing in her presence. She got the sense they were talking about something she wasn't supposed to know, so like any good child in such a situation, she stayed silent, hoping they'd forget her and reveal more.

Bartholomew ground his teeth. He hated when his familiar questioned him, and he hated it even more when Gizmo was right. "So what do you propose then? And not plan C."

"I don't know." The demon's head tilted to either side as he thought. There was frosting stuck to the fur around his mouth. "Maybe we could find a way to see who Mr. Graves is targeting, you know? So we already had a list and weren't just staring into people's eyes looking for something fishy."

"That's not an atrocious idea, Gizmo. Someone will just have to wait outside Mr. Graves' house tonight and follow him through the neighborhood." A slanted smile rose on the warlock's face. "So good of you to volunteer."

TWENTY-NINE

B artholomew spent the night before the election alone, pacing his empty room, worrying about ink quantities, hypnotic side-effects, and the shifting allegiances of short-tempered retirees. Sarah had returned home to ponder over the alluring alcoholic inks and strange conversation between the warlock and his familiar. Gizmo was settled in the tall grass rising around the maple outside of 13B.

Don't know when he heard me offer to stake out a vampire's house alone, the familiar thought bitterly. But Gizmo obeyed all the same. He pressed himself low to the ground, stared at the door, and waited.

And waited.

And waited.

And... you get the idea.

He lay on the grass throughout the night, staring at the vampire's red door until sunrise streaked the sky in pinks.

There was no attempted hypnosis to report, no activity at all. All night, Frederick had remained inside.

Maybe he got sick, Gizmo thought, his eyes growing heavy and tired from all his staring. *Or he's on vacation.*

Neither of those thoughts made sense. Vampires don't get sick. Someone in the middle of a territorial dispute with his supposedly dead neighbor doesn't pack up and fly to Cancun for a weekend.

Something was going on.

But others would learn the truth of it before Gizmo. The poor demon had been awake all night, following his master's orders like a good familiar. Now, the sun warmed his fur, and he yawned.

Then, he thought those famous words that have been the undoing of many a student attempting to pull an all nighter and finish a term paper. *It couldn't hurt to shut my eyes just a little.*

A minute later, Gizmo was asleep.

He had no idea when, in the middle of the day, the door to the vampire's house finally opened.

"Where is he?" Bartholomew muttered to himself, looking around the empty lawns as he fiddled with the collar of his shirt.

The warlock stood in the shade of the functions hall, just beside the door. As a candidate, he'd been allowed to cast his vote early, but now, he had been exiled from the building.

This wouldn't have fazed most presidential hopefuls. Indeed, Dan was nowhere near the functions hall. He'd chosen to devote his last efforts to more door-to-door visits with last-minute pleas to go out and vote, feverish recitations on the importance of democracy, and a few glassy-eyed rants about ridding the neighborhood of the plague of dogs.

Bartholomew, however, was unimpressed with his eviction. Four voters had arrived since he'd been outside. The warlock hadn't been able to detect a hint of hypnosis in any of their eyes when he'd questioned them. But what were the chances that none of the early voters were under Frederick's control?[1] Bartholomew was certain he'd missed some glimmer of hypnosis, fluttering in their pupils. Clearly, he needed to see what happened when they took the pen and paper from Ida, who was passing them out within.

But no amount of sweet-talking would allow the HOA's treasurer to allow Bartholomew into the voting booth. Instead, he was stuck outside with a brown bag full of cheese and jerky cupcakes.

If I'm going to win, I need to know what Frederick was up to last night.[2] Where is Gizmo with my information?

He was too nervous to pace. His foot tapped the sidewalk, twitching almost as much as his hands, which bounced from his pockets to his tie to his hair and back again in an inaccurate mockery of the children's song "Head, Shoulders, Knees, and Toes."

Gizmo should have been back by now. The familiar was supposed to have gathered information so they knew who to give the cupcakes to.

Bartholomew pulled a silver chain from his jacket. His pocket watch spun on the end. He popped the lid, glimpsed the time—already after midday—and snapped it shut. "Useless. Always useless."

But beneath his curmudgeonly grumblings, a repressed fear was bubbling to the surface, accompanied by an unfamiliar twinge of guilt. What if something had happened to Gizmo?

The demon had been weakened by his transformation. Sending him out, unguarded, to spy on a vampire, was dangerous.

---

1. Exceptionally high, of course, but Bartholomew didn't know that.

2. This was quite wrong. Bartholomew would have had a much higher chance of victory had he known what the vampire was doing at that present moment.

Gizmo had been Bartholomew's constant companion since he was a gangly, pimple-faced teenager with greasy hair and pointy elbows. The warlock wasn't certain what he would do without the familiar by his side.

Not because he cared for him or anything like that, Bartholomew assured himself. It was just that, without Gizmo, there was no one to blame when things went sideways.

"Dammit, dammit, damn him back to the underworld," the warlock muttered. He shifted his bag of cupcakes and stepped out of the shade. His focus should've been on the election. Their continued existence in Mills Run Heights depended on its outcome.

Instead, Bartholomew was marching off to find his familiar.

He had no idea that someone was hiding in the shadows, watching him the entire time.

The mysterious individual, skulking in the shade of the parkette trees and spying on the warlock like some dastardly villain, was none other than Frederick Graves.

Since his last meeting with Bartholomew, the vampire had gone through his own spiral of emotions. He needed to cheat. But how? If he hypnotized one person each day he could buy himself three votes and a splitting migraine. He had no knowledge of runes or the magic required to use them even if he did. There were no fairies or djinns nearby that he could capture and force to grant him a wish.

Frederick had mulled on the matter until after sunrise each day, sipping on a delightful mixture of malbec and B-negative[3] until his head grew giddy and his ideas became increasingly ludicrous.[4]

But at some point, it occurred to the vampire, who'd been living among humans for much longer than the warlock and his familiar, that cheating didn't require magic.

The realization caught him quite off guard. It took him a long day's rest and a strong cup of a barista's blood before he could address it.

By then, it was the night before the election, and Frederick needed to plan fast. He paced the dark length of his living room, speaking aloud to the stuffed owl beside his coffin, unaware that there was a demon lying in wait beyond his door.

"What would a human do if they were going to rig an election?" Frederick asked.

The stuffed owl statue did not respond, mostly because it was a stuffed owl, but also because, having spent most of its existence in the care of an undead vampire, it knew very little about how humans operated.

"No, Trevor," Frederick stopped, holding up a finger and lecturing the owl as though it was it who'd just spoken. "The first question we need to consider is how does one win an election."

The stuffed owl knew the answer this time.

"Votes," Frederick said, resuming his pacing. "And how would a human get more votes?"

---

3. Drinking the blood of an alcoholic would've produced a similar effect, but that was surprisingly difficult to come by in Mills Run Heights.

4. He couldn't turn the entire neighborhood into vampires and seize control. It went against his intention of secrecy and was likely far beyond his capabilities. Frederick had never turned anyone. He wasn't sure he even knew how.

Suddenly, he stopped.

The answer had been right before him all along.

"Why, he'd vote more times! Trevor, you genius! We've done it again!" He rushed forward, picked up the stuffed owl and kissed it square on the beak.[5]

So instead of going for his usual nightly stroll, Frederick devoted the rest of his night to the technicalities of his plan. He wrote the name *Dan Miller* in as many ways as he could think: tight-scripted cursive, large loopy letters, scratchy disjointed lines. He changed the shape of the *D*, dotted the *i* with an assortment of shapes, wrote the *a* like it might've appeared on an old typewriter.

By midday,[6] Frederick was ready.

With some trepidation (for his plan required him to brave the sun), he readied himself. He covered as much of his skin as he could, pale blue gloves, pink socks, a thin violet scarf that he wrapped around his face. At the door, he forsook his favorite turquoise coat in favor of a long, dull black one that he'd received as a gift from his former leprechaun associate. It lacked that sense of pizzazz. But Frederick didn't want to draw attention to himself today.[7]

He grabbed his large umbrella, opened the door, and stepped into the deadly field of sunlight that burned the earth before him. The vampire was too focused on avoiding instant combustion to notice

---

5. Trevor felt quite chuffed by the compliment.

6. After an unintentional nap brought about by a combination of fading adrenaline and increasingly large sips of wine.

7. You might already see where Frederick's outfit would not have given this impression. The vampire, however, considered that he'd been quite conservative in choosing his attire.

Gizmo, sprawled on his back, legs twitching in the air so that they rose from the grass like oversized, fluffy mosquitoes.

Frederick scurried between shady oases, making his way toward the community center. He couldn't use the front entrance like the rest of the residents. Otherwise, whoever was outside, monitoring the voting process might realize when he spent a long stretch of time beyond the curtain.

The vampire's plan involved misting through one of the shaded windows[8] and entering the booth without anyone being the wiser. But when he arrived, there was a significant problem. Bartholomew was guarding the door. If he saw Frederick out in the day, the warlock would know something was afoot. So the vampire hid among the trees in the small parkette on the east side of the community center, and waited.

Until finally, Bartholomew left.

Frederick slunk forward, cowering under his umbrella until he reached the shade. He had to act fast. The vampire had no idea why the warlock had suddenly disappeared, nor did he care.

Though he might have had he realized that Bartholomew, a former acquirer, was heading to his house.

---

8. His power wouldn't work in direct sunlight.

THIRTY

W hile Frederick was busy forging handwriting in a curtained voting booth (and listening to William Lee[1] attempt and fail to make small talk with Ida[2]), Bartholomew was racing toward the vampire's house.

The warlock wasn't much of an athlete, but his giraffe-like legs proved useful in these instances. He arrived at 13B in a few short minutes[3], out of breath with a sharpening pain of nagging anxiety. His worry evaporated in an instant, however, when he spotted the black legs rising and sinking in the grass. Anger boiled in its place.

Bartholomew stumbled to a halt on the sidewalk just beyond the grass. He glared down at his familiar. With every breath that the furry

---

1. Who had been convinced to volunteer by Dan as counting the votes would require a second pair of eyes.

2. "Great weather we've been having, isn't it?"
   "Far too hot."
   "Did you see those tomatoes coming up in the community garden. They look delicious." "I suffer from acid reflux." And so it continued painfully every minute or so.

3. A short minute being about 45 seconds, which is of course, the time period teachers actually give students when they say "one minute left."

black chest rose and fell in peaceful repose, the warlock's jaw clenched tighter. Soon, he was at risk of gnawing through to his gums.

"Gizmo, you useless foozler," Bartholomew snapped. When that had no effect, he gave his familiar a sharp prod with his toe.

The demon's eyes burst open. He twisted and hopped onto his feet. "Where did it go? Did you see that?"[4] He looked up, and his gaze fell on the warlock's thick brow and narrowed eyes. Bartholomew's lips were twisted in some hideous, pained version of a smile.

"How was your nap?" he asked.

Gizmo stretched his hind legs, shuffling into a version of up-ward-facing dog. The events of the past night were returning to him. "Quite good, actually."

"Oh wonderful." The warlock's smile dropped into its usual scowl, and his voice rose in fury. "Because we'll both be sleeping outside for the foreseeable future thanks to you! Where's my list?"

There's no need to shout, Gizmo thought. Staring up at Bartholomew, he got the impression that this would not be the correct thing to say. Still, the familiar didn't see what there was to be so fussed over.

"There isn't one," he said, switching his pose into downward facing dog so that he could stretch his front legs.

Bartholomew's hands fluttered to his head. His fingers wrapped around his hair and tugged. Unfortunately, the boyish curls remained rooted to his scalp. "Of course there isn't!" he shouted. "Because you

---

4. It was, you see, an abrupt transition for Gizmo. One moment, he'd been running through a desolate landscape of dark pits and bubbling lava pools chasing a sea of brightly colored butterflies. Then, one of them had flown into his ribcage with considerable force and everything was bathed in sunshine.

fell asleep on the job! You useless, incompetent, no good foozler of a familiar."

Gizmo tilted out of his stretch. He thought this response quite unfair. After all, he'd forgone a good night's rest in his very own bedroom, in the center of his beige carpet, all for the warlock.

"There's no list because Frederick never left his house," the familiar objected. "I watched all night. He never left."

Bartholomew's eyebrows lowered. "Really? Not even once?"

Gizmo shook his head. He watched the warlock, wondering if perhaps an apology was coming his way at last.

One definitely wasn't. Bartholomew was very much of the opinion that an empty list was still a list, and he very much wanted to wring his familiar's neck and yell this fact at him.

However, the warlock was now preoccupied with a greater concern. If Frederick hadn't left last night, he must've done all his hypnotizing earlier.

Bartholomew began pacing the walkway of the vampire's house. He shook the bag in his hands. "How're we supposed to find out who to feed the cupcakes to?"

"I don't know. Maybe Frederick made his own list."

At the demon's suggestion, Bartholomew stopped his pacing. His eyebrows rose. It was a long shot, but maybe...

The warlock's hand slipped into his jacket and around his quill. His head turned toward 13B.

"Woah. This is some spooky décor!" Gizmo said, his head turning around Frederick's living room.

"Shh! Keep your voice down," Bartholomew whispered. He pointed to the closed black coffin in the corner furthest from the windows. It was empty, of course, but neither of them had any reason to believe that a vampire was out roaming the streets in the daytime or stuffing forged papers into a ballot box. There were more dignified ways of handling things when you had magic at your disposal.

A pair of large yellow eyes watched Bartholomew from near the coffin. He jumped back, a small squeak escaping him. It was only a stuffed owl.

"Did you just squeak?" Gizmo whispered.

"Certainly not. That was probably you. You're the one who's taken on a form akin to a large mouse," Bartholomew objected, straightening his tie and keeping an eye on the owl.[5] A small part of him worried it might take to the air or squawk and warn Frederick of their intrusion.

Gizmo, who had little interest in stuffed animals unless they were tossed for him to chase, pouted up at the warlock. He objected quite strongly to Bartholomew's accusation. "A dog is less like a mouse than a cat is," he argued.

"Certainly not," Bartholomew said, tiptoeing toward the kitchen and beginning to open drawers. He was searching for anything that might help him, but his acquiring eye was always on the lookout for valuables. "A cat is the opposite of a mouse, and a dog is the opposite of a cat. Ergo, a dog and a mouse are practically the same thing."

"You wouldn't say that if I was a German Shepherd."

"But you're not. You're a yorkie."

"I've told you, I'm a pomapoo."

---

5. The warlock once had a mentor who'd enchanted stuffed animals. Bartholomew was cautious of them as result.

"You're just making up ridiculous words." Bartholomew opened a cupboard door. There was a supply of food within. The warlock pulled out a black box and opened it, hoping to find something valuable. There was a collection of bags full of dried flakes of blood. Handwritten brown labels were tied to them with a piece of string. He read one.

Type O-, low in platelets, infused with a dash of high caffeine A+.

"What is it? Anything good?" Gizmo asked, standing on his hind legs and trying to peer into the box. "Cheese?"

Bartholomew returned the box to the cupboard. Beside it was a Tupperware full of red cookies. The warlock somehow doubted that they were red velvet. "If there's cheese in this house, it isn't the kind you'd want to eat."

"I don't think there's such a thing," Gizmo said honestly.

Bartholomew flicked his hand at his familiar. Had he really been worried what he would do without Gizmo? His life would be so much easier. He'd be rid of all these pointless debates. Maybe he could even get a proper familiar, one who obeyed without talking so much. "Go search somewhere else. Your brain obviously doesn't function in the kitchen. And watch for traps."

Gizmo would have much preferred to look for cheese, but in Bartholomew's current mood, he probably wouldn't have let the familiar enjoy a slice anyway. *Maybe if I can find something about the hypnosis victims, he'll give me a treat,* Gizmo thought. *Or at least, he might ignore me if I reward myself with one.* He trotted off in search of what he wasn't quite certain, perhaps a list of names or a box Frederick kept with trophies from his victims.[6]

After combing the kitchen, Bartholomew determined there was nothing worth acquiring within[7] and moved toward the living room. He walked on the tips of his toes, throwing nervous glances over his shoulder at the empty coffin and probably unalive owl. There was a black couch, a China cabinet, and a collection of books.[8] The warlock searched everywhere he could think, looking for a list or anything that might be a clue as to Frederick's previous movements. But the longer Bartholomew spent in the vampire's house, the more the profession of his dead self whispered to his soul.

There was something else he ought to be hunting for instead.

Wasn't Frederick in hiding because he'd stolen a leprechaun's pot?

"Barf, Barf! I foun' summin!" Gizmo dashed from the bedroom.

"Shh!" Bartholomew pressed his finger to his lips, but his dark eyes were alight with excitement. "What is it? Wealth beyond our greatest imagining?"

There were a set of papers in the familiar's mouth.

"Oh." The warlock tried not to feel disappointed. "A list of his victims. That's good too."

---

6. This theory was the product of Gizmo bingeing too much television while Bartholomew had left him alone at the motel. Frederick was a vampire, not a serial killer.

7. Which wasn't to say he found nothing of value. In fact, Frederick had quite a few rather luxurious items, including a collection of gold-plated cutlery, a crystal bowl, and a state-of-the-art blender that he'd braved the sun once to get. But Bartholomew found it difficult to be tempted by any of these for he kept imagining them covered in blood.

8. Mostly plays and historical romances.

Gizmo shook his head. He dropped the papers onto the floor near Bartholomew's feet. "It's worse than that. Look at these."

With a furtive glance at the owl, whose eyes he swore were following him, the warlock bent down to examine the pages. There were five in total. He picked one at random, held it up, and his eyes widened.

In the center of the paper was a sketch of the Amulet of the Impaler. Bartholomew's eyebrows lowered. He studied the details. There was the black onyx eye set in the center of the sun. Those were the exact curves of its rays. It even had thin lines to represent the grooves of the many now indistinguishable runes etched into the gold.

It could only have been drawn by someone who'd seen the amulet.[9]

"You don't think..." Gizmo began to say, but then stopped himself. It was too big of a coincidence.

Bartholomew continued to search the papers. Notes on the amulet, a letter from someone giving theories about its previous whereabouts, and an entry that appeared to have been ripped from someone's diary where the writer hypothesized on how it might have been created. The most worrying page, however, was the last that the warlock saw. On it, written in cursive that had opted for elegance over legibility, was all of the information about Bartholomew Whitlock's supposed death.

And circled in red at the bottom of the page—

The current possessor of the amulet? No. Someone else.

"I do think, Gizmo. That's what separates us," Bartholomew said, coming to an incorrect, but understandable conclusion given the ci

---

9. This was not quite accurate. However, it had been sketched by someone who'd seen a drawing done by someone who had seen the amulet. The artist of the work in the warlock's hands had been Frederick's mentor. He hadn't been pleased when his protégé filched it from his possession and *skipped off to dance the jig* with a leprechaun, as he put it.

rcumstances.[10] "Frederick was Otto's buyer. He's the one who killed him."

The warlock said it with such conviction that a lump rose in Gizmo's throat. "If that's true, Mr. Graves is more dangerous that we realized."

Both their heads turned to the coffin. They grabbed the information, turned, and raced from the house. Their hearts pounded in their chests, and both their minds were full of new fears about the vampire.

But that was because they had no idea of the real threat.

In the case of the murder of Otto Ewing, Frederick was innocent. But someone was guilty.

And at that very moment, that someone was preparing to leave the city and take a bus ride out to the suburbs.

---

10. All of these pages suggested that Frederick had been hunting for the amulet for some time, and the stuffed owl still watching Bartholomew gave everything a more menacing feel and inclined him to jump to the most horror-movie-esque conclusion.

THIRTY-ONE

B artholomew and Gizmo were too busy worrying about the imagined threat of the vampire to notice the actual Frederick, who they passed in their frantic dash from his house. But he noticed them.

He had finished his task, stuffing the ballot box with enough *Dan Miller* votes that the human's victory was assured. Frederick was feeling quite chuffed with his accomplishments and, despite the deadly sea of sunshine, already beginning to compose the victorious speech he would deliver to the warlock.

Ask not how I have achieved... Frederick paused. He needed to get the words perfect. *That isn't quite right. What if started with, "Question not my accolades." Or perhaps—*

Frederick's thoughts were interrupted by the sight of the warlock and familiar racing down his street, not running exactly, but walking at a fast enough pace that someone could certainly mistake it as such.

The vampire watched them disappear down the road without even a glance in his direction.

Quite rude, Frederick thought. He was of the opinion that just because someone was your enemy it was no excuse for poor manners. But the lack of decorum was only one part of the vampire's concern.

What are they running for? It seemed obvious to Frederick that the warlock was up to something.

But it couldn't have been better than his idea to stuff the ballot box, the vampire reassured himself, skulking back to his house.

When he opened the door and entered his dark abode, Frederick felt an immediate sense of relief. He'd braved the sunlight and survived. But his calm was short-lived.

Something felt strange.

Had he tucked in his kitchen stool that morning? Were the books on his shelves in a different order? Had he tracked grass onto the carpet?

But it was the afternoon, the sun was high and hot, and Frederick's mind was not at its sharpest.

"I must be imagining things, Trevor," he concluded, addressing the stuffed owl. The vampire yawned, rubbed his eyes, and slipped into his pajamas. He climbed into his coffin and closed the lid over him.

Given his exploits, Frederick was exhausted. He ought to have passed out and not woken until well into the night.

Instead, he tossed and turned. His dreams were full of running warlocks and slightly shifted furniture. He couldn't shake the sense that something was off.

While Frederick was struggling to sleep, Bartholomew was trying to determine his next course of action. He spent another hour loitering outside of the functions hall. Two voters came during that time, both retirees. The warlock inspected their eyes. His fingers hovered over the buckles of his bag, but he waved them in without opening it.

"Not a single person with glassy eyes when talking about voting. Not a one," he muttered under his breath. "What do you suppose that means?"

He wasn't really asking his familiar so much as voicing his own thoughts aloud, but seeing as Gizmo was sitting on the grass beside him, the demon felt justified answering. "I suppose it means Mr. Graves didn't hypnotize anyone."

"Obviously it means that," Bartholomew snapped. Or it might have meant that he was doing a bad job checking, but he didn't dare admit that he was concerned about his own abilities. "But why didn't he? Does he not care about Dan winning? But if he doesn't care about the election, he must have something else planned."

"Or another way to cheat," Gizmo guessed, quite correctly.

But the warlock wasn't listening to his familiar. He was far too busy imagining the worst. After all, if Frederick had killed Otto, he might be coming for Bartholomew next.

"But he can't kill me," the warlock muttered.[1] "Not if he wants the amulet." It was runically sealed in a wooden box, hidden in Bartholomew's built-in closet. But he hadn't checked on it for a few days.

A sudden concern shook him. He'd broken into the vampire's house. How certain was he that Frederick hadn't done the same?

"Dammit! Come on, Gizmo!" Bartholomew stormed toward the road. His familiar, still rather confused, had no choice but to follow.

Of course, Frederick had not broken into the warlock's house. The vampire lacked the skills of an acquirer, the main one of which is a natural disregard for other people's property. When Bartholomew

---

1. For Gizmo, who was not in Bartholomew's mind, this statement came rather out of left field.

retrieved the wooden box, he found his rune unbroken and the amulet rattling within.

But this did little to quell his mounting concerns.

The warlock and his familiar passed the rest of the afternoon locked in their house, trying to figure out their next course of action.

As was his habit now, Bartholomew paced the empty living room. Gizmo sat beside the kitchen island, staring mournfully at the cupcakes sitting upon it. *Such a waste,* he thought to himself. All those delicious beef and cheese desserts ruined by orange ink.

"What's the appropriate response for when you discover your neighbor has killed your associate?" Bartholomew asked.

This time, the warlock was talking to his familiar. But it was very difficult for Gizmo to tell, and he was quite distracted by the cupcakes.

"What, now you can't talk?" Bartholomew snapped his fingers.

Gizmo turned his head and found the warlock scowling at him. "Sorry, what was the question?"

Bartholomew's scowl darkened. Why couldn't the demon hang off his every word like a good familiar? "What should you do when you discover that your neighbor is a murderer?"

"Oh that's easy!" Gizmo sat up, tail thumping, happy to be able to answer. "Assuming he hasn't gotten the proper permits, you call the enforcers."[2]

Bartholomew's jaw clenched. *Why do I even bother asking him?*

---

2. The enforcers were what counted for law enforcement in the magical community. They operated under the command of The Bearded Syndicate, punishing those who hadn't paid the appropriate bribes. Murders committed without Syndicate permission held a penalty of a century's imprisonment within the pits of the underworld. Prior to becoming a familiar, Gizmo had tortured more than a few such guilty individuals.

"I can't call the enforcers, you buffoon! I'm dead."

"Well, I didn't know we were talking specifically about you," the familiar replied. "I thought it was a more general trivia question."

"Obviously we're talking about me! Have you not been paying attention?"

Not for the past hour or so, Gizmo thought, licking his nose as he glanced at the cupcakes.

Bartholomew resumed his pacing, grinding his teeth. "Next thing you'll suggest I just send him to the underworld myself." The warlock could find a way using the orange ink, but then Frederick might be inclined to start telling people about the supposed-to-be-dead Bartholomew Whitlock living in Mills Run Heights. The information would undoubtedly get back to The Syndicate.

"The easiest solution," the warlock said, speaking aloud, "would be to grab a wooden stake, charge into Frederick's house now, and plunge it into his chest before he wakes."

Gizmo didn't think that would be easy at all. For one thing, there weren't nicely carved wooden stakes lying around the lawns of Mills Run Heights, and for another, Bartholomew was seriously underestimating the upper body strength required to ram a piece of a tree into someone's chest. There was an awful lot of muscle and sinew to get through, and the ribs could get in the way if you weren't careful.

There was no need for the demon to voice these concerns, however. He knew the warlock.[3]

Indeed, despite his words, Bartholomew made no movements to rush outside and break a branch from one of the maples. He continued pacing, searching for viable solutions.

---

3. As you might recall from earlier, Bartholomew, for all his flaws, was not a murderer.

"Garlic won't cut it anymore. This house needs protective runes," he said.

"And we need ink," Gizmo chimed in, making an effort to pay attention now that he'd been caught zoning out.

"*I* need ink. You need to obey commands better," Bartholomew corrected. "If we'd found the leprechaun's pot, I might have had the funds to purchase some."

Gizmo's ears perked up. As a rule, the familiar was more interested in cheese than gold, and Spudsy O'Cabbage's stolen pot had slipped his mind. But now that Bartholomew mentioned it, why hadn't they come across it while searching Frederick's house?

The warlock continued, "Not that I could just walk into a store and buy some now anyway. Bartholomew Bartlow doesn't have Syndicate approval. I'll have to start brewing it myself."

"Just like I suggested!"

"No, you didn't. You never suggest anything useful, or you'd know where I could get money for the ingredients now that Otto's gone and we haven't acquired a leprechaun's pot." Bartholomew's pacing brought him to the wall. He turned and surveyed the large, open-plan room before him. There wasn't exactly an appropriate place for a secret brewing room. But it would be a hell of a lot more doable than attempting to brew ink while living in a tent in the woods. "This house is our last hope of protecting ourselves and managing to have a peaceful retirement."

The weight of that thought sent the warlock crumpling to the floor, a heap of long, formally-dressed limbs.

Gizmo abandoned his position by the cupcakes and trotted dutifully across the room to lick Bartholomew's fingers. They tasted vaguely of beef jerky frosting. "Don't worry, Bart. I'm sure the presidency comes with a good paycheck.[4] Once you win, you can kick Frederick out, secure the house, and soon our retirement will be as peaceful as we envisioned."

He was picturing eating cheese in the park, chasing rodents through the community gardens, and peeing on all the maples before coming home to burrow into the blankets of a very large bed for a sixteen-hour nap.

But unfortunately for the familiar and the warlock, their retirement would be far from peaceful, and a few minutes later, a harbinger of doom knocked on their door.

Despite the still shining sun, the hour was approaching night. The votes would have been tallied by now, and Bartholomew answered his door hoping to see Ida Meadows on the other side. She'd promised to bring him news of the election results.

Instead, it was Sarah Miller. The girl had squeezed herself into a black velvet dress that she'd worn to her grandmother's funeral the previous year. In lieu of a veil, she'd clipped a black piece of felt into her already black hair. It had seemed appropriate, for she considered herself to be in mourning. In Sarah's hand was a cell phone.

She held it up toward the warlock. In a somber voice that was much too deep for a little girl voice, she informed him, "It's for you."

---

4. It did not, in fact, come with any money at all. But given that Gizmorgoth of Darkness was a demon, he knew very little about what being president of a Homeowners Association entailed.

The warlock frowned. He put the phone to his ear while Sarah attempted to glide into the house, though it was more of a wobbly skip.

Her eyes went at once to the cupcakes, visible in the open bag on the kitchen island. She'd spent most of the previous night thinking about the ink and the curious shape that Bartholomew had carved on each. The eleven-year-old was beginning to suspect it wasn't alcohol at all. But it was certainly something.

However, Sarah left the cupcakes alone for the time being.

In the doorway, the warlock was engaged in his second ever smartphone conversation.

"Ms. Archer?" Bartholomew guessed.

"No, it's William," the voice responded from the other end.

"Wrong number." Bartholomew raised his hand to end the call.

"Funny, Bart. It's me." When the warlock gave no indication that he had been joking, the voice continued, slightly less confident. "William Lee. Your neighbor. Dan's friend. Come on, you know m e."[5]

"Ah yes. 21B."

William laughed uncomfortably. He was currently sitting in a floral armchair within the functions hall, staring at the empty fireplace and wondering if this entire situation wasn't some elaborate prank that his friend had orchestrated. "Why have you got Dan's phone number listed as your own?"

---

5. They had at this point encountered one another on numerous occasions, including earlier that day when Bartholomew had gone to cast his vote. William, misinterpreting the warlock's disdain for dry wit, thought they had a fairly good rapport.

What a ridiculous question, Bartholomew thought. "Because it's the best way to reach me."[6]

William laughed again, feeling a bit more at ease. He was increasingly certain that this was indeed a joke. "Right, okay. Well, I've got the election results."

Bartholomew straightened. "Why did you waste time with all that pointless chatter then. What are they?"

"Oh, Dan won. By a landslide!"

Bartholomew's chest went cold. He slumped against his doorway, unable to move as he processed everything.

"I don't know what you two were playing at, but somehow you managed to get more people out to vote than ever," William continued. He sounded a bit too cheerful given the circumstances, but he'd concocted his own theory where Dan and Bartholomew had orchestrated this outcome together. "Anyway, I think the stipulation was two weeks to rehome your dog. If you haven't got anyone in mind yet, I have a sister, who would be—"

The warlock dropped the phone onto his lawn and stepped inside. Destitute. Hunted by a murderous vampire.[7] And now, homeless. Bartholomew's retirement was not going as planned.

---

6. His application for president had also required he fill something into the space, and Sarah had volunteered to carry the phone between the houses.

7. Actually, the person with murderous intentions currently hunting him was not a vampire, but this would have been little comfort.

THIRTY-TWO

Only a few things truly panicked Gizmorgoth of Darkness. Bartholomew accepting an invitation to a party with no ulterior motive was one of them.

Dan Miller had come over a few minutes after his daughter. His greatest fear was that someone might dislike him, and it was therefore very important to him to clear the air with his former competitor.

Bartholomew answered the door before he could knock. The warlock's dark eyes were flat. His lips weren't snarled or scowled or twisted or slanted. They were just there, on his chin, only moving when it was essential that he speak.

"Just wanted to say, you ran a hell of a campaign." Dan stuck out his hand. "I hope there's no hard feelings."

Gizmo watched from the behind the door, eyes widening in shock as Bartholomew accepted the handshake.

"None," the warlock said, voice as flat as his expression.

It should have been obvious that he was lying. But sometimes people like Dan Miller[1] hear what they want in these situations. He was all smiles. "Fantastic, so glad to hear. Because I'd still love to be

---

1. Optimistic extroverts with a puppy dog's need for popularity.

friends. I'm throwing a victory barbecue tonight. Not that I knew I was going to win." He held up his hands. "I was going to hold it for either of us, I swear. Anyway, I really hope you'll come over. We've got great food."

"Sure."

Gizmo gasped. The situation was even worse than he'd imagined, and it had already been pretty bad as far as he could see. But the familiar hadn't given up hope that they might've been able to turn things around still.

Bartholomew had.

News of his loss had hit the warlock with a sudden sense of hopelessness. He'd sunk into it like a comfortable mattress and wrapped himself in a blanket of his own self-pity. It was significantly easier than trying to come up with a solution.

Bartholomew wanted to bask in his wallowing. Adding a party to his suffering seemed apropos.

"Well I won't be there," Sarah said, stepping out from behind the door where she'd been standing with Gizmo. The familiar followed at her feet. "Not if you're going to force my friends out of the neighborhood."

"Sarah!" Dan's eyes widened. He had, up until this moment, no idea that his eleven-year-old daughter was hanging out with their adult neighbor and his dog. "What are you doing here?"

Bartholomew and Gizmo looked around, trying to see who this *Sarah* was to whom Dan was speaking.

"I came to tell Mr. Bartlow that you'd won and were going to force him out of the neighborhood," she said, flipping her felt veil out of her face and crossing her arms.

Dan laughed, suddenly embarrassed. "Don't be dramatic. He's only got to find someone to take in his dog." He leaned inside to grab his daughter and saw within. "Have you not got furniture here yet?"

"It's out being cleaned," Bartholomew lied.

Dan had never heard of such a thing, but it didn't seem polite to pry further. His eyes landed on Gizmo, sitting by his daughter's feet. He felt a twinge of guilt that he couldn't quite place. "I am sorry about you needing to rehome your dog and all, but—" His eyes glazed over, and his voice grew robotic. "Dogs are a scourge on Mills Run Heights. The covenants must be changed to ban all canines." He blinked, and the signs of hypnosis vanished. "Well, see you in a bit, Bart! Party starts at seven." He grinned, took his daughter's hand, and pulled her out of the house.

Bartholomew and Gizmo watched the two walk across the lawns toward their own home.

"Do you suppose," the familiar said, head tilted to the side, "that Aurora Moon is actually named Sarah Miller?"

"What does it matter. Life is suffering and Fate is out to get me,"[2] Bartholomew said and closed the door with a heavy sigh.

He left his house for the party an hour later. Gizmo was at his feet.

Neither of them noticed, but in the warlock's current state of depression, he forgot to lock his door.

2. This was, quite frankly, false. Fate had, at this point, paid little attention to Bartholomew. As an acquirer for The Bearded Syndicate, he'd been a pawn in a game of chess. Fate concerned herself with Kings and Queens, and perhaps, occasionally, Knights and Bishops. Luck, however, was still holding a bit of a grudge.

The first stars blinked through the painted pinks and gold of the setting sun, and laughter rose from the Millers' lawn. More people had come to celebrate Dan's victory than had bothered to vote for his success, but they kept that secret to themselves. After all, what did it matter? He'd won anyway.

Children took turns skipping rope and falling flat from aborted cartwheels, curling into giggling balls at their own failure. Friends chatted around the dancing fire of the barbecue, congratulating Dan. Others stretched on the lounge chairs, snuggling tired infants in a picture of happy parenthood.

Bartholomew hated everything about it.

The barbecue was too hot. The children were too visible. The adults were too many.

Most of all, however, the warlock hated that he was going to have to leave it all behind.

He stood at the grill, surrounded by Dans' usual group of friends.[3] There was a cold beer in the warlock's hand. He took a sip as he listened to the new president's plans. Dan wanted to encourage individuality and self-expression, loosen the many rules that made it difficult for children to enjoy the neighborhood's public areas.

In short, he was going to ruin Mills Run Heights.

Bartholomew sighed and took a sip of his beer. It tasted horrid, like fermented barley mixed with yeast that had turned bitter. The perfect beverage to add to his suffering.

Oh, this is growing increasingly concerning, Gizmo thought to himself as he watched the warlock swallow the beer with an expression of great pain.

---

3. Though Joe Baker was noticeably absent.

The familiar lay behind the maple on the edge of the property, hiding in the grass. He'd been banned from the party when he'd tried to follow Bartholomew. According to Dan, it sent the wrong message, given the circumstances. Gizmo took great offense to his rejection. The entire matter of not including dogs in neighborhoods or at parties seemed very species-ist in his opinion.

I'll bet they wouldn't treat me this way if I was a duckling, Gizmo thought. He'd never heard anyone say they didn't like ducklings.

"It's not fair. It's just not fair," Sarah said. She was seated in the grass beside the familiar, glaring at her father. She needed to get his attention so she could make it clear that she was ignoring him. So far, it had gone completely over Dan's head. "Where will you go?"

"According to Bart, somewhere in the woods," Gizmo said. He hadn't believed the warlock when he'd suggested it before. Bartholomew was used to dark, dusty rooms full of books and clutter. He hated mud, bird songs gave him a headache, and he tolerated plants only because they were essential for existence. The thought of him living in a forest was absurd, but then, so was the idea of him accepting an invitation to a party.

While Gizmo was picturing a makeshift cloth tent, meals of sour berries, and a curmudgeonly warlock with a long beard walking barefoot in his suit and trying to sweep dirt out of a forest, Sarah had a much more magical image in mind. She saw the little cottage she'd always envisioned,[4] with friendly deer that helped them gather the bounties of the woods, and chipmunks who taught her to sew. She would spend her mornings performing chores with Gizmo, her days inventing stories among the trees, and her nights seated in a large

---

4. Which had eight bedrooms, eight bathrooms, full plumbing, and electricity. Most adults would have described it as a luxury mansion

reading room with Bartholomew. He would have a book on his lap, a quill in his hand, and his inks shimmering on the table.

Gizmo didn't see it for he was looking at the warlock, but there was a curious flicker of something in Sarah's eyes as she thought of the inks. Something dark. Something dangerous. Something powerful.

"Can I come with you?" she asked.

The question caught Gizmo off guard. His head snapped up. He turned to the girl who, after great deliberation, he suspected was not named Aurora Moon. "You mean to live with us? Wouldn't you miss your parents?"

"I might a bit, but I could always send them letters."[5]

Gizmo considered it for a moment. He'd grown quite fond of Sarah. There was something about her that reminded him of Bartholomew.[6] But even if he'd like to, the warlock would never agree, and they couldn't very well condemn the poor eleven-year-old to suffer puberty while living in a tent with a bearded centenarian.

"I'm afraid we haven't—" Gizmo started to let her down gently, when he was struck by a brilliant idea.

There was a way to leave Mills Run Heights with both money and Sarah. It was the leprechaun's pot.

If she and Gizmo acquired it and brought it to Bartholomew, he wouldn't be able to deny the eleven-year-old's usefulness. Funding would no longer be an issue, and he'd have to agree to take her with them.

It was just a matter of determining where Frederick had hidden the stolen pot. Leaving something so precious outside where anyone

---

5. *That would be much more eccentric than texting!* she thought.

6. Though it certainly had nothing to do with their personalities.

might stumble across it seemed dangerous without runes to protect it, and even those could be broken.[7] But Bartholomew and Gizmo had searched the house. They should have found it.

Unless... The familiar's eyebrows rose. There was one place they hadn't checked. But it wasn't exactly safe to investigate while the vampire was asleep. He glanced at the sky. The sun was almost gone.

"Ms. Moon," Gizmo said, addressing her by the false moniker out of habit. "How would you like to become an apprentice-acquirer?"

Sarah had no idea what that was, but the fact she'd never heard the title before suggested it was something unique and special. "I'd like that very much."

"Excellent. Then follow me," he said, and leaped up at once. "For our first training session, we're going to steal a pot of gold from a coffin."

Bartholomew was too morose to notice his familiar scampering down the street beside an eleven-year-old girl with a square of felt on her head. He moved through circles of party-hell, holding a chicken thigh, no napkin or paper plate, just letting the barbecue sauce sit in the corners of his mouth, a medallion of his failure.

First, there was Dan's crew, who'd switched from a discussion of the subdivision's regulations to tales of when they'd broken them. "Do you remember when—" one would start. And before anyone could explain, the next would chime in with, "The time with the carrots?

---

7. Otherwise, acquirers would be out of a job.

Of course!" Followed by a chorus that meant nothing to anyone who hadn't been there, and fairly little even to those who had been.[8]

From there, Bartholomew wandered, soundless and sulking, to a group of mothers with infants. They were all quite intrigued by the tall, silent gentleman in his suit who sat with them, and were quick to fill him in on everything they were discussing. "Kaiden is one of the boys in kindergarten with our kids, and his mother, Tanya, let him color on himself with markers. Can you imagine the toxins? Did your mother ever let you color on yourself with markers?" "No."[9] "Exactly! See, that's what I'm saying..." And so on and so forth until the warlock had heard and forgotten the names of every child and parent in the kindergarten.

Bartholomew was questioned on the price of all his clothes and his house by a group discussing finances in another corner, made to skip by the children,[10] and regaled with all the sundry details of different sports games when he entered the kitchen. At that point, the refrigerator caught his eye. He'd need to acquire food from somewhere before he left.

---

8. Some examples of responses include: "Hahaha! That was a day!"; "I tell you, I still can't believe what happened!"; "Different times. Different times!"

9. They weren't invented until the early twentieth century, by which point Bartholomew was no longer a child.

10. Even sulking, he didn't last long in this particular circle of hell. After tripping every time he tried, the warlock flung the rope at the laughing children, scowled and stormed back into the party much to their continued amusement. Bartholomew wanted to be miserable. He didn't want to be mocked.

"Did you see last night's game?" asked one of the men.[11]

"Yes, yes. One man caught a ball, another threw it. Someone scored." Bartholomew grabbed a serving spoon, sank it into the mashed potato pie, and brought it to his mouth.

The group of sports enthusiasts stared at him with some confusion as he dropped the spoon, wandered to the fridge, and began unpacking the contents.

"He must be closer to the Millers than I realized," one woman[12] whispered, and the conversation resumed.

Bartholomew was so depressed that he put his familiar's needs before his own and grabbed every type of cheese before selecting a few things for himself. He shoved them all into cloth grocery bags and exited through the backdoor.

As he walked across the lawns toward his own home, the warlock realized that his familiar hadn't loyally returned to his heels.

Useless foozler, he thought. *And when I'm so good to him, acquiring all this cheese.*

Bartholomew had half a mind to eat it in front of Gizmo and not share any.

The warlock was busy grumbling to himself about his familiar. His worries revolved around living in a forest full of dirt and leaves with no functioning toilet, hiding from a vampire who wanted to both kill him and steal the only valuable thing he still possessed, and finding a

---

11. Gregory Lewis, a sixty-year-old former high school linebacker who'd since developed a rather large gut and a need to tell anyone who would listen that he'd almost gone to university on a football scholarship.

12. Rachel Coombs was a forty-eight-year-old single mother of two, whose personality revolved around not wearing makeup, drinking beer, and informing everyone that her closest friends were all men.

way to make the useless demon who'd turned into a dog listen to him for a change!

Bartholomew had no way of knowing that the detection rune in his bedroom was currently blinking, warning of an unfriendly presence within. Otherwise, he might've chosen his concerns more wisely.

He entered his house, letting the door slam shut, grumbling quite loudly about ungrateful familiars. The warlock hoped that Gizmo was within and might hear him.

But it wasn't his familiar who heard.

Upstairs, the intruder dropped the box containing the amulet onto a rumpled pile of suits. He grabbed the shotgun that he'd rested beside the closet and tiptoed down the stairs.

Bartholomew's head was in the fridge. He was unpacking his newly acquired groceries. The warlock had no idea that he was in danger until he felt the barrel of the shotgun press against his neck.

"Hallo, Bart," the intruder said. "I was wondering when you'd get back."

THIRTY-THREE

B artholomew knew that voice.

He dropped the bag of groceries into the fridge, raised his hands, and turned slowly so that the shotgun pointed at his chest.

Before him, dressed in an oversized gray hoodie and jeans, with a large black bag making him appear a bit like a turtle, if reptiles were capable of growing bushy brown beards full of crumbs, was none other than Otto Ewing.

"I heard you were dead," Bartholomew said.

His associate smiled. "Everyone heard the same about you."

"So you faked your death too." The warlock's jaw clenched.[1] He didn't appreciate his genius being copied. It undermined his brilliance if people started thinking that someone like Otto was coming up with the same ideas. "Bit uninspired. But why? Does this have to do with the dangerous buyer you encountered?"

Otto chuckled. It was a deep belly laugh that made the crumbs quiver in his beard. "Don't you get it? I thought you were the smart

---

1. Technically, both individuals in this scene are warlocks, but *the* warlock in this story is Bartholomew.

one, Bart. That's what you reminded me in all of your letters. I thought you would've figured it out. There is no buyer. I set you up."

The warlock couldn't believe it. He was already low, and now his ego was forced to endure such a cruel blow. To be outsmarted by a worthy opponent would have been painful enough, but Otto was a fence, a glorified salesman, pathetic enough that he didn't even have his own familiar! "How?"

Now, should you ever wish to become a villain and find yourself in such a situation, the smart thing to do is to ignore questions like these, and continue swiftly with your nefarious plot. There is no advantage to revealing the truth to your victim once you have them trapped.

Except that it feeds the ego.

And Otto's was ravenous.

Unlike Bartholomew, who had the good fortune of having Gizmo's constant pair of ears to listen[2] to his schemes, his former associate had been forced to pat himself on the back throughout his own plan. Otto was eager to explain the whole thing.

"I suppose you think I was out to get you from the start given the tracking rune I placed on the first note I left in the tree. You found that, I imagine. That's why you left it behind? Were you surprised to learn that I knew such a rune? I'll bet you thought I didn't have a single trick up my sleeve."

Bartholomew had never inspected Otto's note. But he certainly wasn't going to admit that. He scoffed. "It was easy to find. Hardly an impressive rune."

"Well, you didn't find it when I hid it on the bottle of ink that you stole from my apartment."

---

2. Albeit, not as adoringly and enthusiastically as the warlock would have liked.

"Acquired, " Bartholomew corrected him. "Wait, you left that for me to find?"

Otto chuckled, delighted to see the surprise on the warlock's face. But they were getting off track. He'd prepared a monologue to explain everything. It would be simpler if Bartholomew didn't interrupt with questions and only responded with the observations that his former associate had imagined when he'd rehearsed his moment of triumph in his head.

"We have to start at the beginning," Otto said. "When you first came to me for help, I was perfectly happy with the idea of splitting the profits with you.[3] Even when you insisted on me fronting you my savings, I agreed, didn't I? And I only wanted to know your location in case you tried to pull a fast one, you know—try keep my money and the amulet." He paused. When Bartholomew didn't speak, Otto prompted him with the correct response. "This is where you argue that you couldn't have done that, or I might've gone to The Syndicate."

"Well, that's obvious. Why would I bother to say it?"

"Because I can refute it," Otto said, rather pleased with himself. "You worked for The Bearded Syndicate. You might've been planning to have me killed."

"Oh what, so everyone who's affiliated with a morally deficit organization is a murderer in your eyes?" Bartholomew huffed.

---

3. He had intended to lie to Bartholomew about the buyer's price and keep the larger share for himself, but that was beside the point.

"Exactly.[4] And when I received your note demanding that I send more money and inks, I realized that you didn't see me as an equal partner at all. I'll bet you'd have had no problem killing me off. So I decided to fake my own death. But the real brilliant part of my plan didn't come to me until I saw you in the woods that day, taking messages from the tree." He was expecting a gasp of surprise, but Bartholomew was too offended from the previous accusation to react. "I realized you must have been close by. I figured you'd come looking if I stopped responding. That's when I decided to lay a trap for you so that I could follow you back to your house, steal the amulet, and kill you."

He smiled and shifted his gun, letting it rest against the shelf of his stomach. This was where, in Otto's estimation, Bartholomew was supposed to nobly admit defeat, sad to die, but impressed by his opponent's cleverness none the less.

As anyone not basking in delusions of their own grandeur can guess, this did not happen.

Bartholomew's eyes widened, and he looked at Otto's gun with sudden uncertainty. "There was a body that got dumped into the river. Was that really you?"

"Course not. That was a computer programmer I shot. You'd be surprised how easy it was to find one that looked like me."[5]

---

4. This might seem rather a stretch to those criminals with stronger morals. However, Otto, despite his genial nature and appearance of a younger Santa Claus, lacked the same conviction. He was capable of murder if the situation required it, and so assumed others were too.

5. This was true. Otto shared a look similar to almost half of all single computer programmers still living with their parents.

A shiver went through the warlock's spine. That was exactly what he'd been worried about. His hand inched toward his quill. But there was no way for him to draw a rune faster than Otto could pull a trigger. "I don't suppose you'd consider letting me live with the knowledge of this humiliation instead. I really don't think killing me would bring you as much satisfaction."

There was also, of course, the fact that Bartholomew was not keen to die. But while the warlock considered that quite significant, he doubted his former associate felt the same.

"Don't be ridiculous," Otto said, lifting a hand[6] and scratching his beard. It was getting quite itchy. "One person can fake their death without arousing much suspicion, but two people? Someone's bound to look into it. Safer if at least one of us really is dead. But don't worry. I'll make it quick, just need you to—"

He broke off as a dark mist sank through the door, glimmering at the corner of his eye.

This interruption is a prime example of why villains ought not to gloat in monologue at their victims. The longer any speech, the higher the chances of someone arriving.

In this case, it was an irate vampire in a bright turquoise colonial-era jacket.

The scent of garlic had him rather discombobulated, and as he materialized, he held his nose pinched closed. The effect was that his hand obscured most of his vision, and his raspy voice was more nasal than normal.

"See that, Bartholomew. If you haven't the decency to abide by the rules of polite society, then I shan't accord you common courtesy either. I too can enter your abode without invitation." Frederick's

---

6. Not the one on the trigger, or Bartholomew might have attempted an escape.

head turned. He spotted the warlock with his back against the fridge. There was a large, bearded man pointing a gun at him.

Otto stepped back and spun so that it was pointed at the vampire now too.

Frederick lifted his arms. This was precisely why people shouldn't go barging into houses uninvited.

THIRTY-FOUR

F rederick stared at the barrel of the shotgun. It couldn't kill him, of course. He was a vampire. But he didn't fancy having a bullet rip through him all the same.

"My apologies, good sir," he said, smiling at Otto[1] and giving a nervous, high-pitched laugh. "I believe I've misted into the wrong house."

As was already obvious from his pre-prepared entrance lines, this was mostly a lie. Frederick had come to the warlock's house with a very clear purpose.

The vampire, exhausted from his day's scheme but unable to sleep, had awoken as soon as it was dark outside. He'd pushed the lid from his coffin, climbed out with creaking bones and still racing anxiety. There was an old phone that he kept in his study. He thought he might call Dan Miller and learn the fate of the election.

---

1. Whose appearance immediately offended Frederick. The vampire took pride in preening himself. He couldn't abide clothing-stained t-shirts and beards full of crumbs.

However, when the vampire went into his study, he was temporarily waylaid. His desk was in disarray.[2] He searched the contents and didn't find what was missing.

All his information on The Amulet of the Impaler had been stolen. The culprit was obvious.

Frederick and Bartholomew may have been enemies, scheming, plotting, and cheating in order to force the other to leave the neighborhood. But that was no excuse for them not to be civil! Entering someone's house without invitation was a terrible faux pas. Frederick was most offended.

He also wanted the notes[3] back in his rightful possession.

The vampire debated for a moment on the best way to obtain them. He didn't like the idea of bargaining with someone so uncivilized, and the warlock's knowledge of his true name left Frederick fangless when it came to threats.

There was only one option. Frederick would have to stoop to the warlock's level. Vampires were, after all, quite gifted when it came to breaking and entering. He rationalized it as a teaching moment for Bartholomew.

---

2. There were three main clues that alerted Frederick that something was amiss. First were the teeth marks on the drawer handles, courtesy of Gizmo. Next was the rip in his seat's cushion. Finally, there was a muddy pawprint on the papers. Bartholomew would've been aghast to learn of his familiar's carelessness, but Gizmo didn't see how he was to blame. He had to open drawers with his teeth, he didn't have hands. Anyone could've ripped an old cushion, a cat certainly would have. And as for the mud, Gizmo would've wiped his paws before entering the house, but the vampire didn't have a welcome mat.

3. Which he had originally stolen.

Perhaps he'll understand how dreadfully rude it is to invade some-one's private space uninvited if he has it happen to him.

And so the vampire had donned his turquoise jacket and huffed out of his house and down the street, not noticing the eleven-year-old girl and fluffy demon dog that were hiding by his maple tree, waiting for him to leave.

Frederick stormed straight toward Bartholomew's house, imagining himself in the role of the avenging hero in a Shakespearean tragedy. He envisioned himself chastising the warlock for his uncouth act, re-stealing his former mentor's notes, and eloquently persuading Bartholomew to divulge more details on the amulet.

But all heroic fantasies had vanished at the sight of Otto.

Frederick wanted to leave the way he'd entered, in an unshootable mist.

The problem was that, with his arms up in the air, there was nothing blocking the garlic from wafting into his nose. The pungent scent made his eyes water. He couldn't use his powers under such conditions.

"A vampire!" Otto stepped back so that he could swivel the shotgun between his two targets. His eyes flicked between them, narrowing at Bartholomew. "I knew you were plotting to betray me! You found your own buyer for the amulet."

Feeling a bit bolder now that the shotgun was only on him fifty percent of the time, Bartholomew scoffed. "I was never going to betray you, Otto because I'm not a snake. I keep my deals.[4] Mr. Graves is my nemesis." He gestured toward the vampire with his chin.

---

4. This was, for the most part, true, and one of Bartholomew's only good qualities.

At this point, Frederick forgot about trying to mist through the scent of garlic. Two things had caught his attention.

"Beg your pardon, Mr. Otto," the vampire said, "But are you perchance speaking of The Amulet of The Impaler?"

Otto's eyebrows rose. He swiveled the shotgun to Bartholomew[5] but turned his face toward Frederick. The vampire had used his name. That didn't' bode well for someone who was attempting to fake their own death. Frederick had just become a complication. He'd have to be killed.

But what was that old saying? Otto knew it: *the enemy of my enemy is an easy mark.*

He smiled, revealing a speck of ham stuck between his teeth. It had been sitting there since lunch.

"I am indeed, Mr. Graves," Otto said. "And I'm looking for a buyer. Do you have any interest?"

"Certainly!" Frederick responded.

"Now wait a minute," Bartholomew said, interrupting this deal. If the vampire wanted to give someone money for the amulet, it ought to be him. "I've got the amulet, not Otto!"

"Not for long," his former associate objected. "Upstairs. Hands up. Otherwise, I'll shoot. This'll only take a minute, Mr. Graves."

Bartholomew didn't like taking orders, but he wasn't a vampire, and a bullet could kill him. And so, much to the warlock's embarrassment, he was forced to comply with Otto's request. He marched up the stairs, feeling the gun pressing into his spine whenever he hesitated.

Bartholomew's mind was spinning, simultaneously attempting to plot an escape and cursing everything else for his current predicament.

---

5. Whose hands had been twitching toward his quill quite by accident.

Damn Otto for not sending me enough ink to defeat him. Damn Frederick for not having a soul. And damn Gizmo! Damn him most of all! What's the point of having a damn familiar when he's not here when I need him?

THIRTY-FIVE

I t was true. Gizmo and Sarah were on their own mission. The moment Frederick had turned the corner from his house, they'd hurried from their spot behind the maple.

"Quick, open the door," Gizmo said, standing on his back legs and batting at the knob. The familiar might've been able to tap it if he jumped, but he couldn't have turned it anyway, so he didn't bother trying.

Sarah was a few steps behind, one hand clutching her felt veil so it wouldn't fall off. She grabbed the knob. It wouldn't turn. "I think it's locked," she said.

"Drat!" Gizmo hadn't seen Frederick turn a key, but the vampire was in the habit of locking the door and slamming it shut when he left. The familiar stretched up, pawing at the hinges with a little whine of desperation. Without Bartholomew to draw the correct rune, he couldn't think of a way into the house. He glanced at Sarah. "I don't suppose you have any ink."

She reached into her pocket and retrieved her sparkly pen. "This writes in purple. Could that work?"

"Violet or indigo?" Gizmo asked, then shook his head, dropping to the step. "No, it doesn't matter. That won't work. Unless you have the skills to fashion it into a makeshift key?"

Sarah shook her head.

Gizmo sighed and flopped, belly first onto the ground. "Then that's it. I don't see how we could possibly ever get into a house on our own. How do human thieves do it?"

"Usually with a rock, I think, to break the window."

Gizmo bounded up. "Ms. Moon, you're a genius! We'll make an acquirer of you yet."

It wasn't easy to find rocks lying around Mills Run Heights. They had to make an impromptu trip to the community gardens near the front entrance. A group of parents had insisted on involving their children over the summer. They'd had them paint rocks, which now displayed messages like *LOVE <3, Do not touch,* and *this is dumbledore.*[1] Sarah grabbed the closest one,[2] raced back to 13B, and with a lot of goading from Gizmo, chucked it through the window.

The glass shattered, and the girl squeaked. She slapped her hands over her mouth and looked around, expecting one of the neighbors to appear. Sarah had no issue ignoring rules that she considered silly or superfluous, but *don't break other people's things* was a sensible one.

"Are you sure this isn't a bad thing we're doing?" she whispered.

"Of course not. We're helping Bart!" Gizmo, who shared none of the eleven-year-old's guilt, trotted happily toward the broken glass.

---

1. Though with this one, it should be noted that the "*ledore*" was in a different font.

2. It had toddler fingerprints with an adult's script on top that said, *Always smile!* Which is terrible advice for many obvious reasons.

The hole was small, but Sarah could reach through and unlock the window so she could climb through.

When no angry adults appeared to chastise her, Sarah's conscience eased a little. She slunk forward and lifted the little demon onto the sill so that he could slip through. Once he was inside, she followed.

The window led them onto the kitchen counter. Gizmo hopped down on his own[3] and ran toward where he'd concluded the pot of gold must have been.

Sarah was slower. Unlike the demon, she couldn't see in the pitch-black interior, and she stumbled through the kitchen to the light switch. It wasn't difficult to find. 13B's living area shared the same open plan layout as the rest of the subdivision's houses.

But when Sarah flicked on the overhead lights in the living and dining area, her eyes grew wide. Identical layout or not, this couldn't be Mills Run Heights. She'd been transported to a room in a dark gothic manner, with a black lace couch, matching lamp shades, dark wooden tables, and a tawny stuffed owl. Except, the design had been at odds with the decorator's soul. That was the only way Sarah could think to explain the bright pink throw pillow, smiling yellow plant pot, and bright blue bowtie around the owl's neck.

She might have taken a few moments to stand and ponder on the precise nature of Mr. Graves' eccentricity, were it not for Gizmo, sitting and barking at a dark piece of wood that was tucked into a windowless corner on the far side of the room.

"Is that a coffin?" Sarah asked as she approached.

"That's not all it is." Gizmo's front paws were on the edge of the wood. His chin peered over, tongue hanging out in a big grin while

---

3. Though he regretted it afterward given the height.

his tail fluttered behind him, as fast as a hummingbird's wings though less capable of flight. "It's also a hiding spot."

Sarah looked within and her jaw dropped.

At the base of the coffin was what looked to her like a small black cauldron. Only instead of a bubbling potion or cream of carrot soup, it was full of money. But the most bizarre thing was that, while she watched, she saw a new dull green bill grow amidst the pile as though it were a leaf on a tree.

THIRTY-SIX

B artholomew was forced to enter his own room.

The doors to his cupboard were flung open. Their shelves were empty, his books and suits tossed onto the floor.

Not enough to kill me, he's got to make a mess of my things too, the warlock thought. He was quite fond of his belongings and felt they deserved better treatment. One of the books had fallen badly. It would take ages to straighten the folds being pressed into its pages.

A dark thought crossed his mind: If Otto were to shoot him, he might not have a chance to fix it.

That would be terrible. What if one of The Syndicate discovered his body here? They might change his tombstone to read, *Bartholomew Whitlock. Ill-treater of books.*[1]

The warlock could think of few worse monikers.

"Open it," Otto said behind him, pressing the gun into Bartholomew's spine once more.

---

1. For warlock criminals who died before they could be justly punished in the underworld, it was common practice to have cruel addendums engraved on their tombs.

"It already is," Bartholomew objected, gesturing toward the empty shelves and open doors. He assumed that his former associate was talking about the closet, which was all he could see.

Otto, however, thought it was quite obvious that he was talking about the box with the amulet. He assumed Bartholomew was trying to be clever and gave him a sharp poke with the shotgun. "I'm not that stupid."

Bartholomew winced and rubbed his lower back. Although the wooden box was technically visible, it was hidden in the folds of his suits. Without knowing where to look for it, the warlock continued to be confused and more than a bit frustrated with his former associate. If Otto was going to kill him, why didn't he get on with it?

"What's wrong with you? Are you daft? Look!" Bartholomew said.

"You're the idiot if you think I don't know there are runes."

"What runes?!"

Their back and forth went on for another few minutes. Downstairs, Frederick hunted through the empty drawers and cupboards. He was looking for something.[2]

The sound might have given both Bartholomew and Otto concern. But they couldn't hear the rattling over their own voices.

By the time the warlock finally understood what his former associate wanted him to open, Frederick had finished searching the cupboards and come up empty.

---

2. Actually, he was looking for a couple things, one of which was the notes that Bartholomew had stolen. He would also have accepted other worthwhile magical artifacts, golden trinkets, or a good book. What he didn't want to find was something he might use as a weapon lest he felt obliged to assist.

Bartholomew knelt down.[3] His hand fluttered toward the crumpled book, flattening the pages as quick as he could.

There was a bang and the warlock jumped as a bullet ricocheted from the roof and buried itself in the floor a few inches shy of his knee.[4]

"Try anything funny and I'll bury it in your head next time," Otto said, genial tone not matching his threat.

"I was only fixing my book," Bartholomew muttered, but he didn't dare straighten his suits. He retrieved the box.

"You've got your tricks," Otto said, still sounding more amused than one would expect a man threatening murder would. "I'm not going to make it this far just to have you outsmart me."

"I wouldn't dream of trying," Bartholomew said. He inspected the box. His own name was crafted into his runes. It would be easy for him to flip the latch and retrieve the amulet. "I'll need my inks to break the seal."

Otto's eyes narrowed, but he nodded.

This is my chance, Bartholomew thought. He withdrew his quill and inks. Now, he was going to do something exceptionally clever and escape.

But what?

Bartholomew needed to stall while he figured out what the details[5]

.

---

3. Not out of any deference for Otto, obviously. It was simply easier to craft good runes when there was something to press on.

4. It was a warning shot from both Otto and Luck, who was still hoping the warlock would realize how much he needed her.

5. And the generalities, and abstractions, and concepts, and everything else.

"You're going about this entirely the wrong way, you know," the warlock said.

"How so?" Otto asked, scratching his beard.

The warlock quietly debated which ink he might use in his eventual scheme. Orange made him a tad nervous. Indigo might be better. What would happen if he wrote *lock* on the gun?[6]

"Honestly," he replied, "you ought to have threatened to kill me *if* I didn't give you the amulet. I've got no incentive."

Otto balanced the shotgun on the shelf of his stomach. "How about, if you don't give me the amulet, I'll hand you over to The Syndicate instead?"

"Quite effective actually." Bartholomew's stomach turned. It wasn't fear, of course, just a healthy sense of panic. He looked at his inks again, all nicely lined in their box: white, indigo, blue, and orange. There had to be something.

In the kitchen, Frederick was battling with his own conscience. The vampire had a romantic ideation of himself as a tragic hero. But actual heroic acts had never been in his nature. He was much more adept at running and hiding and muttering passive-aggressive comments.

He'd heard the gunshot. There was a very good chance Bartholomew had been killed.

---

6. Nothing good. Given how a gun's lock functions and the fact that indigo ink weakens, you may well imagine what effect this might have had if Bartholomew had been careless enough to try it.

And why should I care? Frederick thought. *He was my nemesis. And besides, there wasn't anything I could've been expected to do.*

It was at this moment that his eyes landed upon Bartholomew's brown bag, lying on the kitchen counter.

And, much to the vampire's despair, he had an idea.

"Hurry up! You're stalling!" Otto barked. "Choose an ink."

"I have to think," Bartholomew argued, looking up. There was a strange black mist seeping through the door behind Otto's back. The sight made the warlock jump.[7] His quill dipped into the white ink quite by accident.

What the bloody hell is Frederick doing? Did he come to witness my murder? Bartholomew wondered as he saw the vampire starting to coalesce. *And what's that brown thing he's holding? Did he steal my bag strap?*

As the warlock was watching him, trying to piece together what was happening, Frederick did the strangest thing. He winked.

Had Otto been watching the warlock's face, he might've realized that something odd was happening and turned around. However, his eyes were wide, glittering with greed, entirely focused on Bartholomew's quill. He knew how talented the warlock before him was and was practically salivating at the thought of learning a new rune. As such, he had no notion as to what was happening behind him.

---

7. Obviously not in fear, if you asked Bartholomew, just surprise.

"Did you curse it?" he asked, trying to guess why white ink would be useful for opening a box as opposed to sealing it. He craned his head forward.

Behind his back, Frederick flicked his eyes. Bartholomew understood the gesture.

Three things happened in quick succession. Following the vampire's hint, Bartholomew dove to the side. His former associate and current captor, finally aware that something was amiss, released the safety on the gun. But before he could aim, Frederick grabbed Otto's arms.

The result was that the gun dropped to the ground and fired. A bullet shot clean across the floor, burning a hole in the pile of clothes.

Not my suits, Bartholomew thought. And he half wondered if Frederick had planned that somehow.

"A little help, Mr. Whitlock," the vampire shouted. Otto was quite large and was rudely resisting. It made it difficult to tie his hands with the strap, to say nothing about his feet!

Bartholomew bounced up, as spry as he was awkward with his long limbs. He hurried forward, quill in hand.

And together, the warlock and the vampire bound Otto like a hog on a spit roast.

Thirty-Seven

You might believe that now, having vanquished a common foe, Bartholomew and Frederick were ready to cast aside their animosity for one another and become friends. That is because you have never met centuries old magical beings.

The warlock and the vampire stared at one another from opposite ends of the kitchen island. Each held a mug of coffee. Neither of them was drinking.

Bartholomew knew quite well that Frederick had just saved his life. Custom dictated that he was now in his debt. To break it would mean ill-luck, though the warlock had never worried much about such traditions. *Debt* was taking this a bit too far in his opinion. A thank you of some kind would be sufficient.

But expressions of gratitude were as foreign as French to the warlock.

For his part, the vampire knew precisely how he'd like the debt repaid.

Bartholomew's fingers crawled like ants over a thin wooden box. Within was The Amulet of the Impaler. A fitting gift for someone who'd saved your life in Frederick's estimation.

But it would be a bit rude to just come out and say it. So instead, after a moment, Frederick cleared his throat and lifted his pale eyes from the box and toward the mug in the warlock's other hand. Written in big blue letters on the white ceramic were the words *World's Greatest Dad*.

"I didn't know you had children," the vampire said, offering a thin fluttering smile in an attempt at polite conversation.

Bartholomew's dark eyebrows lowered, and his eyes narrowed. *What's he playing at?*

In his haste to make the coffee for Frederick,[1] he hadn't paid attention to the mugs. Like most items in the kitchen, they'd been acquired from the Millers.

"I can think of nothing more detestable," the warlock said and took a sip of his coffee, waiting to see what curious, borderline insult the vampire might hurl at him next.

Frederick was equally perplexed. "I suppose your demon got that for you then." He pointed to the mug.

It must be noted here that the vampire knew very little of the relationship between warlocks and familiars or he would never have made such a comment.

As it was, Frederick's innocent suggestion sounded like an insult to Bartholomew. Gizmo was an ancient being; the warlock not yet two centuries. His jaw clenched. "How old do you think I look?"

"Late twenties?"

Oh that does it! Bartholomew's fingers curled into a fist around the handle of his mug, so tight his nails dug into his palm. It was one

---

1. The warlock was of the belief that the polite thing to do for guests was offer them beverages and as such normally never did so, lest any unwanted visitors grow comfortable and decide to linger. But he made an exception in this instance given that the vampire had saved his life.

thing to imply he looked old, but to suggest he looked young was unforgivable.

Enough with this charade of politeness! Bartholomew had played nice (or as nice as he could) for longer than necessary.[2]

"What do you want, Frederick?" he snapped.

The vampire, who had a significantly higher tolerance for these sorts of things, was taken aback by the warlock's bluntness. Frederick was prepared to pass the next few hours exchanging pointless pleasantries and artfully dancing around the issue, before guiding Bartholomew to the obvious conclusion.

"Why, whatever do you mean, Mr. Whitlock?" Frederick said, hoping to get them back to civil discussion. "You have a lovely"—he looked around the room, hoping to see something that he might compliment. But, of course, there was still no furniture.

The vampire's eyes fell to the brown bag. It wouldn't do to mention its appearance given that he'd torn off its strap.

But what was that within? He caught glimpses of brown and yellow.

"Cupcakes!" Frederick concluded, reaching into the bag and pulling one free. The scent was unusual, but the vampire found that of most foods and beverages that lacked blood. "You gave no indication that you were such a skilled baker!"

Bartholomew saw the vampire lift the ink-laced cupcake into the air, and a feeling of utter relief washed through him. He flung himself across the island and whacked the dessert free from Frederick's grip.

---

2. Not including the time they'd spent dealing with Otto, the two had been together for five minutes and twenty-four seconds. This was indeed a record for Bartholomew when it came to tolerating company without displaying open animosity.

"Hah!" the warlock announced proudly as he rolled back onto his feet. "We're even now. I owe you nothing."

Frederick might not have understood what had possessed Bartholomew to slide across the countertop on his belly (as though he were a penguin and not a warlock in a black-and-white suit), but he understood what that meant.

"I beg your pardon," the vampire said, resting down his mug of coffee and pressing his hand to his chest. "I saved your life."

"And I just saved yours. Those cupcakes are laced with ink. One bite and you would've been gone."[3]

"But I wasn't going to bite it," Frederick objected. This was true for much the same reason that the vampire hadn't sipped his coffee. None of it had been flavored with blood. "So we aren't even at all."

"Hardly relevant. I might've freed myself without your assistance as well."

"You would not."

"Would so," Bartholomew muttered, barely suppressing his desire to scowl. "Anyway, I'm not putting myself in your debt because you did a decent thing. And I've certainly nothing to give you."

You might compose a sonnet of gratitude or write an ode to my chivalry, Frederick thought. That was what he might've done if their situations were reversed. But he kept those ideas to himself lest the warlock take him up on the suggestion. "I'm certain you have some means of expressing your thanks."

The scowl broke free, and settled down on Bartholomew's lips like a grumpy old man might sink into his armchair and refuse to move.

---

3. Bartholomew had no reason to believe this was true, but he did want to be rid of the debt he now owed Frederick even if it meant paying it off with a bit of a trick.

His hands waved at the empty space around him. "Perhaps you haven't noticed, but death hasn't left me flush with cash. And I won't be around long enough to do you a favor thanks to your little scheme with the election.[4] So thanks for saving my life, now get out my house while it's still mine."

Throughout Bartholomew's rant, Frederick had been flicking his cold eyes toward the wooden box. It wasn't exactly subtle. But somehow the warlock still wasn't getting it.

Or perhaps he just wants me to suffer the indignity of asking aloud, Frederick thought. *Well, let him have his wish.*

"The Amulet of the Impaler, you fool!" The vampire said, waving his hands toward the box. "You can repay me by giving it to me."

Bartholomew's hands stopped fluttering just long enough for him to give Frederick a dark glare. The warlock snorted with more than a hint of derision. "Don't be ridiculous. That's worth a fortune."

"More than your life?"

No, but Bartholomew's life was no longer at risk, which made it much easier to refuse. "I need money more than I need to ease my conscience."

"Ten thousand then," Frederick said.

"Ten thousand million?"

"What? Are you out of your mind? That's more than it's worth." And significantly more than even the very wealthy vampire possessed. Bartholomew could never have gotten that price for it. "Ten thousand dollars. Straight."

The warlock's eyes narrowed. He'd been the best acquirer The Bearded Syndicate had. They didn't waste his talents fetching trinkets.

---

4. He wanted to ask how Frederick had managed it, but he didn't want to admit that he couldn't figure it out on his own.

The amulet would be worth millions to the right buyer. It must've been worth more than that to Frederick too.

Indeed, it was. The vampire had been dreaming of the amulet for centuries. Under normal circumstances, he would have been more than happy to pay millions.

But Frederick had a nose for sniffing out two things: blood and bargains. Bartholomew was penniless and desperate, in no position to decline an offer of ten thousand, even if it was a rip off.[5] The vampire wasn't about to offer more than necessary.

Especially considering I just saved his life! Frederick thought. In his estimation, he was the clear hero of the story. If he wasn't to be gifted the amulet in a denouement of his selfless deed, he was at least entitled to a generous discount.

"Think about it," he said, leaving his untouched coffee on the island and inclining his head in a mock bow as he walked toward the door.

Bartholomew glowered at him, his teeth grinding loud enough that it was a wonder he heard Frederick's parting words at all.

"I'll give you twenty-four hours before I change my mind," the vampire said, offering a wan smile before he opened the door. "Always a pleasure, Mr. Whitlock."

Frederick stepped into the night, feeling pleased. He'd won this round and, as far as he could see, the entire battle.

Had he passed either of the two humans who were separately making their way toward Bartholomew's house, however, Frederick might not have felt quite so confident.

---

5. This was technically true, but Frederick had no idea just how petty Bartholomew could be. The warlock might have owed the vampire his life, but that didn't mean he was going to let himself be conned out of gratitude.

THIRTY-EIGHT

"Curse him," Bartholomew muttered to himself as he glared at the vampire's back, disappearing down the road. "Curse him, and then I can save him, and we can be even."

The warlock kicked his wall in frustration. He wouldn't sell Frederick the amulet for ten thousand, not even for ten million if the vampire upped his offer.[1]

"Probably saved my life just so he could lord it over me!" Bartholomew shook his fist toward the window and noticed a torchlight moving across the lawns. It was heading toward his house.

His first assumption was that it must have been Gizmo.[2]

Useless familiar! This is all his fault. If he'd been here, he could've saved me instead of that damned vampire!

Bartholomew stomped to the door, and flung it open with a scowl, ready to unleash his rage onto the demon.

---

1. At least, this was what he told himself in the moment. The truth was that, even the warlock's pride had a price. In his current situation, it was considerably lower than ten million.

2. How his familiar would have managed to hold a flashlight so high he couldn't have said, but in his current mood, the warlock didn't notice such details.

It wasn't a fluffy black dog on his doorstep. Instead, it was an old lady in a floral skirt and frilly white shirt with a pair of cat-eye glasses perched on the edge of her nose. Ida's notebook was tucked under one arm, while she attempted to wield a cumbersome old flashlight.[3]

With some effort, for his scowl was quite comfortably embedded on his lips, Bartholomew forced his mouth into the closest proximal shape to a smile he could muster. It was a jarring sight, particularly with his face illuminated by the old woman's flashlight.

Seeing the handsome young gentleman sneering like a haunted jack-o-lantern might have snuffed Ida's growing admiration for the warlock. But with her glasses balanced on her nose, she couldn't see him clearly enough to have been bothered and was luckily saved from the ghastly sight.

"How good to see you," Bartholomew lied. He had no interest in seeing the old woman at the moment, but still mistaking her for an individual of importance, the warlock was cautious to avoid offense. "I'd welcome you inside, but I'm afraid I'm not able to be a very good host given the circumstances."

He was referring of course to several things. The lack of furniture was the most obvious. But there was also Bartholomew's current fouler than usual mood thanks to Frederick. And the occasional muffled screams from his former associate, now trapped in his closet, might raise suspicion.

However, Ida, who knew none of this, assumed he was referring to the election.

"That's just what I've come to speak to you about," she said, struggling with the weight of her flashlight. It was cumbersome and heavy,

---

3. Her phone was capable of performing the same task, but Ida had never mastered that (rather simple) feature.

and she was growing a bit peeved that her young neighbor hadn't offered to hold it. "Though I shouldn't have had to walk so far if you'd come to the functions hall yourself. Didn't you worry when you didn't hear from me?"

Bartholomew frowned. The old woman hadn't crossed his mind since he'd learned of Dan's win. He'd been far too busy feeling sorry for himself, dealing with the betrayal of his former associate, and, worst of all, trying to accommodate for the single good deed on the part of his nemesis.

Just thinking about it made the warlock's expression sour, and he snapped, "I was otherwise occupied."

This would have greatly offended the old woman, and given her own prickly nature, she would have left without delivering her news. But, quite accidentally, luck assisted Bartholomew.

The light was tilted up into his eyes. It was very annoying, and in his frustration, he snatched the bulky device from the old woman.

Ida mistook his irritation for chivalry.

Finally, she thought, *that's the gentleman I met.* Her small, shriveled heart swooned. Any impudence in Bartholomew's tone was immediately forgotten.

"Well, I didn't forget about you," she said, tossing a curl of her perm over her ear with what she considered girlish charm. The muscles in her hunched shoulders clicked at the motion. "There was something off with the votes. I noticed it when we were tallying them, but that fool, William, wouldn't listen." She gave a haughty sniff.

Bartholomew pointed the light toward the ground. His dark eyes narrowed with suspicion. A flicker of hope was sparking in the pit of his stomach. The warlock wasn't used to positive feelings, however, and mistook it for indigestion.

"I wrote down the name of everyone who voted."[4] Ida brandished her notebook before her. "Twenty-seven in total. But do you know how many votes came in? Seventy-seven!" She lashed the banister of the staircase with her book remembering fondly the days when she could've done the same to a child's wrist with her ruler.

"Are you saying someone shoved fifty additional votes with Dan's name into the box?" The warlock scowled, not because he was offended by the cheating. He was only annoyed not to have thought of such a simple solution himself. Frederick had bested him at his own game, the damned hornswoggler!

Ida's eyes were just able to detect the look of displeasure on Bartholomew's face. She assumed he was much a stickler for the rules as she was.[5] "Precisely! No doubt it was Daniel himself, the dirty crook. But don't you worry, I won't allow the integrity of our HOA to fall under scrutiny. In my capacity as treasurer I'm declaring all of today's votes ineligible to be counted."

There was that indigestion again. The warlock pressed a hand to his stomach. "But then, who will be president? Will you stay on in the role?"

"No, no. We'll have a redo tomorrow. I'm going to put notices in all the mailboxes right now."

---

4. There was nothing inherently wrong with this, but the old woman intended to send sternly worded notes to every resident who'd ignored their civic duty. Nothing prohibited this act either, but had it ever gone to a vote, people might have turned up just to ensure that it was in the future.

5. She wasn't wrong, given that Ida enjoyed enforcing rules more than she saw the need to personally follow them herself.

Bartholomew's eyebrows rose. Another election meant another chance. Perhaps he and Gizmo weren't going to be leaving Mills Run Heights after all. The slant of a smile slashed the warlock's chin.

"What excellent news, Ida. Allow me to assist you with this task." He slipped out the door, took the old woman's hand and led her down the stairs.

Bartholomew intended to ensure that there was at least one mailbox that wouldn't hear about the change until it was too late.

Arm in arm and both happier than usual, the pair began their rounds of the neighborhood. Bartholomew was sure to avoid any road where he glimpsed a bright turquoise coat out for a stroll.

Thirty-Nine

At this point, if you have been paying attention, you will remember that there were two humans making their way toward the warlock's house.

The other was Sarah Miller, stumbling along, looking very much like a witch without the hat, dressed in black and carrying the thin handle of a cauldron. Money flew out of the rim, so that she left a trail behind her, much like Hansel and Gretel might have if they'd been the children of stock-traders from Manhattan instead the children of an alcoholic[1] widower.

Running behind her, mouth full of green bills that he scooped from the ground, was Gizmo. His entire butt wagged in delight.

In order to avoid being spotted by Frederick, they walked through the patches of trees[2] that sequestered the neighborhood before dash-

---

1. The original tale doesn't explicitly state that he's an alcoholic, but one must assume. His new wife suggests abandoning his two children to starve in the forest. Clearly, someone in that household is a monster. Most assume it's the wife, but (as Bartholomew himself was fond of arguing) it could easily be that the kids were hellions given that he goes along with it. In any case, be it his wife or his children that were horrid, the man probably sought solace in a bottle.

2. Which the residents generously referred to as a forest.

ing down the street toward 42A. As such, it took them longer than usual to arrive, and Bartholomew was gone by this time.

The warlock had locked the door, but Sarah was, by now, an expert at tossing rocks through windows. They climbed through the kitchen, just as they had at Frederick's house, and waited for the warlock within.

It would be fifteen minutes before Bartholomew returned, at which point the warlock would find a pile of broken glass in his sink and a familiar that looked far too pleased with himself all things considered. He'd yell and scream and holler at Gizmo, who would slowly deduce what had occurred while he'd been gone. And only when Sarah interrupted would the warlock stop and finally learn what his familiar had been up to.

But in that brief, seemingly insignificant fifteen-minute window, at least one noteworthy thing occurred.

Trying to be clever, Gizmo sent Sarah to hide in Bartholomew's room with the pot of gold. The familiar thought it would be a fantastic surprise to cheer up the gloomy warlock. He had no idea that Otto Ewing was currently bound and gagged in the closet.

Sarah arrived in Bartholomew's room and dropped the cauldron to the carpet with a dull thud. Her dark eyes gleamed as she surveyed the previously forbidden space. Like any typical eleven-year-old in such a situation,[3] she was eager to snoop, hoping to discover some great secret that she was (quite rightly) certain that the warlock was hiding.

Ideally, she would have liked a room cluttered with strange artifacts and full of bookshelves that, if she pulled the right object, would shift

---

3. Though she would have been terribly offended to have her behavior called *typical*.

to reveal mysterious passageways.[4] The lack of furniture was a bit of a disappointment.

Her eyes moved from the small pile of books, now neatly arranged in the corner, to the suits spread out on the ground. There were holes in two of the jackets. Maybe that was something worth investigating, but it didn't grab her curiosity the way she'd hoped. The built-in closet was the same as her own room.

Sarah's eyes fell on a massive black backpack. She'd never seen that before. Bartholomew always used his brown saddlebag. Was this a secret sack?

She skipped across the room, bent beside it, and wasted no time before pulling zippers open.

It was, of course, not Bartholomew's bag at all, but Otto's. He'd packed it full, planning for his new life on the run.

Sarah pulled out packages of dried meats, boxes of crackers, two pairs of large underwear,[5] a stained gray t-shirt, a pair of sweats, more bags of cookies. It was all feeling very mundane and more than a bit disappointing, until she reached the bottom and discovered a large wooden box. The key for the small brass lock was stuck to the top.[6]

Inside was a collection of fifteen glass vials.

---

4. In this, she and Bartholomew were in total agreement. This would have been the warlock's preference as well.

5. Which she quickly dropped and pretended not to have seen once she realized what she was holding

6. Unlike Bartholomew, Otto didn't know any runes for locking or unlocking items so was forced to secure his inks the usual way. Only, he'd lost his key so many times that taping it to the box had seemed the safest solution. That this made locking it at all quite pointless somehow escaped him.

Flames of curiosity seemed to dance in Sarah's eyes. There was, once again, that flicker of something dangerous and powerful. But no one was there to see it.

She pulled out the vials and inspected the inks within. Eight colors. White, brown, blue, indigo, pink, gold, orange, and red. What did each do? Were they different? How many more colors were there?[7]

Sarah would be delighted to know that she studied the inks for longer than most children would have considered normal. She watched how the light danced on their surface, examined the viscosity of the liquid when she turned it in the glass, undid the little corks and inhaled the scent. They made her head spin, and she giggled with giddy delight.

Each color smells different! She wondered if this was what drinking alcohol was like for adults.

It was this passing thought that gave her a life-altering idea.[8] She began to think of her mother mixing cocktails for her friends.

What if I mixed two of these? she asked herself.

A vial of red was in her hand. Perhaps because she'd seen it added to the cupcakes, she reached for orange. Playing scientist, she mixed the two, pouring them back and forth between bottles. Nothing seemed to be happening.

Still, she might've added a third, just to be certain, were she not interrupted by a muffled scream from the closet.

She pulled the door open and discovered a very round man with a bushy brown beard full of cracker crumbs. He'd been hog-tied, limbs

---

7. Had Bartholomew been present, he wouldn't have told her the answer, but he might have thought to himself, *Thirteen*. And he would've been right in a literal sense, while also being mistaken.

8. Though it would be quite some time before that would become clear.

pulled behind his back, so that he writhed on the floor like a worm. There was a black sock shoved into his mouth.

"Mmhff mmhff mmhff," Otto said. Translated, that meant, *Help me, little girl!*

"Huh." Sarah blinked at him for a moment. Then a smile spread across her face.

At the sight of it, Otto became more than a little anxious. There was something off about a child grinning because they've found someone hog-tied in a closet.

Sarah, however, was thrilled to have found Bartholomew's hidden human. How delightfully eccentric!

"Who are you?" she asked, stepping forward and pulling the sock from Otto's mouth with more bravery than wisdom.

Luckily for her, Bartholomew had used a rune to seal his former associate's limbs with his bag strap. The only thing Otto could have managed was to wiggle forward and snap at Sarah with his teeth.

"I'm a kind, traveling salesman," Otto said. "An absolute sweetheart."

"But what's your name?"

Otto hadn't decided on a fake name to use for the rest of his life yet, though he'd whittled it down to three top contenders: Dirk Dangerfield, Brock Handsome, and Sterling Strong. "Never mind that. The cruel man who lives here trapped me. If you bring a very sharp knife up, you should be able to cut me free."

Sarah crossed her arms and narrowed her eyes. As far as she knew, there was no cruel man living in the house, only her eccentric friends. "I'm not allowed to handle sharp knives," she informed him. "I'm a child."

"A strong pair of scissors then?"

"Not allowed to use those either. My parents make me cut everything with my teeth." Sarah curled back her lips and nibbled the air, like a rabbit with a piece of lettuce.[9] She was quite amused by her own lie, thinking it made her sound like a tortured heroine from a children's novel.

Otto thought it sounded like Sarah might have been a werewolf or a vampire or some other creature with sharp canines, and he had a momentary rush of elation before he noticed that her teeth were quite human.

Those would never cut through the thick fabric of the bag strap.

Otto sighed, and his stomach rumbled beneath him. He hadn't eaten since lunch. "Bring me a snack then? There's a package of cured ham in my bag."

Sarah paused. Then, after a moment, she said, "Sure. I can bring you something."

By now, Bartholomew had returned home. He was downstairs with Gizmo, quarrelling with the familiar, who was desperately trying to interrupt and explain himself.

"Saved by Frederick Graves! My nemesis!" the warlock was shouting as Sarah crept down the stairs. "Have you any idea the indignity I suffered?"

---

9. Not a carrot. Rabbits are not nearly as fond of those as popular culture would
    have you believe.

"I thought you said that you were about to escape," Gizmo said, sitting in the center of the empty living area while Bartholomew paced around him.

"Well, yes, obviously, I was going to do it myself," the warlock lied. "But he got there first!"

"I just don't see how I could've been more useful here considering I was—"

"Are you serious? You useless foozler! You don't see how saving my life would have been the most important?"

"But Frederick—"

As you can see, they were going in circles by this point and might have continued to do so until morning were it not for Sarah's interruption.

She slipped into the kitchen on the tips of her toes. Her hand slipped into the brown bag that was now missing its strap and pulled out a Tupperware container that had once belonged to her family.

At the sight of her, Bartholomew froze.

"Don't mind me," she assured him, feeling the warlock's eyes on her. "I'm just taking a cupcake."

She waved the yellow and brown questionably flavored dessert, smiled sweetly, and retreated up the steps.

Bartholomew and Gizmo were both quite stunned. It took them a moment to realize what she'd done.

"Ms. Moon, wait!" the familiar shouted, worried for her safety as he followed her up.

The warlock followed, scowling and shaking his fist. He was more concerned about what the hell she was doing in his house.[10] "You can't eat that, you little guttersnipe," he shouted.

Of course, Sarah had no intention of eating the cupcake herself. She took it into the cupboard and held it before Otto's unsocked mouth.

"Here you go. Eat it quick," she said, with a smile.

Now, given that Sarah is an eleven-year-old girl, you might want to be generous and interpret this act on her part as one of kindness and sympathy for a poor, hungry, hog-tied man. It was not. Quite the opposite. She'd heard Bartholomew and Gizmo's many warnings not to eat the cupcakes. There was, she figured, a good chance that their consumption would have an adverse effect.

But Sarah didn't care. She needed to know what the ink did.

And there, yet again was that flash of something hidden in her dark eyes.

Otto recognized it.

His eyes narrowed at her as he chewed the cupcake. If he'd had a more refined palate, he'd have spat the desert back onto the floor. Unfortunately, as a fan of beef jerky and an eater of many ill-advised meals, Otto continued to indulge, not objecting as Sarah pushed the cupcake further into his mouth.

"So did Bartholomew take you in as—" he started to ask, but then the magic took effect.

---

10. Though, deep down, the warlock was concerned for the eleven-year-old's well-being too. He didn't like her, of course, and still firmly believed that she ought to stay out of sight until she reached maturity sometime in her mid-thirties. But he'd grown accustomed to her in the sense that while he didn't want her there, he would've felt a twinge of sadness if something bad happened to her.

In writing memory in orange ink, the warlock had hoped it would eliminate only a small recent fraction of such. This was not the case.

The orange ink had worked its way to Otto's brain and begun destroying indiscriminately.

There was nothing left.

Bartholomew and Gizmo arrived at the doorway in time to witness the consumption of the laced dessert. They saw the empty, blank look in Otto's eyes and realized what had happened.

"Well, that's another problem solved thanks to Sarah," Gizmo said, trying to play off his discomfort at watching a man have his entire memory erased. Even when he was torturing his enemies, the demon had allowed them the dignity of maintaining their identity. "Don't suppose you've got to worry about Otto saying anything to anyone now."

"Who is Sarah?" Bartholomew asked, his fingers clenching and unclenching. He was trying to find a reason to sustain his anger, but it was difficult. Especially given the large supply of inks that were suddenly in his possession, neatly lined on his floor.

"Aurora Moon! I told you that, but you never listen to me. Or you'd know we'd also stolen you a leprechaun's pot." Gizmo pointed toward the cauldron beside the door, still full of money. "Though, I suppose you can return it now since you're staying, and you do owe Frederick your life."

Bartholomew's dark eyes glittered at the sight of the wealth that was now his.

This is how my retirement was supposed to go! he thought, a cruel smile lifting one corner of his lips. The warlock rubbed his hands together in glee.

Gizmo looked at him and sighed. "You're going to keep it, aren't you?"

Bartholomew laughed. It was deep and low and ominous.

From the edge of the closet, Sarah's laugh, higher and less certain, but equally sinister joined him.

The warlock was pleased because he'd won. He'd bested Frederick, and tomorrow it would be official.

Sarah was cackling because she was now certain, without a shadow of a doubt, that magic was real.

FORTY

A nd what of poor Frederick?

The vampire, full of false confidence in his victory, strolled the neighborhood, composing in his mind a theatrical script of his rivalry with the warlock. He was busy counting syllables in the lines of the climatic soliloquy[1] that he would deliver when making the decision to rescue Bartholomew.

Then the first hint of light burned his eyes. Daylight was creeping up on him.

Frederick opened his umbrella and hurried from the community gardens where he'd been admiring the plants,[2] retreating to the safety of his home.

It was only then that he discovered the broken window.

He hurried inside and noticed at once that the lid of his coffin was open. His eyes grew wide.

---

1. For he wanted at least his speeches to echo the great iambic pentameter of Shakespeare.

2. The rocks, he thought, looked as though someone had gone riffling through them.

"That brute! That cad! That lout!" Frederick exclaimed as he raced forward and discovered only a few hundred-dollar bills.

His precious pot of gold, the source of his wealth, had been stollen.[3]

"And after I saved his life! This is how he thanks me? Can you believe it, Trevor?" He asked turning to the stuffed owl.

Trevor, as always, remained mute. His beak was permanently shut, after all. But Frederick was certain that the owl was agreeing in his own way.

"Yes exactly! Imagine stealing something that I've already rightfully stolen for myself. There has to be a limit to how many times an item can illicitly change hands, or we'll be living in anarchy," the vampire declared. "But I'll get it back. Wait and see."

Trevor would, but only on account of the fact that he couldn't move and his eyes were stuck open.

Frederick, in a huff, turned to leave, but then he noticed the thin line of deadly light sneaking into his kitchen through the broken glass. A lump rose in his throat. Facing a warlock, who was likely expecting him now, in daylight was probably not the best idea.

"I'll get my revenge tonight," he informed his stuffed companion, inching away from the kitchen and cowering near his coffin.

As the vampire prepared to sleep, he spoke boldly of what he might do. But his plans would never come to fruition.

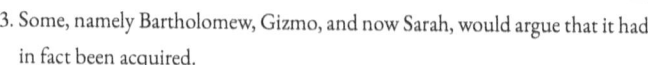

3. Some, namely Bartholomew, Gizmo, and now Sarah, would argue that it had in fact been acquired.

That night, he awoke and dressed in darkness before slipping out his door and making his way toward the warlock's street. The smoky scent of barbeque filled the air.

Might taste quite nice with a good blood sauce, Frederick thought, stopping to sniff for a moment.

He looked toward the Millers' house, expecting to see the usual crowd of suburbanites laughing and lounging on the fresh mowed lawn. But the yard was empty. The peal of smoke was wafting out onto the street from two houses down.

No, that can't be right, Frederick thought, slinking closer. *That's Bartholomew's house.*

But sure enough, as he approached, he saw the warlock standing on the corner of his lot before a shiny new barbecue. Behind him, a modest party was in progress. Ida Meadows sat on an expensive lawn chair, rolling the cube of ice in her Manhattan and feeling like a proper socialite. It was the first invitation she'd ever received from someone under the age of sixty.

Opposite the old woman, in a less comfortable seat, was Dan Miller, wearing his signature baseball cap and jeans. He leaned forward, a forced smile on his face, which had more to do with his current conversation partner than any awareness that he'd purposefully been given a plastic chair.

Hanging on the wall was a large banner that read: *Congratulations, President Bartholomew!*

Frederick peered out from behind the corner of the house next door. He was utterly baffled. As far as he knew, the warlock had lost. *Have I woken up in a parallel universe?*[4]

"There you are, Mr. Graves," a cheerful voice said, followed by a high-pitched bark.

The vampire stumbled backward, caught off guard. When he looked down, there was a fluffy black poodle-mix at his feet.

"Demon," he hissed.

"Gizmorgoth of Darkness. But I prefer Gizmo,"[5] the familiar reminded the vampire, assuming he'd forgotten his name and not that it had been a gasp of shock and fear. The familiar's tongue lolled from his mouth in a smile that only made Frederick more concerned. "Now, come along. Bart's expecting you."

Without looking to see if Frederick was following, Gizmo trotted forward.

"Why?" the vampire asked, apprehensive as he slipped from the shadows. But there was no sense attempting to retreat now that he'd been discovered by the familiar. It would only be a show of weakness and might make Bartholomew's next strike even bolder.

If he hadn't already secretly delivered the killing blow.

"Probably to gloat," Gizmo informed him.

---

4. During his time with Spudsy O'Cabbage, Frederick had heard a few of the leprechaun's victims claim that they'd awoken in different universes, and had already paid their debt where they'd come from. He'd rightfully never put much faith in the claims, but now he was starting to wonder if his skepticism had been unfair.

5. Gizmo didn't like being addressed as *demon* any more than you might appreciate being shouted at as *human.*

The warlock looked up from the barbecue. Flames danced in the darkness of his eyes. His lips quirked into a twisted, slanted grin as he closed the lid and stepped from the lawn.

Bartholomew and Frederick met in the center of the road. The stars glimmered above them just as they had on their first meeting at the pool.

"How are you, Mr. Graves? I saw someone sent a rock through your window. Terrible luck. I'd be happy to reinforce the glass for you in the future," the warlock suggested. He meant it. Now that his supply of inks had been refreshed, he could afford to be generous. Especially if it meant rubbing his good deed in the vampire's face.

Frederick's cold eyes narrowed. He adjusted the collar of his black coat, wishing he'd worn his usual turquoise instead. It gave him a good deal more confidence. Perhaps then, he could've thought of some clever retort or turn-of-phrase.

Instead, the vampire was forced to lower himself to a level better suited to Bartholomew with unrefined bluntness. "Cut the crap. I saved your life, and you stole my pot of gold. There'll be a special place in the underworld for you when Karma catches up."[6]

"What a dreadful accusation," Bartholomew said, savoring the aggrieved expression on the vampire's face. "My associate[7] acquired something from 13B, but I assure you, I stole nothing."

Frederick's heart would have beaten faster, if it were capable of beating at all. He was feeling nervous now, though he didn't want to

---

6. Fortunately, or unfortunately, Karma is rather a slow jogger.

7. He wasn't entirely sure if it was Gizmo or Sarah who he was purposefully forgetting, but he certainly wasn't going to give both of them credit.

show it. The fact that the warlock wasn't bothering to deny being in possession of the leprechaun's pot made him uneasy.

Why is he so confident I won't be able to get it back? Frederick wondered.

The reason was that Bartholomew, thanks to Otto's inks, had now been able to properly fortify his house. No vampire was misting in, and even if they did, the leprechaun's pot was protected behind a number of enchantments.

Frederick found himself without a good response, so he pointed to the banner hanging from the wall instead. "How's that possible?"

The warlock glanced over his shoulder, and his mouth grew increasingly lopsided as half his smile rose. "Your illegal votes were discovered. There was a reelection today."

"And you cheated."

"Naturally." Bartholomew'd had the brown ink required for his original plan. "But I didn't get caught."

Frederick nodded. He was beginning to understand what was going on now and why the warlock was so calm. If tinted windows and heavy curtains were now banned, the vampire would have no choice but to venture elsewhere.

"Oh ho!" Frederick gave a wry, raspy laugh. There wasn't much else he could see to do for the moment other than wag a long pale finger at the warlock. "I see how The Syndicate operate now. No honor!" He licked his tongue over the top of his mouth. It took him a few seconds, but eventually he mustered enough saliva to spit at Bartholomew's boots. "You rob me *and* now intend to forcefully evict me from a neighborhood I discovered first. Does the code of conduct mean nothing to you? Well, congratulations, Mr. Whitlock. You may have won, but at least I have my dignity." Frederick flipped an imaginary scarf about his shoulders and pressed his nose into the air.

To Bartholomew, who cared very little about meaningless concepts like dignity and principles and justice, this attempted insult had little effect. His twisted grin only grew toothier as he basked in his victory. Hearing the vampire admit defeat filled him with a deep sense of satisfaction that most people only manage to experience when they've stolen a piece of bubble wrap before their siblings notice and can hide away in a closet popping it all by themselves.

The warlock was so pleased with his own gloating that he'd probably have allowed Frederick to leave without saying anything else were it not for a little paw stamping on his foot.

It didn't hurt. Gizmo was much too light in his current form. But still, Bartholomew scowled at the audacity of his familiar.

"Eh hem!" The demon cleared his throat, continuing to nudge the warlock.

"I know. I was getting to that," Bartholomew muttered, snarling at his familiar and pulling his foot away. He reached into the pocket of his suit. His hand wrapped around a chain, and he pulled out a pendant. The eye of the sun winked at them.

Frederick, who'd started to turn away, froze. His head snapped toward the artifact. "Is that—?" He didn't dare to speak the words.

"The Amulet of the Impaler," Bartholomew said. He held out his hand. "Take it. Go on. It's not like I need to sell it at this point."

No, I imagine not since you've stolen my money-growing pot, Frederick thought, but this irritation was short lived. His hands reached out and grasped at the amulet, clawing the warlock's palm like a raccoon reaching for food[8].

---

8. If you're thinking that this is an odd comparison, you've clearly never made the mistake of letting a raccoon grab dog chow from your bare palm.

Frederick held it before him. His eyes grew wide with reverence. For centuries the vampire had dreamed of possessing the power of the amulet. Now, it was his.

He hurried to slip the chain over his neck before the warlock could recant and snatch his gift back. Frederick hid his own gleeful smirk. He was under the false impression that Bartholomew had just made a grave misstep.

"You realize that with this, you haven't won at all. I can walk in the sunlight without fear."

"I know," Bartholomew said. "That's why I gave it to you. I want you to stay."

"You beef-witted warlock. Now you—" Frederick stopped. He'd been so excited to retaliate now that he no longer felt outwitted that it took him a moment to process what Bartholomew had just said.

"In my magnanimous nature,[9] I've decided to offer you a deal," the warlock said. "Now that I'm President of the Homeowners Association, Frederick, things are about to change. I want you to join me. Help me make Mills Run Heights the most inhospitable place for anyone with even the slightest magical inclination."

Bartholomew laughed. It sounded deep, threatening, vaguely evil. He offered his hand.

Frederick considered it for a moment. "Me, a member of the Homeowners Association?" he mused softly. Then his wan smile appeared over his papery face. "This place could use someone to give it an air of gentility."

---

9. The decision was more a result of the incessant whining of his familiar and Bartholomew's own reluctant awareness that an ally might be more useful than a nemesis in his current situation. (Only because Gizmo was so useless, of course, as he made sure to point out to the demon.)

The vampire clasped the warlock's hand. They shook.

"So it will just be us," Frederick said, feeling relieved to find himself now with a confidant instead of a foe. "No one else with any magic."

"Precisely," Bartholomew agreed. "Just the two of us."

"Three," Gizmo corrected them. He was going against custom and counting himself separately to the warlock. Which would have been a bit ridiculous to most, given that they were a package deal.

Nonetheless, the familiar was correct.

There were, at least, three magical individuals disguised as human residents in Mills Run Heights.

And, despite the worst intentions of Bartholomew, more would surely arrive.

Note from A.J. Renwick

Thank you so much for exploring the magical world of The Warlock's Homeowners Association!

If you enjoyed *Subdivision Battles of the Dead and Undead*, please tell your friends, or leave a review in the place where you purchased it. It would mean so much to me!

More information about me and my series is available on the Plotworks Publishingwebsite. If you sign up for the newsletter, you get a discount on your first purchase! You can also follow me on Instagram: @aj.renwick

About the Author

A.J. Renwick is a lover of all things fantasy, from mermaids and unicorns to vampires and dragons. She writes young adult paranormal romance in the *Castor's Grove* Universe, and comedy fantasy in *The Warlock's Homeowners Association*.

When she's not writing, A.J. Renwick enjoys reading (duh!), baking (sometimes more successfully than others), and spending time with her three dogs (the Dragon Squad).

More Titles by A.J. Renwick

For a sneak peak into A.J. Renwick's first novel, *Orphan's Egg*, turn the page—

ORPHAN'S EGG

F rances West stood, frozen on the sidewalk, staring at the familiar gray door.

It was the first thing she'd recognized since returning to Castor's Grove three weeks ago. Though she'd been born in the city, Fran's time in it had felt less like a homecoming than she'd secretly hoped. The streets were easy to navigate with buildings organized in square grids, her temporary apartment on the edge of downtown was clean and conveniently located, and there was nothing lacking in the environment. With the ocean on its south and east borders, forest to the north and west, and dense urban high-rises in its center, Castor's Grove was a city that boasted something for everyone.

But there was nothing special about a city that everyone could enjoy. Fran liked it, but it was in the same way any visitor might. While waiting to hear back from the adoption agency, she'd wandered the streets, avoiding the usual tourist activities, waiting to see something that sparked some long-buried memory or wander into someone who would recognize her.

Now, it was happening.

But instead of the sense of belonging she'd imagined, Fran's chest tightened, and her breath caught. Her anxiety buzzed in her brain.

There was an image of a sword burned into the door. It stretched almost the entire length of the door, its hilt hovering only a few inches above a sunflower welcome mat that looked far too normal in the context. Who lived in this house?

Your foster parents. Fran grappled with her anxiety to take control of her own thoughts. *They're probably into Dungeons and Dragons, or one of the kids they cared for did it.*

Either way, it was nothing to worry about.

Fran took a deep breath and pushed her hands into the pocket of her large black jacket. It wasn't cold, but she wrapped it around her as she walked up the steps. There was no doorbell. She tapped her elbow against the wood.

No response came from within. Fran could've tried again. It had been a light knock.

This is too weird. They might not even live here anymore. What was I thinking just knocking on their door?

She should just leave a message. There was paper in her pocket; she could buy a pen somewhere nearby, write a letter, and slip it into the mailbox.

"Upon my honor."

Fran spun around to see a thin middle-aged woman with olive skin. Short gray hairs frizzed around her temples, narrowly escaping the band that pulled the rest into a black ponytail. She wore an oversized green dress with a canary yellow jacket that matched the shopping bag in her hand.

The woman took a few steps closer, keeping her eyes on Fran. There was a wariness to her expression.

"Um, I was just—"

There was nothing suspicious about knocking on someone's door in broad daylight, but Fran felt suddenly guilty. "Do you know if the Franklins still live here?"

"We do." She narrowed her eyes, glancing between Fran and the door as though she thought the teenager was blocking her path. "Is this a university project? Are you doing a census?"

Fran was tempted to lie, tell Mrs. Franklin yes, and bolt, but she'd made it this far, so she shook her head. "No, I'm not with the university. I'm actually, well I was, one of the kids you fostered. It was like fifteen years ago. You probably don't remember—"

"Frances Buckler."

The sound of her original name rang like a bell in Fran's ears. Her lips mouthed the word *Buckler*, trying to wrap themselves around the harsh first syllable and the slur of the second. She'd whispered it to herself every night since she'd learned it, but it still felt like it belonged to someone else.

"It's Frances West now, actually."

"You've dyed your hair." Mrs. Franklin reached toward her, and Fran flinched away, but she was too slow to stop the woman from grabbing a clump of black hair. She ran a finger along it as though testing if the dye would rub off. Then she dropped the hair, pulled a set of keys out from her bag, and turned to the door. "Come inside. You shouldn't be out here."

"Oh." Fran pulled her jacket tight again. Her first instinct was to refuse. Stranger danger and all that. But how did she expect to get information about her parents if she didn't talk to Mrs. Franklin? "Maybe for a minute, but I can't stay long."

The strange yet familiar door led to a normal and therefore relatively forgettable living area. There was a fireplace in the corner with olive green couches and a squat brown coffee table. Paintings of flowers hung on the walls.

Fran's stomach tightened as she stepped in. *Why doesn't it match the door?*

"Sit." Mrs. Franklin instructed, pointing at the couch.

Fran hesitated, but the woman kept smiling and staring. Eventually, she gave in and sat on the edge of one of the chairs. Mrs. Franklin didn't join her.

"You must tell me about your life, dear. What's brought you back to the city?"

"Nothing in particular," Fran said, fingers crumpling stray pieces of paper in her pockets as she tried to guess what Mrs. Franklin's angle was.

There's no angle. She's just a nice older lady who took care of me for six months when I was a toddler. Don't listen to your anxiety.

"Although, I was wondering if you knew anything about my parents," Fran forced the truth out. "I wouldn't bother you about it, but there's no record of them anywhere, no birth certificate on file for me, but you're the one who recorded my last name as Buckler, and my dads said you sent that gift with me, so I just thought, maybe you'd known them?"

Fran held her breath as she waited for Mrs. Franklin's response. This was it. Her former foster parents were her last chance of learning the truth about her birth parents. Who had they been? What had they done? Had they loved her?

The woman before her might have those answers.

Mrs. Franklin's smile faltered. "What gift?"

"You know," Fran said. If the woman had been able to recognize Frances after fifteen years, she must have remembered it. "The Fabergé egg. It's purple with gold details."

Mrs. Franklin's smile stretched so tight that it looked like her skin would snap. "You still have that?"

"Obviously." Sarcasm leaked into Fran's voice before she could stop it. Did the woman really think she'd have thrown away the only gift she'd ever received from her parents?

"It's here with you? In the city?"

Fran stiffened, feeling her heart thump in her chest. That was a strange question. It wasn't just her paranoia.

"No. I left it back in Lansing."

"Excuse me a moment. I need to make a call." Mrs. Franklin spoke with the smile frozen on her face.

Fran nodded. Her eyes flicked to the front door. It was close, but not so close that the older woman couldn't grab her before she got to it.

Mrs. Franklin didn't leave the room. Eyes trained on Frances, she pulled a phone from her pocket, pressed a button, and raised it to her ear.

Fran struggled to keep her breathing steady as she stared at the woman.

"Dammit." Mrs. Franklin's smile finally dropped as she lowered the phone. She knelt on the carpeted floor before Fran and rested her hands on the teenager's knees.

Fran was small, but the woman before her was frail. She could push her off. But her body was frozen. All she could think about was the fact that she should've hidden her knife in her pocket instead of her boot.

"Listen, Frances, I have the answers you want, okay? But we need to be honest with one another. What's the address of your home in Lansing?"

There was no way Fran was telling her that.

"Never mind. Two dads, West? I'll look it up. Just wait here until I'm back, okay? I'll tell you about your parents then."

Before Fran could fully process what the woman had said, Mrs. Franklin had raced out of her own house. The tension in Fran's body slackened as she realized that she was alone, but her heart continued to quiver. This was all far too weird, and try as she might, Fran couldn't pierce through her anxiety to come up with a logical reason for Mrs. Franklin's actions.

I need to leave.

But Mrs. Franklin knew her parents. Fran could finally learn who they were, who she was.

The longing burned within her, begged her to stay, just as her anxiety screamed at her to run. The result was that Fran sat on the olive chair for a lot longer than most sane people would have. And she might have remained there until Mrs. Franklin returned were it not for the noise.

A loud twang shook the floor beneath Fran's chair.

That settled it. She leaped up and grabbed the door handle without hesitation. But it wouldn't budge. Mrs. Franklin had locked her in.

Crap.

Trustworthy people didn't lock teenagers in their houses. Whatever claims Mrs. Franklin made about her parents could easily be false. She couldn't stick around.

But how could she escape?

The Franklins' house had only one entry, and there were bars on all their windows. Except for the ones in the basement.

It was the design of all the houses in this area. Fran had noticed it while walking through the neighborhood. But the strange noise had come from the basement.

Fran reached into her boot and pulled out her knife. Fingers trembling, she managed to get the blade free. She held it before her, afraid to breathe as she searched for the basement door.

It didn't take her long to find it in the kitchen.

Cold sweat trickled down Fran's back as she stared down a long flight of steps. There was no sound now save Fran's own pounding heart.

Maybe the noise she'd heard was a cat. People owned those. They knocked things over. At least, they did in television shows.

And I think I'm too smart to die in a horror movie? This is the dumbest thing I've ever done.

But waiting for Mrs. Franklin would've been just as foolish. So Fran tiptoed down the stairs, knuckles white around her knife.

A stream of light from a high window illuminated the bottom of the staircase. The tension eased from Fran's body. It was too high for her to climb through, but there might be a ladder or something she could stand on down below. Maybe she wasn't about to die.

"Dust!" a boy's voice exclaimed.

Or maybe she was.

"Couldn't you at least give me a few minutes to try to escape? Maybe we could make a trade?"

Fran's legs turned into metal rods, anchored to the ground, unable to move. Her heart did its best to escape them. It took all her effort to turn her head toward the voice.

Her mouth dropped open. The only thing that stopped her from gasping was that her chest was too tight to let the breath escape.

Trapped underneath a silver net was a boy about her own age with a mass of red curls. But it wasn't the net or the color of his hair that made Fran feel as though she were about to faint.

He had wings.

Thank you for reading *Subdivision Battles of the Dead and Undead*. If you enjoyed this work, please visit plotworkspublishing.com to find more of our titles!